© Copyright 2017 Kenneth Guentert

All rights reserved. No part of this book may be reproduced in printed, digital, or any other form without written permission from the author.

Contact the author:
ken@thepublishingpro.com
www.thepublishingpro.com

The Publishing Pro, LLC
511 Custer Ave.
Colorado Springs, CO 80903

More book info: evilspeakg.blogspot.com

ISBN 13: 978-1973908180
ISBN 10: 1973908182

Cover photo: Robert Stephens
Cover and interior design: The PublishingPro, LLC.

*To the class of '66
and the men who taught us.*

Disclaimer

Evil Speaking is a work of fiction. At the same time, it is set in a real place and a real time: Holy Cross Seminary, 1964-65. I was a junior in that school year. However, the characters mentioned in this book were not there and the events mentioned in this book did not happen there. Some events, one in particular, inspired me to create this story that did not happen. I borrowed personality quirks and certain behaviors to create characters who never existed, except in my imagination. This is the fun of fiction.

Chapter 1

Monday, August 10, 1964

I thought I had hit bottom three months before I wound up in Hank Grieshaber's office. Hank was a classmate from seminary days. We had roomed together in this same building—before I went off to war and he went off to novitiate. He was a good guy. Brilliant. Funny. Honest. He should have been in the theology department at Notre Dame, teaching Scripture. I'm not sure why he wasn't. Instead, he was the rector of Holy Cross Seminary, where one of his first moves was to sit behind his blonde oak desk with a glass of scotch in his hand and offer me a job teaching English.

Oh, I forgot. My name is Bert, and I'm an alcoholic. To be rigorously honest, my full name is Englebert Aloysius Foote, three reasons why I prefer to be called Bert. A year ago, I had been doing fine. I had a wife, two kids, a decent job as editor at Spes Unica Publishing House near the university and a modest 1920s home. Then I got in my own way. I had always liked to drink, and it had never seemed much of a problem. Then one night, after spending some time drinking with my colleagues, I came home and got into an argument with my wife. I hit her—or so she told me the next morning in a most matter of fact way—along with the promise that she would leave me if I ever did it again.

I was stunned—and mortified, especially because I couldn't remember anything. I believed her though. She didn't play games, and I was so embarrassed I didn't have a drink again. For a week. When I felt in control again, I went back to my bourbon, came home and hit her again. I guess. I don't really remember that episode either, and she never said. She just left before I woke up the next morning, taking the kids with her. I knew that was it. Being married to a drunk—and getting the crap kicked out of herself every night—was not in Sarah's plans. She was a tough cookie. That's why I married her. That's why I lost her.

I did not pass go. I did not collect $200. And I did not go to jail. Instead I went to AA, thanks to a kindly judge who offered to throw my butt in jail if meetings didn't work. The meetings did work, after a fashion. I haven't had a drink since then, which has so far served mainly to make me acutely aware that every single day I meet someone whose brainless melon I want to smash to bits.

Nowadays, you'd say I had anger issues.

My sponsor told me I was making progress because I had stopped acting on the impulse, but that was before I took a swing at Mother May-Eye and broke his nose. Mother May-Eye's real name was Monsignor Albert Mayer, but he had acquired his nickname because of his officious airs. That and his ability to stare down an alligator, especially when the alligator wanted something. Like a raise. Mother May-Eye was my boss. He was the publisher. I was the editor. I wound up in jail for that one, two nights. Mother May-Eye dropped the charges after I promised never to go near his publishing house again. I was out of a job, and my name in the Catholic publishing world was mud. In one sense, that was okay. I was past the point where I could edit church stuff with any credibility. It was time to leave. Maybe that's why I hit him. I didn't have the guts to leave outright. I had to work myself up into a rage to make something happen. Still, if I had to hit someone, I was better off doing it sober. At least I could enjoy it—over and over again. My sponsor had taught me to count my blessings.

So, having burned my bridges in the world of Catholic publishing, here I was getting offered a job teaching in a seminary.

"You know I almost wound up in jail for decking a priest," I reminded Hank. I knew he knew. Everybody in the community knew.

"Ego te absolvo," Hank said, moving his glass of scotch in a sign of a cross. "To be honest, I lifted a glass to your name when I heard. Mother May-Eye is the biggest jerk in the order, and that's going some. Wanted to hit him a few times myself, the last time for helping put me on this path to oblivion. He lobbied to get me this assignment."

In the cold light of my own sobriety, I stared at Hank's scotch and wondered if he might be doing a good job of putting himself on the path to oblivion. I didn't say say so. Instead I said, "So you're getting even in a way—by hiring me."

"That's a plus, but it's only icing," Hank said. "The real reason is that I have an opening that I need filled, and I want someone I can trust. Someone, um, not from the community."

"Why?" I asked, surprised. I thought he had been trying to do me a favor. He wasn't. He was using me. I felt better already.

"There is some ugly gossip about one of our incoming faculty members, a Bernard Fox. Do you know him?"

"I assume he's a priest," I said. "Never heard of him. I haven't poured over the provincial newsletter in quite a while."

"Right. He's a history teacher," Hank said. "He comes off a bit arrogant sometimes—but he's popular with students, some of them anyway, probably just because he's different. An odd duck."

"Being an odd duck should be no problem in your pond," I said helpfully. "What's the gossip about?"

"He taught at Notre Dame High School in Niles for years," Hank said. "Last year, the principal started hearing noise about Bernie and, um, boys."

"Hmm, boys in general or boys of the high-school persuasion," I asked.

"The stories seemed to be coming from the students," Hank said, "but there was no formal complaint, and there was no evidence you could hang your hat on."

"Why, in the province's infinite wisdom, did they send him here?"

"Because the order doesn't have a girls' school," Hank said, with just a trace of irritation in his voice. "To give the community the benefit of the doubt, there is no real evidence against the guy. Only story. He's a good teacher, in spite of his quirks, and most students seem to like him. So the provincial figured they would get him away from the gossip and ..."

"... and he told you to keep an eye on him."

"Right. I didn't much like it, but he told me I could hire whomever I wanted to teach English."

"And that's where I come in."

"Right again," Hank said. "If he's dirty, I want him out of here. If he's clean, I don't want the young men here telling stories about him."

"And of course, you want me because of my extensive background in private investigation," I said neutrally.

"I didn't know you had any," he said.

"Geez, Hank, you're on the job for a week, and you've already lost your sense of irony. I wouldn't know an investigation from a dissertation. I've never taught school a day in my life. I don't need any more teenagers in my life. I'm not Catholic anymore. I didn't like this place when I was here. I beat up the last priest I spent any time with. So maybe you need a better grade of hootch."

"You're hired," Hank said.

Chapter 2

Monday, August 17, 1964

My new digs could have been worse. The room wasn't much—fifteen by fifteen feet, green vinyl tile, a twin bed, a wooden desk, a chest of drawers, an armoire, a red easy chair that proved to be rather comfortable, and a serviceable bathroom with a shower. The upside was the view, looking down the hill out over St. Mary's Lake to the golden dome and the spire of Sacred Heart Church. The downside was that I was up on the third floor, sans elevator, between the freshman dorms. The climb and the proximity to the freshmen made it undesirable to the other faculty members, all priests. Bernie Fox, the new guy, had the only other faculty room, adjacent to mine. Hank had thought ahead.

However humble, the free room and board was the reason I had jumped at the seminary opportunity. After the second episode with my wife, she had left in the middle of the night but returned in the cold light of day and told me to get the hell out. I didn't argue. I was appalled at my behavior, the more so because I couldn't remember it. However, I still had a job at that point and was able to book a motel room on Dixie Highway at monthly rates. Lacking anything better to do in the evenings, I started attending AA meetings every night. This had a stabilizing effect on me. Sort off. The incident with Mother May-Eye had happened when I was sober. Apparently, I had anger issues. Rick, my temporary sponsor, said not to worry. I was what they call a dry drunk. Great.

On the plus side, Rick at least had some understanding of the issue. When I lost my job and any wherewithal to pay for a room, Rick offered me space above his garage for as long as I stayed sober. He didn't need to worry about me staying forever. The place lacked amenities. No electricity. No water. If I had to pee in the middle of the night, I had to climb down the stairs, walk from the garage across the sidewalk, unlock the door to Rick's house, creep up the stairs to Rick's only bathroom, trying not to wake up Rick or his wife. Or I could opt for a leak in Rick's hollyhocks. I tried to think of it as camping, but it didn't help much. Ever since the war, I didn't have much use for camping.

Hank's job offer had come in the nick of time, When I told Rick about it, noting that the offer included room and board, all Rick said was, "Good thing. You're killing my hollyhocks."

Unpacking my suitcase, four boxes of books, and one box of odds and ends shouldn't have taken long. The problem was I had to hike them from the parking lot up the two flights of stairs. By the time I made it two trips up the worn slate stairs—one for the suitcase and the other for my trusty Underwood typewriter—I was breathing hard and decided to leave the boxes in the Edsel for another day. I made a mental note to give up smoking.

Then I sat down in the easy chair, lit up a Lucky Strike, and wondered if I could learn how to teach English and be a detective in three weeks.

Chapter 3

Saturday, August 22, 1964

"Good-looking kids," Brother Rufus said, looking out at Butch and Sissy goofing around on the raft. Rufus had caught us taking a swim and asked us if we'd help him put the raft out in preparation for the arrival of the seminarians.

We were glad to help out. It gave us something to do. Kids their age—Butch was 14, Sissy was 16—don't want to hang around their parents, and I had given them some legitimate reasons for not wanting to hang around me. Someday, I'd need to reach out and apologize for what a bad parent I had been. Now was not the time. They didn't want to hear about it; they didn't need the reminder. When I tried to talk with them about any matter of substance, they resisted. Butch retreated into stony silence. Sissy, ever the extrovert, talked. And talked. And talked. About nothing—and anything, mainly I gathered to keep me from talking. I didn't worry that much about it. I figured I had enough on my plate just staying sober. Anyway, things were looking up. At least, I had a job and a room with a bathroom. My wife and I still weren't talking much, but she had agreed to let me take the kids every other Saturday. So here I was. It wasn't much. It was the best I could do. It was better than I had ever done.

"Hmm, thanks," I responded finally. "Must be my wife's doing. Er, we're separated."

"Well, I assumed there was no wife in the picture."

"What with me taking on the life of a monk and all."

"Yeah, that too. Anyways, the life of a monk ain't so bad. Of course, this year promises to be a lee-tle different." He strung out "lee-tle" like it was a piece of taffy with an accent.

"You're not entirely in favor of the changes," I said. My buddy Hank might have been fond of his scotch, but he managed where I hadn't. He had things he wanted to do. Inspired by John XXIII and the Second Vatican Council, Hank had decided Holy Cross Sem needed a few open windows of its own. He planned wholesale changes. Big stuff. Seminarians would no longer have to keep silence in the halls. He was going to abolish "visiting Sunday" and let seminarians have visitors any weekend, once their chores were done. He was going to be more liberal about letting seminarians go off campus. In fact, he wanted them off campus at times, to work on what he called their apostolates. The idea was to do service—working with retarded children, poor folks, Negroes, which was still the politically correct term in 1964. He announced he was going to throw out the music code—now even the freshman would be able to listen to the up-and-coming Beatles instead of Peter, Paul, and Mary. He changed the dress code, allowing sweaters in the classroom instead of the traditional blazer. Finally, he thought the seminarians should be able to interact with other students, including and especially girls. Some of the faculty were ecstatic. Traditionalists like Brother Rufus were uneasy.

"Not my call," Rufus said, as if reading my mind. "But truth to tell, I think it'll be trouble. Leastways, it'll be interesting."

"Yeah, I guess it will be different all right," I said, moving the conversation ahead, oh, a quarter of an inch.

"Yep," he said. An eighth of an inch.

"New faculty, too," I said. Half an inch.

"You and that Fox," he said. An inch.

"Know much about him?" I asked. Whoa, a foot.

Rufus grunted. "Just what I've heard." Bingo. A yard.

"And what's that?"

"Well, you know, I really shouldn't say." He was dying to tell me. "Put it to you this way," he said staring out to the raft, where Butch and Sissy sat with their feet dangling in the water. "If I had a daughter as pretty as yourn and Br'er Fox came around, why…" He paused, enjoying his own suspense.

I waited and finally gave in. "Why-y what?"

"Why it wouldn't bother me a bit," he said, his eyes twinkling as if telling a dirty joke. "Now if he got near the boy …"

Br'er Fox hadn't even shown up yet. Rufus was right. It was going to be an interesting year

Chapter 4

Thursday, August 27, 1964

Eli Bonpere was my lawyer—and one of God's little jokes on me. After my wife served notice, I had enough sense to get myself a lawyer but not enough to do more than pick one out of the Yellow Pages. I stuck on Bonpere because I didn't have enough energy to get past the "B's" and Eli Bonpere sounded like somebody who'd grown up wrasslin' alligators in the bayou. With a talent like that, I figured he'd have a shot at my wife.

Eli was every bit as interesting as I thought, just not in the way I thought. He came out of Louisiana all right—Bourbon Street. He was black—or Negro as we still said back in the early sixties. Eli was Creole born, Chicago raised, Jesuit educated, and a Jew by choice. Orthodox no less. He knew more living and dead languages than I had fingers—and he could speak in several dialects that don't have names. When he got married to a doe-eyed Moroccan Jewess named Leah, he added Arabic and Ladino to his traveling suitcase. I couldn't wait to get him into a courtroom—I figured he could talk to any judge or jury, didn't matter their language or culture. Maybe. But he didn't talk to them. He talked to me in my vernacular. Told me he'd take my case as long as I got my ass to AA and stayed there. Then he worked out a separation agreement that included limited visitation rights, child support, and a payment schedule for him that he said would be good for my sorry soul.

The man got my attention. Right after I popped Mother May-Eye a good one, I didn't call my sponsor first. I called Eli. Good move. He persuaded the good monsignor not to press charges. In return, I had to give up my job, my pension, and the rights to all the books I had written. Eli said the deal would be good for my sorry soul. The man was beginning to get on my nerves, but I signed the necessary papers and was mostly glad to have another part of my life behind me.

Today I wasn't in the same kind of trouble I had been in a few months ago, but I was troubled. I didn't feel equipped for my job, not the teaching part, not the detective part. Don't get me wrong. I was grateful to have a job, not to mention a place to live, and the wherewithal to continue child support. But I felt like I was being sucked into something soft and slimy, something even creepier than my own life, and it terrified me. I was drawn to talk to Eli about it, maybe because of his moral confidence, maybe because of his background. I was in a swamp that would have done his ancestors proud, and I was looking for firm ground.

I had explained the situation in a general way in a phone call the day before. New job. Some moral complications I wanted to talk over. I didn't need legal help. Would he mind seeing me? No problem, he said, and found an open half hour for me.

I was right on time. It was one thing I was good at. Eli's office was in downtown South Bend. His setup made it look like he was part of larger firm. He wasn't. He and four other attorneys, who also worked for themselves, had one-room offices and shared a secretary. She was a stern looking, sixtyish white woman in a ruffled blouse and a gray skirt. She looked at me blankly when I asked for "Mr. Bonpere," which forced me into a stuttering description of him as "um, Mr. Bonpere, my lawyer, the, um, Negro."

"Oh, him," she said and rose to usher me into his office.

Eli was on the phone, talking to a client and waving me in at the same time. He excused himself quickly, hung up, and reached across his desk to shake my hand.

"Good to see you, Bert. Coffee?" I nodded. He got up, walked around his desk, leaned out the door, and said. "Trudy, bring us two black coffees, please."

"She brings you coffee," I said, puzzled. "She doesn't even seem to know your name. Either that or she's a racist."

"Neither," he said. "She's sweet as pie to the colored folk who come in here, and she called me 'Mr. Bonpere' until last week when she found out I used to be Catholic. In her world, you don't leave the church. She expresses her displeasure by pretending not to know my name."

"Why don't you get rid of her?" I asked.

"She's not mine to get rid of," Eli said. "I share her with the other lawyers on the floor—and, as it turns out, she's a good secretary."

"And she gets your coffee."

"And she gets my coffee. What can I do for you?"

"I need a moral compass," I said.

"Better late than never."

"Thanks. Are you this polite to all your clients?"

"No, I have to be tough on some of them," he said. "Better get on with it. I have to be in court in a half hour."

I filled him in on my recent career change and new home address. He seemed amused and congratulated me for being able to pay child support again and for already having gotten my wife to agree to some informal arrangements for spending time with Sissy and Butch.

"Here's the problem," I said. "I wasn't hired for my non-existent teaching skill. The rector wants me to shadow one of the faculty members and find out if he's been molesting some of the students."

"Sounds like good work," said Eli.

"Molesting the students?"

Eli laughed. "Trying to find the truth. Your rector has heard rumors that one of your colleagues likes boys. He doesn't trust the rumors, but he can't ignore them either. So he hires you to get beneath the scuttlebutt and find out what's what. Your rector sounds like a good man."

"And I'm not scum?"

"Oh, man, you gotta quit leaving me openings like this," Eli laughed. "Why would you have trouble with this? You were a journalist."

"An editor," I corrected him. "But I get your point. It just feels like, well, spying."

"Of course it's spying, but so what? If your new colleague is diddling with his students, that's a terrible sin. But there's something worse."

"What's that?"

"Spreading the rumor that someone is diddling with his students—when he's not. Your rector knows that."

"But what if he is?" I asked.

"Well, then," Eli said, "I guess you better get busy."

Chapter 5

Monday, September 7, 1964

I didn't meet Bernie Fox until Labor Day.

By then, the upperclassmen had been around for a week—alternating painting and scrubbing with playing and goofing off. Normally, upperclassmen pointed out, preparation week had a camp feeling—with most of the usual rules held in abeyance until the freshmen came and classes started. This year the place was abuzz with the news that the usual rules weren't going to be instituted at all. The upperclassmen had spent more than their usual time in the chapel, listening to Hank Grieshaber (immediately dubbed "Father Grease") drone on about Vatican II and how the winds of change were sweeping through their seminary before any others. This was a source of pride to most, though some of the seniors expressed discomfort.

The freshman had begun arriving on Saturday with almost everyone on board by Sunday, just in time for the annual bunco party. The upperclassmen passed on the news about the big changes with an enthusiasm that was lost on the newbies, who, after all, had never experienced the bad old days. They were more caught up in surviving their few days away from their mommies.

The camp feeling—days spent playing softball, swimming, watching movies—was meant to distract them. By and large it worked. Only one homesick freshmen had abandoned ship by Monday.

The corn roast, to be followed by a hootenany, was the last part of the fun before classes began on Tuesday. Brother Rufus and three burly juniors had spent Monday morning digging the corn pit. They loaded it up with wood at noon and spent the afternoon burning the bonfire down to glowing goals. A small truckload of corn, unshucked, was dumped on top of the coals and devoured before sunset with chicken, cole slaw, and potato salad.

Bernie Fox showed up just in time to get his share. I'd accuse him of making an entrance, but in fairness he just stuck out in a crowd. He was a few years older than I—mid-forties—and tall, maybe six -feet six inches, with a blonde flattop, a ruddy complexion, and a noticeable scar that started just under his left eye and proceeded down almost to his mouth. He was wearing a tennis outfit, white shorts, white v-necked sweater with blue trim, and white tennis shoes. He didn't smile and looked diffident, hovering on grumpy. He greeted his fellow priests with little more than a nod and grabbed himself a Dixie Cup of "bug juice" from a thermos on a picnic table.

Father Grease—I loved Hank's new handle—went over to him, said something, and brought him my way. "Bert, Bernie Fox," he said with feigned enthusiasm.

"About time, " I said, shaking Bernie's hand. It was softer than I expected. He wasn't feigning any enthusiasm. "I've heard a lot about you."

"I bet," he said. "And I've heard you have a knack for punching out priests." Mr. Charm.

"All true," I said with a smile, thinking I could have said what I heard about him. But I didn't. Mr. Charm Squared.

"Okay, you got me Bernie," Hank said. "I hired him to be my

enforcer."

"I assumed it wasn't his teaching experience," Bernie said, looking right at me rather than Hank. "If you'll excuse me, I'm going to introduce myself to some of the boys."

"Bert, I think he likes you, " Hank said.

"My lucky day. Let's get some of that corn."

Chapter 6

Tuesday, September 8, 1964

"Well?"

"Deep subject," I said.

My wife cocked her head and looked at me, probably marveling that I had been a teacher for a day and my humor had already descended to the level of a fourteen-year-old. Deep subject, indeed. Sarah and I had barely spoken since I'd left her house, touching base mainly to confirm arrangements for picking up and dropping off Sissy and Butch.

I wanted to blame Sarah for our lack of communication, but it wasn't as if I had nothing to do with it. I was embarrassed about my behavior, frustrated that I couldn't remember the worst of it. For the past three weeks, I had avoided the newly opened university library, where Sarah worked as a reference librarian. Today was different. After my first class, I was hyped. I wasn't sure if I needed a walk to decompress or needed to talk. After some meandering around campus, I found myself in the library, half hoping to run into Sarah.

And so I did—at the reference desk. A reference librarian at the reference desk. Go figure.

She was ten minutes from a break and suggested we go outside and sit by the reflecting pool. It was a kindness that allowed me to smoke.

"Well?" she repeated. "How did it go?"

"I had only one class today," I said while reaching into my shirt pocket for a Lucky. I offered her one, which she waved away."Freshman English, but maybe it was enough to break the ice. I wasn't really sure how to begin, but I talked with the other teachers and settled on a three-point plan. First, I handed out the syllabus and went over it with them. Then I had them take out their copy of *Sound and Sense*, one of their textbooks, and had each student read a paragraph. My idea was to identify anyone who had trouble reading. Other than the two guys who read more slowly than the others, there were no issues."

"No surprise," Sarah said. "Unless there's been a big change, you're getting the cream of the crop in a seminary."

"In fact, this year does represent a big change," I said, pausing to strike a match and light up. "But no, not in the academic sense. These are bright kids. Anyway, after the reading exercise, I assigned them to write a few paragraphs about what they liked to do for fun. Basically, I wanted to get an idea of their writing skills and to learn about what interested them."

"Sounds like a decent plan."

"It did what I wanted," I said. "Unfortunately, the upperclassmen need a more sophisticated approach."

"And you have how many classes?"

"I have five classes," I said. "Two freshmen classes, and one sophomore, one junior, and one senior. That's about fifteen hours of class time, which is a little short of a full load but plenty for me."

"Any other English teachers?"

"I'm it."

"How did you manage that?"

"I didn't," I said. "The truth is, the rector, who was a classmate of mine in the seminary, had an ulterior motive when he hired me."

"Which was?"

Oops. I wasn't sure I should have brought up the subject, wasn't sure I shouldn't have. "I can't tell you right now," I said after a pause. "Hank and I are the only ones in on it. It has to stay that way for a while."

"Really? Aren't you the one who used to tell me that there can be no secrets between husband and wife."

"I am," I admitted. "But our status as husband and wife is a bit up in the air at the moment."

"There's that."

"That." I said. "On the other hand, I think you'll find out about it sometime, perhaps sooner rather than later."

"And why is that?"

"I may need your help."

Chapter 7

Thursday, September 10, 1964

I had been a teacher for three full days and hadn't beat the crap out of a single priest. Not that I didn't want to. As far as I could tell, Father Bernard Fox didn't exhibit any signs of being a sexual predator, but he was a first-class prick. He was scornful of me, none too friendly with his colleagues, and diffident with the seminarians.

Nevertheless, he seemed to be capturing their imagination. On the first day of his sophomore class, he announced that he was bored with teaching U.S. history the normal way and had decided to teach it backwards, beginning with World War I. This pushed a lot of buttons—but it fascinated the rebels.

When Hank invited him to say the Mass in the main chapel yesterday, he did it in fifteen minutes. Record time, again pissing off the traditionalists and cheering the rebels. The Fox, which quickly became the nickname of choice, was a hot topic—right up there with the altar turned around to face the people, no silence in the halls, and the end of the music censorship committee.

Right now, in fact, "I Want to Hold Your Hand" was blaring over the rec room sound system, something unheard of the year before. Or so I was told. Last year, the seminarians had a committee that decided what music to prohibit, which tended to limit the playlist to folk music, some show tunes, and a bit of classical music.

With the censorship committee gone, the Beatles and the Rolling Stones were fair game.

I was engaged in a bridge match, partly for something to do and partly as a reasonably safe way to interact with the Fox. My mistake. I wasn't much better—or much more interested—than our partners, two freshmen who were singing along to the Beatles tune. This irritated the Fox, my opponent, who had opened the bidding with a heart and appeared to be far more serious about teaching bridge than he was about teaching U.S. history.

"Mick, we're waiting," said the Fox.

"I want to hold your h-a-n-d," sang Mick Clark, shaking his head and sorting his cards.

"I bet you do," giggled Louis Dzinski.

"Not my hand," I said, looking at Louis out of the corner of my eye and my spread, which contained a single counter.

"No table talk," the Fox said, glaring at me over his half glasses, which accentuated his scar.

"Umm, I dunno, a spade, I guess," said Mick.

"Two hearts," said Louis.

I passed. The Fox made it four hearts, which gave him control and made Louis the dummy. This was fine with Louis, who laid down his cards and started singing along with Mick.

"Why did you jump to four hearts?" I asked, more to make conversation than anything else.

"Because four hearts is game," the Fox said, with a tone that suggested I should have known better. He began to draw trump.

"And what's game?" I asked.

"Never mind, we're not counting points anyway," he said, pulling an ace of hearts from the dummy.

"Does that mean you should have settled for three hearts?" I said, tossing my lone trump, the king of hearts, onto the pile.

"Only if I didn't give a damn," he said, flipping out the jack of hearts.

"Oh, I don't give a damn about a greenback dollar," Mick sang, repeating a tune he had heard at last weekend's hootenanny while the record player changed Beatle tunes. He almost shouted the "damn."

Louis giggled again. I was trying to figure out which of the three was getting on my nerves more.

"Mick, play your queen," the Fox said.

"Hey, how'd you know I had the queen?" Mick said. Bernie Fox looked at him as if he were dumber than ratmeat—and Mick muttered, "Oh, wow!"

Chapter 8

Friday, September 11, 1964

Thank God it's Friday. I had survived the week—barely. The freshman were still trying to remember their teachers' names, but the upperclassmen were reveling in having their world turned upside down. As a group, the juniors had a bit of mean streak. They had already identified several freshmen to target for Halloween hazing, and they decided that Friday's English lit class would be a good place to test my mettle.

When I arrived for English lit five minutes before the bell, most of the class was already in their seats, snickering at the six-pack of Drewrys on my desk. How anyone came up with that on a Friday I didn't know. And I didn't care. This was their idea of going for the jugular. The amateurs. I didn't know a damn thing about teaching, but being accused of being a drunk—now that was familiar ground.

I opened my briefcase, took out a set of papers and asked a lad in the front row to pass them out. I set the rest of the papers on the desk and planted the six-pack on top like a paperweight. Then I lit up a Lucky and waited for the rest of the class to show up.

When the bell rang, I made a calming gesture to indicate the beginning of the moment of silence that I had established two days ago as our beginning ritual. I broke the silence by saying, "Mounty piss," gesturing with my cigarette to the local brew with a red-coat-ed Canadian policeman on the label. "Anyway, when you get to be as good at drinking as I am, beer doesn't do it. Bourbon does—but I guess you guys couldn't come up with a bottle of Jim Beam."

I paused. "Here's the deal. You've heard that I've got a little problem with drinking, and you think it's funny. Maybe so. Getting drunk, falling down, and puking straight up—that's a load of laughs. Getting so drunk you beat your wife and can't remember doing it, that's another story. So, hey, maybe I should kill this six-pack and see what happens when I lose control in front of a bunch of clowns that just tried their best to insult me."

Their eyes were getting bigger, but I was on a roll. "But I won't—at least not for the next five minutes—because I happen to know a secret. Half of you guys are here because you're trying to escape from your old man who's a bigger lush than I am."

Their eyes expanded to the size of manhole covers.

"So if you want to talk about alcoholism, let's talk about it." I said, "but let's skip the stupid props. You're not freshmen anymore."

That turned out to be the best class of the week.

Chapter 9

Saturday, September 12, 1964

Saturday was a quiet day, at least for the faculty. The local boys had gone home on Friday after classes. On Saturday morning, the other seminarians were wrapped up doing their weekly chores, same as in years before. But afternoons were free, really free, a big change under the new regime. They could go into town to catch a movie or entertain themselves on the seminary grounds or on the Notre Dame campus.

I had to check in with Hank and invited him for a walk around the lake. No dice. Walking wasn't his cup of tea—or scotch—but talking was fine. We sat at a picnic table overlooking the lake.

"How's it feel to be a high-school teacher?" Hank asked me.

"It's not easy, but I'm getting there. Yesterday, I noticed I might be enjoying it."

"You sound surprised," Hank said.

"I am," I said. "I didn't ask for this job. I don't have the background for it. I could have been a real flop."

"But you're not," he said. "What's you're secret?"

"Well, it's only been a week. The juniors tried to rip my covers off, but I turned the tables on them."

"Apparently your lesson plan had to do with mixed metaphors," Hank said.

"More like mixed drinks," I said. "Anyway, I handled it and it came out well. The freshmen are easier. The secret has been to do as little actual teaching as possible. I invented a project for the freshman—turning a short story from our text into a radio play. They're having a ball."

"That explains why I found a crew in the handball courts with tape recorders."

"Yep, sound effects," I said. "Those unbreakable dishes you make the seminarians use may be unspeakably ugly, but they mimic the sound of a subway when you rotate them around on a handball floor."

"You've managed to stumble on a good teaching technique in your first week," Hank said. "Or did someone give you the suggestion?"

"Nope, everyone seemed keen on leaving me to my own devices."

"Even Bernie?"

"Oh, c'mon," I said. "You knew he wasn't going to give me any help."

"Pretty much, but I thought you should ask. You never know. Have you gotten to know him?"

"More than I care to," I said. "You know, he's a little hard to take. Teaching has been a piece of cake compared to trying to warm up to this guy."

"You think he's got a problem?"

"Yeah, he's got a problem, but maybe not the one you're worried about."

"How so?"

"Well, he's a jerk. I'm not sure he likes his job."

"Being a priest, you mean," Hank asked?

"Right," I said, "But I don't make him for a pedophile."

"Why is that?"

"He's not likable enough," I said.

"He seems to be a hit with some of the boys," .

"You're right," I said, "and it's odd. The other day, I played bridge with him and a couple of the freshmen. He was hard on them, but they seemed to like him. I don't get it. Some of the other fellows like him for his rough edges. He's a rebel. He says Mass in fifteen minutes. He teaches history backwards. He's rude. He's sarcastic. But he's not universally popular either. In fact, some of the seminarians seem to despise him for these same qualities. Pedophiles—at least according to my research—seduce their prey with charm. Bernie is way short on charm."

"So he's just a garden-variety bastard," Hank said.

"That's my take,"

"Well, that *is* good news."

Chapter 10

Sunday, September 13, 1964

So much for my instant wisdom. Not a day later than my conversation with Hank, I started picking up scuttlebutt about the Fox and the boys.

"Hey, batter batter! You can't hit."

Swoosh.

Loudmouth was right. Louis Dzinski couldn't hit. The twelve-inch ball coming in at a slow arch might as well have been an atom bomb to the batter. He had no intention of hitting the thing. He hunched over, about four feet away from the plate, made a face and held out the bat like it was a three-foot turd. A fresh one.

The pitch. The turd moved in a half-hearted arc. Strike two.

"C'mon, Whiz, you can do it," yelled Jack Carter, a junior monitor standing next to me behind the backstop.

"An encouraging word," I observed. "Good for you."

"Yeah, well, I guess that's my job," Jack said. "Dzinski's a twerp, but look around. Half of these freshmen never picked up a bat until September."

"Hey, batter batter! Better get your fairy godfather to hit it for you." The loudmouth again. It was Dan Johnson, a sophomore, about ten feet away, grinning like he had said something brilliant.

The pitcher wound up, underhanded a loop that Louis missed by three feet.

"Oh, fudge," exclaimed Mick Clark from what passed for the on-deck spot.

"Oh, fudge yourself," giggled the Whiz, relieved to be handing off the bat to someone else. .

"Fudge?" Carter queried.

"Fairy godfather?" I repeated, glancing over at Carter. "Where did that come from?"

"Hmm, probably a reference to the Fox. Some people say he's taken a shine to the Whiz."

"Really," I said, trying to keep my tone even.

"The Whiz has been playing bridge with the Fox. He and Mick," Carter said, keeping his voice low. "No big deal until the Fox ripped some of the guys in my class for picking on the Whiz. Now they're paying him back."

"So the guys are just having a little fun at the Fox's expense?" I asked.

"Something like that," Carter said.

"You said anything to your mates," I said. "This kind of talk can get out of hand."

"Oh, they don't mean anything by it," he said.

"Right," I said.

Chapter 11

Tuesday, September 22, 1964

"Oh, shit!"

That was my response, and I didn't even know the poor guy. Jimmy Parker, a new college seminarian at nearby St. Joe Hall, had been found dead that morning. Hank told the faculty at a stand-up meeting after lunch.

"All we know at this point is that he was found hanging from a tree near St. Joe Lake," Hank said. "Probably suicide. This is all too common at the university—every couple of years an ND student crumbles under the pressure of grades, homesickness, or God-knows-what—but Jimmy was one of us. He wasn't professed, and he was new, but it'll be tough on the community all the same. Especially the guys at St. Joe Hall."

"Tougher on the family," I said. When you don't know what to say, state the obvious.

"God, yes," Hank said, looking down at his shoes. He was in control, but barely. It was just past 1 P.M.

"Any word on arrangements?" I asked. As an ex-seminarian myself, I well remembered the custom of having Holy Cross seminarians "wake" the body of the recently deceased member of the community all night in hourly shifts until the funeral. The thought of two high-school boys staring for an hour, in the middle of the night, at the body of a young suicide gave me the willies.

"No word yet," said Hank. "Because Jimmy wasn't professed, the arrangements almost certainly will be handled by his parents—and they're not from the area. We won't have deal with wake duties—or even attending a funeral mass or burial. My guess is we'll have a memorial mass somewhere, probably Moreau's chapel. That'll be it. This will limit the impact on our guys."

"Except for the seniors who met him Friday night," said Brother Rufus, alluding to what we all were thinking. The seniors had gone over to St. Joe Hall last Friday for a soiree with the St. Joe Hall seminarians. They had entered the seminary as collegians and were expected to go on to novitiate the following year with the current seniors from Holy Cross. The Friday night soirees were supposed to be a monthly affair. The idea was to let the two groups get to know each other.

"Yep, that's a problem," said Father Aloysius Hopfensperger, known to the students as Father Hop, a play both on his name and his ever-present cane. He was the assistant rector and, unlike Hank, didn't mind his nickname. "They know who the guy is, and they'll spaz."

"True. And so will others, depending on how we handle it." added Hank. "Let's play this straight but low key. I'll make the announcement about Jimmy's death at Vespers. We'll pray for his soul, just as we do for any member of our order."

"But what about the seniors?" Father Hop reminded him.

"Right," Hank said slowly. "We can't exactly low-key them. Let's you and I meet with the seniors in the chapel, just before Vespers. We'll give them the news, some basic information, and give them a chance to ask questions, to share what they know about Jimmy, and whatnot."

"Are you going to mention suicide?" I asked.

"Yes," said Hank. "Well, probably. I think I have to tell the seniors. And if I tell the seniors, I'll have to tell everyone else. They'd find out anyway. It doesn't sound like there's any doubt about what happened, but I need to make sure."

"They're all going to want to know details," I said.

"Try not to get into it," said Hank. "Let 'em talk, but steer them away from motive and especially methods. Tell them you just don't know. Stress the impact on the family. Your main job is to listen, not lecture. In a way, it's easy."

"Yeah, easy," I said.

The stand-up meeting broke up, and we headed out. I caught up with Bernie Fox and said, "You were pretty quiet."

"So? What was there to say?" the Fox said.

"No questions? No words of wisdom?" I said.

"No. I have to prepare for class." And with that Mr. Warmth hurried up the stairs toward his room.

I went outside to have a smoke and stare at the lake.

"Those things are going to kill you," said Hank, coming up on my blind side.

"Easy for you to say," I said. "You've still got your scotch, which by the way would be mighty comforting at the moment."

"I hear you," Hank said "I'd like you to walk over to St. Joe Hall with me after dinner."

"Why? You think we're not depressed enough over here?"

"There's a wrinkle," he said. "We have to have a chat with Father Perry, the rector over at St. Joe Hall. He thinks he might have a free minute after seven."

Twilight

By the time dinner rolled around, none of the teachers wanted to talk about the suicide. It wasn't a topic of discussion at dinner among the students either. Hank was pleased but not surprised. When he talked to the seniors, he treated them as adults, enlisting their aid in steering any discussion in appropriate directions: compassion for Jimmy, his family, and his classmates at St. Joe Hall. Hank's theory was that getting the seniors on board, as older brothers in effect, would bring out the best in them. It worked. In the short free period after Vespers, the seniors had fanned out and answered inquiries about what Jimmy was like, confessed to not having any details to share about the suicide itself, and admitted sadly that the best they could would be to pray for Jimmy's soul and his family. At dinner, the seniors steered the conversation back to chatter about classes and ND's prospects in Saturday's football game against Wisconsin. the first to be coached by Ara Parseghian.

Hank buttonholed me after dinner, and we set off in the Indiana twilight down the cinder path toward St. Joe Hall.

"This must be the most walking you've done in a year," I said to Hank, who was known for driving everywhere, not a good thing considering his affection for Lady Scotch.

"Yeah, well, I need the air," he said. "I guess it went okay this afternoon. Considering ..."

"Thanks to you, Mr. Psychology."

"Yeah, there's that," Hank said, pausing to catch his breath. "Maybe we should have taken the car."

"Nah, the walk has got to be good for our health," I said, removing a Lucky from my shirt pocket and lighting up. It was a good excuse to stop. "All things considered, things went pretty well. But I heard something after Vespers that stopped me cold."

"What was that?"

"Something about Jimmy being one of 'the Fox's boys.' "

"Oh! Who said that?" Hank stopped in mid-stride.

"Dan Johnson, I think. It was said sotto voce when I had my

back turned, so I can't be sure."

"Dan Johnson? He's a sophomore. The seniors have met Jimmy. The juniors don't know him from Adam."

"Curious, isn't it."

"And unnerving."

"What did he mean by it?"

"Got me," I said. "I caught up with him as we were going in for dinner, but he denied saying it. Maybe I'm crazy."

"Maybe not," Hank said, starting to walk again. "Jimmy Parker was a graduate of Notre Dame High School."

"In Niles? So?"

"So ... that's where Bernie taught last year."

"Oh, yeah, right. So Bernie probably knows, er, knew, Jimmy."

"No probably about it. He was Jimmy's reference for getting into St. Joe Hall."

"Oh-oh. Bernie told you this?"

"Nope, Bernie hasn't said much more to me than he has to you. Joe Perry told me," Hank said. "And that's what he wants to talk about."

St. Joe Hall was a three-story yellow building, rather stodgy compared to its immediate neighbor, the curvaceous Moreau Seminary that had been completed just seven years earlier and housed the professed seminarians attending Notre Dame.

Father Perry's combined office and living quarters were on the first floor. He met us in his office and ushered us into the intimacy of his living quarters. He was a small man with a crewcut, a ruddy complexion, wire glasses, and an expression that would have been jovial under other circumstances. He looked at Hank and said, with more of a question than an accusation, "I thought you'd be coming alone."

"I know," Hank said, "but I have my reasons." And he proceeded to fill Father Perry in on why he had hired me.

"That solves one mystery," Father Perry said. "The word in the faculty lounge is that you were bent on tweaking Mother May-Eye."

"Well, there's that," Hank said. "But that's not why I brought him along tonight."

"I could really use a drink," Father Perry said. "You fellas want something."

"Scotch rocks for me," Hank said, without missing a beat. "And Bert will have … "

"A broken heart," I said. "Also known as a club soda."

"You're a teetotaler," Father Perry said, getting up to fetch the drinks. "Probably a good idea from what I've heard."

"Word gets around," I said.

"Word does that when you smack a monsignor upside the head," he said.

"Yeah, well, the next time I do that, I'd like to be sober enough to remember it."

"I love that joke," Hank said.

"You think it's a joke?" I asked with a straight face. "You mind if I smoke?"

"Mmm, your man is a poet," said Father Perry, handing us our drinks.

"And don't he know it," said Hank. "But then he teaches English."

"Hmm, if you're going to be proper English teacher, you should give up those cancer sticks and smoke a pipe."

"I tried," I said. "But it burned my mouth."

"Could be your pipe wasn't broken in," Father Perry said. "Could be your tobacco."

"Cherry Blend," I said.

He made a face. "Nasty shit. Here try some of this." He threw me a half a pouch of Iwan Ries Three-Star Blue. "I get it from a store on Wabash in the Chicago Loop. They've got six blends, all good. And get yourself a decent pipe. A good pipe and good tobacco—people will think you're a good teacher, even if you're not."

"It's all about the right props," said Hank.

"Spoken like a true liturgist," I said.

"Chasubles and chalices," Hank said.

"See, editors like me get off course thinking it's all about what you know and what you have to say."

"Naw, what you need is a good costume," Hank said, showing off his cincture, a cord that served as a belt around the priest's cassock.

Father Perry took a sip of his scotch rocks, let out a big sigh, and sunk into his easy chair. I sensed that I had passed some kind of test.

"Been a helluva day," he said and began to fill us in.

Nightfall

"Whew, that was hard to watch," I said.

"Joe's crying or his drinking?" Hank asked.

"Both, I guess." We started walking again down the asphalt road back to Holy Cross. The crickets were screaming.

"I've never seen Joe drink that much," Hank said. "He's more of a hobby drinker."

"Not a professional, like you and I?"

"You're retired, but yes, the liquor was a big part of it."

Father Perry didn't lose it for a good half hour. He went through most of his story in meticulous and chronological detail. He had become concerned when Jimmy Parker did not show up for mass or breakfast, both required of the new college seminarians. Jimmy was on his watch list because he seemed moody, which the rector attributed to homesickness. In his experience, there was always one who couldn't handle being away from Momma. Usually they didn't disappear. They just asked to go home. When Jimmy disappeared, the priest had a bad feeling. He went down to the cinder path along the lake, walked north to the swimming pier and then south to the opposite shore of the lake. Nothing. On a hunch, he doubled back and walked up the path toward the stations of the cross. At station fourteen, he found Jimmy Parker hanging from a tree behind a bench and opposite the life-sized crucifix.

As he told this, he spoke with control, the only symptom of his discomfort being his steady sips of scotch rocks. Jimmy was wearing the school clothes expected of the young seminarians, khaki pants and a blazer. He had used three ties to hang himself. Father Perry's first instinct was to take the body down, but he knew he shouldn't, and anyway, he couldn't manage by himself. Instead, he turned around and walk-raced back to the cinder path, south along the lake, past the grotto and to the ground floor of the administration building into the security office, where he reported his discovery to Chief Ziolkowski, the man in charge. The chief immediately called the coroner's office, buttonholed another officer, and the three of them drove to the scene, parking on the road to St. Joe Hall just above the stations path.

The priest was glad about this because his seminarians would be less likely to see any commotion as they headed along the lake to their classes on campus. At this point, Father Perry asked if he could help take the body down, but the chief told him that he would have to wait and get permission from the coroner.

In the interim, the priest went back to his office, thinking he should call Jimmy's parents. He was loath to do that, thought better of it, and called the principal of Notre Dame High School. As he had hoped, the principal knew the parents better than he did—which was not at all—and volunteered to break the unhappy news to them. Father Perry, still dry-eyed, looked at each of us and said the principal must be a saint.

By the time he came back to the scene, the coroner was there. After a rather perfunctory check of the surrounding area, the coroner shrugged and agreed to allow Father Perry to help get the body off the tree. The second security officer managed to climb up the tree and cut the ties while Joe Perry held the body.

At this point in the telling, the priest lost it. His eyes filled with tears, he started to blubber, and then we heard a sound that seemed to come from the bottom of the earth.

I had heard this sound once before, during the war just outside the German city of Ulm. We had been under artillery fire all afternoon. Soon after dark, I had been assigned to climb a telephone pole and cut the communication lines—for which I would be awarded a bronze star. Fair enough. I didn't like climbing a pole, much less doing it under fire. I was scared shitless. By the time I got back to my unit, I could hardly stand up. The gunfire had died down, and it was my turn to stand first watch. It hardly seemed fair, and I wasn't in shape to face it. A guy named Ralphie, who was what passed in combat as a best friend, volunteered to swap places with me. I was grateful. I thought I might have my act together in a couple of hours.

When I went to spell him two hours later, I found him dead—a clean shot right through the front of his helmet into his brain. I dropped to the ground and made a sound just like Joe Perry did. The guys in my unit didn't know what it was until three of my guys, M1s at the ready, found me heaving and sobbing while I held Ralphie's body.

"It wasn't the first time you looked death in the face," Hank noted.

"No, but by then I was numb to it—or so I thought," I said. "Maybe it was the guilt. Maybe it was that he was the guy I was closest to."

"But you got over it," Hank said.

"Yeah, sure, maybe, but I'll tell you one thing."

"What's that?"

"I never wore a helmet again." I stopped and fumbled for a cigarette.

Hank waited a bit and finally said. "It took Joe a while to get his legs back."

Yes it did. We waited, saying nothing. Finally, between snuffles, we learned that the coroner inspected the body and, in a businesslike manner, declared Jimmy dead, called the time of death less than two hours before—probably during mass, we guessed—and declared that Jimmy had died by suffocation, typical of suicides who failed to create enough drop to break their necks. "Tough way to go," the coroner said. "It might take twenty minutes to die when you're neck doesn't break."

It had taken Father Perry another fifteen minutes or so for his snuffling to abate, enough for him to get to the most important detail—at least for us.

"What do you make of the book?" Hank asked me, emphasizing "the book."

I said nothing for a minute or so. We had stopped to catch our breath before we climbed the driveway to the seminary parking lot.

Finally, I said, "That he found it and kept it, for one thing." The priest had found the book on the park bench, underneath Jimmy's body, thumbed through it—thinking it might reveal something about Jimmy's motive. And it did. He didn't say anything. He just opened it to the title page, which included a handwritten note, and handed it to Hank.

Jimmy,
Food for thought.
Father Fox

Hank and I had just looked at each other, then looked at Father Perry. He said nothing.

I asked him why he hadn't given the book to the coroner. He said he wasn't thinking. I got that, and I didn't ask why he had picked up the book in the first place. I would have picked it, paged through it, looking for a suicide note. I didn't say it then, but I slowed down once we reached the parking lot, lit another cigarette and told Hank that the book, signed by our own Father Fox, was as good as a suicide note.

"How so?" he wanted to know.

"*The Charioteer* by Mary Renault. Are you familiar with it?"

"No, not at all."

"It's set in England, about a young man coming to terms with his homosexuality. It's quite good. I picked it up because I liked her other novels, which are mostly related to ancient Greece."

"Oh," he said, pausing for a good ten seconds. "I guess that does say something about what the young man was struggling with. And given to him by Bernie, no less."

"Are you sure it was our Father Fox."

"Jimmy went to Notre Dame High School. Bernie taught there until last year," he paused again. "Yep, I'm sure. Dead sure."

Night

By the time Hank and got back to Holy Cross, it was pushing 10 p.m. The house had quieted down. We parted company in the lobby, Hank taking the stairs to the right and I taking the stairs to the left, to begin the climb up the three flights. On the top floor, I paused, out of breath, and aghast. The door of Bernie's room was covered with a collage, composed of beefcake images, pretty boys, and a large torso wearing a roman collar whose head was Queen Elizabeth. Clever enough. And mean.

I began pulling the pictures off of Bernie's door, marveling at how fast word was getting around.

Chapter 12

Wednesday, September 23, 1964

Wednesday dawned, hinting of mugginess to follow. Or maybe it wasn't so much the weather as the way Hank and I felt. At breakfast, I could see he was having trouble getting off the dime. On the way out, I told him about the collage, which helped his mood not at all. He hadn't talked to Bernie Fox about Jimmy, mumbled something about confronting him later that morning. By mid-afternoon, he still hadn't talked to him.

I decided to do what I could do. My schedule called for the usual classes and a meeting with the *CSC* editor in mid-afternoon. The *CSC* was the school's "newspaper," one of those hybrid things printed on slick newsletter paper but designed in three columns to mimic a newspaper. With my background in publishing, I had inherited the job of moderator for all three of the school publications: the *CSC*, the *Windhover* (yearbook), and the *Anchor* (literary magazine). The *CSC* was a publicity vehicle for the school, sent by the order's development department to donors and potential students. As such, it had always been harmless, but this year's editor had a genuine interest in journalism and wanted to do "real stories." Because he was a senior, I didn't expect him to know much about the collage on Father Fox's door. It smelled like an underclassman prank, and seniors had their own rooms well away from the sleeping dorms provided for the other three classes. Still, if he really wanted to be a journalist, he'd have his ear to the ground.

Not bad thinking on my part. Sean O'Hara, the editor, was the first to arrive at *The CSC* office, a converted storage room in the school building. Knowing the others would show up shortly, I got down to business

"Sean, I got in late last night and found a rather creative collage on Father Fox's door."

He didn't say anything, just grinned a little.

"Okay, fess up," I said. "What's going on?"

"Why would you think I know anything?"

"Because you look like the cat that ate the canary. Because you're a journalist—or want to be. Because you're an upperclassman. The sophomores and freshman probably don't have the chutzpah to do anything like this. So I'm thinking juniors or seniors. I doubt if it's seniors—you've got your own rooms—but I bet you know about it."

He paused, thought. "Okay, you're right. I wasn't involved."

When he paused some more, I said "Sean, what do you know? Out with it."

"Okay, here's what I can say. My sources tell me some of the guys wanted to send the Fox a message."

"About ... "

"I didn't see the collage," Sean said. "I heard it's obvious."

"You think Father Fox is a homosexual?"

"Some of the guys do. They're nervous about it."

"Why? What's the evidence?"

"He hangs out with Lois and Clark," Sean said.

"Who?"

"You know. Louis Dzinski and Tom Clark."

My ear to the ground was not as sensitive as I thought. Louis

Dzinski was a whisp of a kid, under five feet tall, and a little effeminate. Tom Clark was a big boy with horned-rim glasses, also on the effeminate side if you were looking for such things. Both were freshmen, and they hung out together. Apparently there was talk. Lois and Clark. The seminarians had a passion for nicknames. This one was unfortunate.

"What do you mean? Hangs out?" I asked, realizing too late that I had fallen into Sean's double entendre. He registered a gotcha grin, but I glared at him, and he thought better of pursuing it.

"They play cards together. And Lois and Clark both chose the Fox as their spiritual director."

"And ... "

"And what?"

"That's it?" I said, sensing with relief that he didn't know about Bernie's connection to Jimmy Parker.

"Well, he keeps talking in class about what the Nazis did to Jews, gypsies, and homosexuals."

"He's a history teacher," I said, a little impatiently. "The Nazis did things. I saw one of the camps."

"You did?" Sean said.

"Another time," I said. "It doesn't sound like you have much reason for doing what you did."

"Hey, I didn't do it. I'm just a reporter," Sean said. "I'm not the one who put those pictures on his door."

"Well, maybe," I said, "If you fancy yourself a reporter, you'll deal with facts. Nothing he's doing—playing bridge with two freshman, teaching sophomores about the persecution of Jews, gypsies, and homosexuals—constitutes misbehavior. Does it?"

He looked at me and hesitated. "No, I guess not."

"All you've got, as I understand it, is a suspicion that he's a homosexual, which you don't know for sure. Correct?"

He seemed to be looking at his shoes.

"Even if you did know for sure, which you don't, you shouldn't be spreading that information unless there's a really good reason or he gave you permission to do so."

"Why not? If it's true?"

"Look, your grade-school catechism taught you about gossip, including something called detraction. That's the sin of harming someone by spreading true stories. Now if you know that he's harming students—that I want to know about. All you've got is that his freshman bridge partners really like him. Gosh, stop the presses."

"So you want me to do a story on this?"

"In your dreams," I said. "But keep your ear to the ground and let me know if you find out who put those pictures on Bernie's— hmm, Father Fox's door—or who's spreading rumors about him, or ..." I stopped.

"Or what?" Sean said.

"Or ... if you find out something else that I need to know about."

Smart kid. I wanted to smack him. Fortunately, another member of the staff arrived and we turned our attention to a story about the school's presidential straw poll. Lyndon Johnson had beaten Barry Goldwater in a landslide.

Late Afternoon

After the meeting, I gave Eli a call. He was busy but invited me to his house the following evening for a barbecue.

Then I went on a hunt for Hank and found him in the faculty lounge, having a scotch. He had confronted Bernie Fox finally and, as expected, hadn't gotten much satisfaction. Bernie did admit admitting knowing Jimmy Parker, giving him The Charioteer, signing it as Father Perry had reported to us, and little else. He denied doing anything inappropriate with the boy and clammed up.

Hank was at a loss. I had nothing to add and changed the subject. "Have you heard from Joe Perry?"

"About an hour ago. He's planning a memorial service, not sure when yet, mainly for the folks at St. Joe Hall. But I'll send the seniors over. They had at least a nodding acquaintance with Jimmy."

"No wake or anything?"

"Not here," Hank said. "Jimmy was from Chicago, and his body will be released by the coroner to the family, maybe tomorrow, presumably after formally ruling that his death was a suicide. Good thing our guys won't have to do the all-night wake. It's spooky enough when they have to sit up with one of our old farts, but imagine them staring for a half-hour at the body of a classmate."

"I assume he's getting a regular funeral, with a mass and everything," I said.

"Depends on the bishop, but I haven't heard of anyone refusing a Catholic funeral and burial to a suicide in years. Vatican II finished off the practice, may it rest in peace. However, I will tell you, that just to be sure, Joe called the provincial, who called the chancery in Chicago. So, yes, they'll be having a funeral mass for Jimmy in his home parish, and he'll get a Catholic burial. If Jimmy had been a professed member of the community, we'd bury him out back in the cemetery you pass every night on the way to your Fatima shrine."

"You know I don't do that."

"Maybe you should," he said, taking another pull on his scotch.

"And maybe you should drink Kool-Aid instead of scotch," I said.

"How do you know this isn't Kool-Aid?" he said, not missing a beat. "And I'm just trying to keep a clear head without sacrificing my image as Papa Hemingway."

"Something's clear, and it's not your head," I said. "Too clear for Kool-Aid."

"Wanna check?" he said, holding up his glass and rattling the ice.

"Your father was a demon," I said.

"At least he wasn't a Protestant," Hank said.

"You don't even believe that, but thank you for reminding me I need a meeting."

"Suit yourself," Hank said. "I think I'll have another glass of Kool-Aid."

I liked Hank. He was the closest man I could call a best friend, but he wasn't always good for my sobriety. The AA meeting was at 7 P.M. in nearby Little Flower Church. I looked at my watch. It was pushing five Dinner was at six, which wouldn't leave me enough time to make the meeting unless I left early. I needed a meeting and would make other arrangements for dinner.

I went upstairs to grab another pack of smokes, in self-defense if nothing else. It was an unwritten rule that AA members substitute nicotine and caffeine for the alcohol they had forsworn. Meetings that allowed smoking were conducted in conditions that nowadays would set off smoke alarms. Meetings that didn't permit smoking were small. Very small.

After getting my valuables, I set off along St. Mary's Lake toward the Huddle. I was addicted, among other things, to their hamburgers. Flat little things on soft buns with the requisite mustard, ketchup, onions and dill pickle. If I had the money, I'd order two, along with an order of fries covered with salt and a dollop of ketchup on the side. It wasn't especially healthy, but no one worried about such things.

The Huddle was the main campus hangout, with comfy nondescript surroundings and waitresses who had worked there for twenty years. On-campus students dropped in sometimes, mainly for Cokes, but the bulk of the business came from off-campus students who didn't have cafeteria passes. The waitresses knew most of them by name. I didn't frequent the place enough to merit that treatment, so they just called me "Hon."

Before buying my meal, I went to the counter at the north end of the room and bought a copy of the *Chicago Sun-Times* and a package of Hav-a-Tampa Jewels. I wanted to get off of cigarettes, but I had no intention of doing it cold turkey. I had tried a pipe, but the Cherry Blend tobacco I bought at first burnt the hell out of my mouth and the bitterness of the taste was directly proportional to the sweetness of the smell. Joe Perry's premium tobacco, on the other hand, was a different world entirely, but I had run out and hadn't had a chance to go to Chicago to buy more.

My meal was predictable but welcome. I finished off my Coke, went to the counter for a cup of coffee, came back and lit up a Jewel. Like any confirmed cigarette smoker, I inhaled. Still, it wasn't bad, and it had a wooden tip that I could chew on without getting tobacco in my teeth. If it weren't for the expense—they were cheap cigars but they were more expensive than cigarettes—I would switch today. That and the ridicule I'd get from the kids for lighting up bad cigars in class.

The meal and the smoke did wonders for my mood, even if it did nothing to help me resolve my Fox quandary. I headed back down the hill, toward the lake, the sem, and my Edsel.

Twilight

The speaker was a rough-looking character wearing a leather motorcycle jacket in spite of the heat in the room, sunglasses in spite of the dim light, and a ducktail hairdo in spite of a strange bald spot on the crown of his head. He had five years in the program and, theatrical get-up aside, sounded like it. Had I been wearing my standard school uniform—Harris Tweed jacket and rep tie—I would have made a stunning contrast to him. In deference to the muggy Indian summer, I had left the coat and tie at home and rolled up the sleeves of my pinpoint Oxford shirt. I still didn't look like I knew much about motorcycles, but I understood the man's story. His drinking—and related fisticuffs—had cost him a half-dozen jobs and two of his "old ladies." I was in the right place.

After the speaker finished, he opened the podium to others in the room. I opted to keep my mouth shut, which was my custom in any case. And tonight, my mind was preoccupied with the situation at the sem, and that wasn't something I wanted to get into from the podium.

For that matter, I realized I didn't want to get into the particulars, even with my sponsor, Rick Doogan, who happened to be at the meeting. Afterwards, he bummed a cigarette from me and asked how it was going.

"Life is good," I said. "I have my own bathroom."

"With a toilet?"

"And a shower."

"Thought you smelled better," he said, excusing himself to talk to another of his pigeons. Good old Rick, always building up a man's self-esteem.

His departure left me in my usual socially awkward position, trying to work up the courage to talk to someone or to just leave. I was opting for leaving when a thirty-ish woman came up to me and asked if I would like a hug.

"Um, yeah, sure," I said, trying to give her a pro-forma embrace while she hugged me like a long-lost friend.

"My name is Laura," she said.

"Bert," I said, giving her a lookover. Laura was middling height, with a wholesome housewifey look that one of my friends liked to describe as "juicy." She wasn't rode hard enough to be AA. "I didn't see you at the meeting."

"Across the hall. Al Anon," she said. "I don't usually come to this meeting, but I was the chair tonight."

"You must have some time in the program, then."

"Just a year," she said, laughing the way women do even when nothing is funny. "But I'm not shy about sharing my story, so I get asked to chair a lot of meetings."

"Well, I am. Shy about sharing my story, that is, and I have to work myself into a froth to speak up."

"You get into a froth much?" she said, laughing again.

"Not if I can help it," I said. "Froth pretty much got me here."

"Well, you do have a problem then," she said, laughing some more. I tried looking at her sundress to take my mind off her laughter. It was starting to work, so I stared some more.

"Maybe you need Al Anon."

"Um, yeah, maybe," I said after a while. "I'm not sure I qualify."

"Do you have family or friends whose drinking bothers you?" she asked, not laughing this time. That was a relief.

"I expect I could rustle up somebody," I said, thinking of Hank and his ubiquitous glass of scotch.

"Well, there you go," she said. "Why don't you try my regular meeting—Wednesdays, seven o'clock, at the First Methodist on Eddy Street.

"Okay, maybe," I said. "At least it's close."

"Do," she said. "Meantime, I've been invited to coffee with the group here, over at Walgreens on 20. Would you like to join us?"

"Can't. I have some papers to grade," I said, staring at her dress some more, wondering if I should go.

"Oh, you're a teacher," she said.

"At Holy Cross Seminary," I said.

"A priest?" she asked, the light going out of her face just a tad.

"Not hardly," I said. "I'm their first ever lay teacher. What's worse, I live there."

"Sounds like an experiment," she said, laughing.

"You have no idea," I said.

Chapter 13

Thursday, September 24, 1964

"Yow!" I exclaimed as I examined the strange-looking structure in the Bonpere's backyard.

"This thing looks like your marriage."

Eli barked a laugh. "Exactly. Made the outside all by my lonesome. Leah did the inside."

"Well, thank God for Leah," I said. The outside was definitely his. With its polyglot of old doors, corrugated steel, and plywood sections, the structure looked like something you'd find in the swamps of Louisiana, perhaps after a hurricane had destroyed all the permanent buildings. The inside was right out of *1,001 Arabian Nights*. It was a cozy riot of color, patterns, and soft material. Exotic pillows surrounded a low circular table, itself on a Persian rug. The four walls, with a tent-like opening in the front were hung with batik and paisley drapes.

This remarkable blend of wildness and domesticity was a sukkah, the centerpiece of the eight-day celebration of Sukkot that Eli, Leah, and their two children were in the midst of celebrating. The sukkah, Eli explained, evoked the temporary living quarters of the Israelites during their sojourn in the wilderness as well as the temporary shelters for harvest workers in biblical times. Sukkot was like most Jewish festivals a celebration of liberation but also a harvest bash. The Bonpere's sukkah was decorated with a cornucopia of Midwestern and Middle Eastern produce—pumpkins, squash, Indian corn, pomegranates, along with strings of figs and dates.

"You like it?" asked Leah.

I said yes, of course, adding that the blend of Bayou and Morocco was quite charming.

"Oh good, I'm so glad," said Leah. "But I confess that I miss the palm branches. In Morocco, we covered the roof with palm branches."

"Palm branches are hard to come by in northern Indiana," Eli added, as he spread some coals around the grill. "Leah has to settle for a centerpiece composed of her tropical houseplants."

"And don't forget the children's drawings," she said, pointing to the crayola and finger paint décor on the walls. "See, they all have palms. Yosi and Yehudah both remember palm branches from their visit to Israel ..."

"More likely from their visit to Disneyland," Eli mumbled.

"I heard that, Eli," Leah said. "Do you see any Disneyland rides on these pictures?"

"One of them sure looks like a picture of the Matterhorn," Eli said.

"That happens to be a portrait of you and your pointy little head," Leah said as she rattled the silverware onto the table.

Eli uncovered skewers of lamb kabobs, a trace of a grin on his face.

"How did you ever become a successful courtroom lawyer?" I said. "You're getting hammered."

"Fortunately, I never had to face Leah," Eli said. "Besides, we've worked out a system. I give her just enough grief to keep the Morroccan fire burning, and then I let her have the last word."

"Always?" I asked.

"Always," Eli said, removing the kabobs from the fire. "I'm just a guest inside her tent, and frankly I rather like it that way."

"Yeah," I said. "What's the reward?"

"That Moroccan fire I mentioned," he said, his eyes twinkling. "This life you see—it's because of her."

And a good life it seemed to me. Eli's house, set inside one of the better sections of the city, was less ostentatious than its neighbors on the outside but more comfortable, I guessed, on the inside. Because of Leah. She was born in Morocco to Jewish parents, who had immigrated to Chicago before the war. This would become Eli's good fortune.

Eli, born in Louisiana to Creole parents, had grown up in Chicago. His working-class parents had moved north during the depression in hopes of finding work. They settled into the Lawndale neighborhood on the West Side of Chicago. Eli's father found janitorial work in a factory, squirreled away enough money to send his only child to Blessed Sacrament Elementary School, St. Ignatius High School, and Loyola University. In spite of his impeccable Jesuit Education, Eli had a lifelong attraction to Judaism, owing he said to the influence of a particular Jewish storekeeper in his Lawndale neighborhood. Abe, owner of a Jewish deli, was a kindly olive-skinned man who seemed to take a natural interest in children of all races and creeds. They in turn gravitated to the store, both for its array of candy and snack food and the good-natured ribbing by the man with the funny accent and a memory for every child's name. The store was closed on Saturdays, which the adults but not the children had gotten used to. When the store occasionally closed on other days of the week, the children were bereft and wanted to know why. Only then did Abe mention his religion. The store was closed, he explained, because it was Passover, or Sukkot, or the High Holy Days and he could not work. They all asked questions, but young Eli asked far more than the others.

One time, young Eli came to the store with his mother and, noticing the sign that said the store would be closed for two days, began drilling Abe with questions. Eli's mother was embarrassed and tried to shush him, but Abe admitted to her that he was flattered by the questions and admired the boy's intelligence. In fact, he wondered out loud with uncharacteristic shyness, if Eli and his mother would be interested in coming to his house the next afternoon for a little show-and-tell. The holiday was Sukkot, which was a particularly fun festival. Eli's mother was reluctant, but Eli begged until she relented and agreed to take him for a visit after school the next day.

To young Eli, Abe's sukkah was magical, a tree house on the ground. Eli asked a dozen questions, which embarrassed his mother and charmed old Abe. Eli never forgot that visit, citing it as the dawning of his interest in Judaism.

When WWII came around, Eli would have served a military hitch in 1944 if he hadn't been a Negro. Knowing through the grapevine that Negroes were taken for service only grudgingly and then mostly deployed for the duration to places like Alabama, Eli opted for college. His draft board was all too happy to accommodate. Feeling only the slightest bit guilty, Eli got his sociology degree from Loyola University and then went to Marshall for a law degree. He began studying Judaism casually during college and got more serious during law school as he discovered that Judaism was, at least in part, a legal system. By the time he passed the bar, he was praying regularly at an Orthodox synagogue. Two years later, he began taking a conversion course. Three years after that, Eliyahu Ben-Avraham (nee Eliyahu Bonpere) was fully converted to Judaism and living in Rogers Park within walking distance of a Sephardi synagogue.

In 1956, he provided some legal help to a visitor to the synagogue, a Moroccan Jew who had escaped with his family from Paris in 1942 and was living in South Bend, Indiana. The man's name was Joe—or more precisely Yosef. He had four daughters, one of whom was Leah.

Eli's legal help was invaluable, his Louisiana French hardly understandable, and his attentions to Leah proper but insistent, especially considering the 100 miles between the north side of Chicago and South Bend. In the end, Avraham came to see this Eliyahu Ben-Avraham, in spite of his exotic background, as a good match for his daughter. Eli's willingness to move to South Bend sealed the deal, especially with Leah's mother.

This was the seventh sukkot that Eli and Leah had celebrated together.

Considering that Sukkot was a religious festival, the meal was blessedly light on religious fru-fru, except for an after-dinner blessing in Hebrew that seemed to go on forever. The children were part of the meal, and I guessed that no one could get away with too much piety while the little ones were carrying on.

The food was exotic and tasty. Leah started with tabouleh, a blend of mostly parsley and bulghur that she called a "salad" but which bore little resemblance to the iceberg lettuce creations I was used to. When we had finished this off, she brought out bowls of soup.

"This is delicious," I said, after trying a couple of spoonfuls. "I've never had anything like it."

"Well, I'm not surprised," said Eli with a chuckle. "For lack of a better description, it's Moroccan seafood gumbo. I tried to get Leah to do a kosher version of the gumbo I grew up with, but she insisted on adding lentils, cinnamon, coriander, and who knows what all Moroccan spices."

"Well, it works," I said, sopping up the soup with pita bread.

"And look, there's some okra right here."

"*Laissez les bontemps roulez*," said Leah, with a twisted grin and in Morrocan French.

Eli's kabobs were terrific, though I allowed as how the spicing seemed to come from a different place than that of the soup.

Um-uh," grunted Eli. "They were marinated in what amounts to Louisiana crab boil. I can't have the crab, but there's no reason I can't have the spice. Especially, when I'm doing the grilling."

"I thought I tasted a hint of cinnamon though," I said.

"You know, I did too," said Eli. "I think my lovely wife frenched the marinade."

"Just a little," laughed Leah. "To tie it together with my dishes."

We finished with fruit cocktail, which combined dates, bananas, and grapes. After the closing prayer, Leah began to clear the table—the kids had long disappeared into the house—and Eli brought out a couple of fat cigars.

"Don't ask me what these are," he said. "I only smoke these things in the middle days of sukkot. With the barbecue and this delicious cigar smoke, I'm reminding myself of the Temple. Anyway, every year I go into Iwan Ries and ask for their most expensive cigars. When they tell me what they cost, I ask for an alternative that costs half that. These are a bit less expensive but still good."

"This is the second time I've heard about Iwan Ries," I said, lighting up my cigar and inhaling deeply. I coughed—and thought I had died and gone to heaven.

"You aren't supposed to inhale these things," Eli said. "They are food. They have a taste."

"Sorry," I said. "I have gone three hours without a cigarette."

"You didn't have to," Eli said, blowing a cloud of smoke into the air.

"I know," I said. "But you served grape juice when I happen to know you dearly love wine and liquor. If you can do that for me, I can resist blowing cigarette smoke in your family's face."

"So how's it going," Eli asked, "as a seminary spy?"

"There are complications," I admitted, filling him in on some of the details of the suicide. "Let me ask you a legal and ethical question."

"I'm your attorney," he said. "Ask away."

"Okay, but I'm going to keep this hypothetical for now," I said. "Suppose someone took some, uh, evidence from a, uh ..."

"Crime scene?"

"Well, that's the thing. It's not an exactly a crime scene. There's a pro-forma investigation, but the police are pretty sure they are looking at a suicide."

"And this someone took something before the police arrive for a keepsake? Or to protect someone?"

"Either. Let's say to protect someone."

"The murderer?"

"No, almost surely not. But maybe the victim had a relationship with this person that, if known, would have led to further investigation by the police and complication and ..."

"Let me get this straight. Someone took something from a crime scene. You may not want to call it a crime scene, but if the police are investigating, it's a crime scene until they clear it. This someone didn't take this something to cover up a murder but to cover up an embarrassing relationship."

"That's about it."

"Well, as an attorney, I'd have to say it's wrong."

"Here's the moral complication," I said. "They didn't do it out of malice, in my hypothetical example, but to protect someone from gossip that might contaminate their own internal investigation of this person."

"You're making this up."

"I'm pleased that you think so."

"Well, it is an interesting dilemma," he said. "In Judaism, gossip is a big deal. We call it *lashon hora*, which means 'evil tongue.' In most cases, you can't even spread tales that are true if it it will injure the person. We go to great lengths to avoid *lashon hora*. There is a well known story that illustrates the issue.

"A man spreads gossip about a member of his community and realizes that in doing so he had damaged the man's reputation. He regrets what he did and goes to a great rabbi and asks how he can make amends for his misdeed.

" 'Here's how,' the rabbi tells him. 'I want you to take a pillow, cut it open, and shake it in the wind until all the feathers escape.'

"The man was puzzled, but he did as he was told and went back to the rabbi. 'I don't see how this exercise makes amends for my misdeed,' the man said.

" 'Oh, but you're not done,' the rabbi said. 'Now you must put all the feathers back in the pillow.'

" 'But that's impossible,' the man said.

" 'Ah, now you see,' said the rabbi."

"So you shouldn't spread tales about another person," I said, "even if the tales are true."

"Unless ... " said Eli.

"Doing so would protect innocent people from serious harm."

"... in which case tale-bearing is required by Torah. Moreover, not spreading the tale in such instances could put a person in legal jeopardy for tampering with a crime scene and obstructing justice," Eli said. "Good thing this is just a hypothetical."

"Good thing."

Chapter 14

Friday, September 25, 1964

The next day I went through the motions during class. I was talking about diagramming sentences in one class and Mark Twain in another, but I was thinking about tonight's memorial service for Jimmy Parker and whether I should attend Jimmy Parker's funeral in Chicago.

By lunchtime, we got the word that the coroner had ruled Jimmy's death a suicide, that his body had been released to the family, and that plans for a Monday funeral were going forward.

The plans for the memorial service had been worked out, knowing that only the seminarians from St. Joe Hall knew him and those not very well. It was to be just a mass, with a homily by Father Perry, and a simple gathering afterward. The Friday night soiree at Moreau was legendary because beer was served, the better to oil the relationship between the seminarians from Moreau and St. Joe Hall. It was the main way they got to know each other. On this night, in deference to the occasion and the fact that the seniors from Holy Cross were invited, beer was not in order. Hank suggested to the faculty that we attend if we were available, both out of respect and to keep an eye on the seniors—and, for my part, Bernie Fox.

The funeral in Chicago was another matter. Jimmy's parents had asked Bernie Fox to give a eulogy at the wake, and I wanted to see how that went. However, no one else from HCS was going, and I didn't know Jimmy from Adam. My appearance there would have raised questions in some quarters.

After the sems broke for recreation in the afternoon, I found Hank in the faculty lounge and asked his advice.

"Don't go," Hank said. "People—Bernie to name the most important—will wonder why the hell you showed up."

"Frankly, that's a relief," I said, "but we can use some eyes and ears in the church. I'd like to know what he says in the homily and how he behaves."

"Joe Perry is going. I'll tell him to wear his strongest antenna, and we'll grill him when he gets back."

"Sounds good," I said, hoping Father Perry's antennae were as sensitive as his taste in tobacco.

"Anything new to report?" Hank asked.

I told him what Sean O'Hara had to say about the collage on Bernie's door.

"Hmm, so we've got a tale-bearing problem," he said. "Is the tale true, or is it just a tale? That's what you're here to find out."

"Sorry," I said. "I've got nothing solid to go on. And the problem is—if the tale isn't true, we'll never have anything solid to go on."

"I can't believe I understood that," said Hank, getting up to pour himself another scotch. "I must need another drink."

"What's the next step?"

"Oh, keep your ears on and your eyes open," Hank said, taking a good swallow. "See if you can find something solid. In the meantime, I'll hope you don't."

"Which will leave us in the dark. Did you study this kind of moral quagmire in Rome?"

"Probably, but I mostly remember the food and drink. Got anything else to tell me."

"Before one of my classes, I overheard one of the sophomores referring to one of their teachers as 'BJ.' "

He stopped. "Okay, BJ? Gotta be ..."

"Bernard J. Fox," I said.

"Okay, so."

I looked at him. "BJ—think about it."

Another pause. "Oh, Christ. If this gets around ..."

"And it will."

"Do what you can to keep a lid on it."

"Sure, right. One more thing. A more entertaining tidbit for you. I went down to the locker room yesterday and found one of the freshman parading around in white cassock."

"So ... he fancies himself as a missionary?"

"More like the pope," I said.

Hank laughed. "Ambitious little bugger. Usually you don't see guys in that kind of getup until theology school."

"Not only that, one of the sophomores was following him around in a monsignori cassock and lace surplice."

"Okay, that may be a red flag," Hank said with a straight face. "Keep your eyes open. If the monsignor starts walking around in a Gypsy Rose Lee outfit, let me know."

"And the pope ... ?"

"Never mess with the pope."

Chapter 15

Saturday, September 26, 1964

Yesterday's memorial service for Jimmy Parker went according to plan. It was low-key. A mass, a homily, and a gathering. The absence of beer helped, as did almost everyone's unfamiliarity with Jimmy Parker. By all accounts, he was a loner. He kept to himself, caused no trouble, created no interest. After he died, the seminarians did their best to remember him. And couldn't. The seminarians from St. Joe Hall were left with a vague feeling of guilt. The seminarians from Holy Cross had nothing, except that icky feeling you get when someone you know—or are supposed to know—commits suicide.

Joe Perry gave a true homily, focusing on Scripture rather than personal remarks about the diseased. He focused on the Christian basics—the suffering of the Christ, his death, and his resurrection. Even so, the priest's voice halted in spots, where I imagined him thinking about Jimmy's body hanging across from the life-size crucifix in the woods.

My weekend turned out to be all about family. I was supposed to have Butch and Sissy all day Saturday, but I arranged to have the morning to myself in exchange for keeping the kids through the evening, when we were scheduled to have a movie and a soiree for those not going home to their families.

I picked them up, just in time to catch Notre Dame's first football game of the season on the radio. Hopes were high, though a little reserved in light of a truly terrible season the year before. Thus, some of the seminarians wanted to follow the game and some didn't care. Sissy went out to the ball diamond with a few who didn't care and got involved in a game of 16-inch softball, which didn't require gloves. I wasn't sure how this was going to work, but I found out later that Sissy became the pitcher for one side. I'm not sure how she managed this, but it made her the center of attention, something she was good at. I gathered she got the ball across the plate on occasion.

Butch and I went downstairs to the auditorium, where some of the guys were listening to the game. I've always had an intense interest in Notre Dame football, but I've never been able to sit and listen to the game. I had to be doing something else. Ditto for Butch and, as it turned out, several of the other guys. They commandeered the pool table, and Butch and I were stuck listening to the game. At half-time, Butch and I took a break and went outside where Dave Johnson, a junior, was readying the rowboat for action.

"That looks like fun," Butch said.

I wasn't sure if he thought it really looked like fun or whether he thought it had to be better than sitting on a folding chair, listening to the radio. Regardless, I had ulterior motives. Butch was a shy boy, and I thought it might be useful if he got to know one of the seminarians one-on-one. I wasn't sure if Dave was the right choice. He was a bit of a stranger in his own class, a loner himself who was obsessed with Australia. Apparently, he had spent his early childhood there, until his mother divorced his Australian father and moved back to the states. He always seemed to wear an Aussie ranger hat and affected an Australian accent.

"Hey, Dave!" I yelled, just before he got away from the pier.

"You mind taking Butch out for a spin? He's a little bored with the football game."

Dave didn't appear to be interested in the football game either. He just shrugged and maneuvered himself back to the pier. Butch clambered in. When he didn't appear to be donning his life jacket, I said. "Hey, Dave! You mind putting on your life jacket. Butch is going to feel like an idiot when I order him to wear his—and you're not wearing yours." I watched Butch cringe, his shoulders nearly disappearing into his ears.

Dave stopped rowing and, with a trace of grin, said, "No worries." He picked up a life jacket and put it on.

Butch followed suit.

I went back to the football game and listened to Notre Dame beat Wisconsin 31–6. A good omen, what with a new coach and all. By the time the game finished, it was time for the seminarians to clean up for dinner. Basically, this was free time, but some of them needed to shower and others needed to change into casual wear, which was a notch above jeans and dirty sweatshirts. This was Saturday, after all.

Butch and Sissy needed to clean up, and I had prepared for that. They had a change of clothes, and I had a room with a shower. Sissy wasn't supposed to be in anybody's room, but a father (the biological kind) had a waiver. It took me fifteen minutes to gather them up, climb the three flights of stairs, and decide who was going to shower first. Given that my recreational activity that afternoon consisted mostly of sitting on my rear end, I took a pass. Sissy agreed that she should go first, being both the oldest and prettiest. Butch just grunted.

While Sissy went to work in the bathroom, I had a chance to talk to Butch about his afternoon, particularly the time he spent with Dave Johnson. He was unusually talkative, perhaps because he couldn't figure out what else to do with me in my room.

"It was fun," he said. "I like being out on the lake."

"Even if you're not fishing?"

"Even if ... except we did fish, sort of. Dingo Dave likes to troll the shore, looking for goldfish. Then he tries to spear them."

"Ugh, does he ever get one?"

"He's pretty good at it. If you walk along the lake and see goldfish floating in the rocks, you can spear them. He let me have a go at it, but I didn't get anything. Still it was fun."

"This doesn't seem like you," I said. "Random fish killing. You're more of a catch-a-bluegill-for-dinner kind of guy,"

"Dingo Dave says he's doing a service," Butch said.

"That's the second time you called him Dingo Dave."

"The guys gave him the name. He talks like he's an Australian—calls me 'Mate' and all that. It's a little phony but kinda fun. Anyway, he says the lake used to be filled with bluegill, but the goldfish have crowded them out."

"True enough," I said. "I used to catch dozens of bluegills in the early morning off the swimming pier on St. Joe Lake. Now the gills are almost gone. So maybe Dingo Dave is right. Is this what you did all afternoon?"

"Much of it," Butch said. "But first he took me to the island on the other side of the lake and showed me his camp."

"Camp?"

"That's what he called it," Butch said. "He built a cool shelter out of yew branches."

"You branches?"

"Yew branches, from a yew tree."

"Oh, y-e-w branches."

"Sorry, now y-o-u get it," Butch laughed. Butch was a sourpuss much of the time, but he liked to play with words. "There are a couple of y-e-w trees on the island, and Dingo Dave broke off some of the lower branches for his fort."

"Sounds cool," I said.

"It was," Butch said. "He had a way of cooking. Well, sort of. He has a Boy Scout cooking kit stashed away, so he can do some simple cooking."

"Surely, you can't get away with a campfire on the island."

"Naw." Butch looked at me like I was an idiot. "This is supposed to be a hideout. Dingo Dave doesn't want to call attention to himself."

I suppressed a laugh. The hat, the accent, the nickname were hardly the work of someone who wanted to hide in the bushes. He had made himself something of a mythical figure among the seminarians, who enjoyed following his aqua-antics and inventing stories about him. "So how does he cook?"

"He has a supply of half-full sterno cans," Butch said, "courtesy of the priest waiters. They use them to keep the coffee warm."

Yes, indeed. The myth of Dingo Dave was a community project. "Very smart," I allowed. "Sterno cans. No smoke. What's he cook?"

"Mostly teas and soups," Butch said. "He made me tomato soup, using little packages of ketchup and crackers that he swiped from the Huddle."

"Oka-ay," I said.

"And he makes tea," he said.

"Tea bags are easy enough to get, I assume."

"Yeah, but he's experimenting with making teas from things on the island," Butch said. "It's a survival thing."

"Ever the Boy Scout," I said. "What kind of tea?"

"Different plants. There's some sassafras on the island. He said you can make a tasty tea from the roots, but it takes a long time. For today, he suggested we try some pine needle tea."

EVIL SPEAKING

"And you did that?"

"Yes, but it was kind of funny. When he suggested pine needles, I got up and started grabbing needles from the y-e-w tree, thinking it was close enough to a pine and might be tasty."

"It's a conifer," I said, "but not a pine."

"Pine. Yew. I knew they were different, but I thought they were all related."

"Sure," I said. "Needles and all."

"But he stopped me cold," Butch said. "He said we couldn't make tea from the yew needles—they were poison."

"No kidding?"

"No kidding. He tried some last spring and got really sick. He wanted to blame the nun's cooking, but nobody else got sick like he did. He guessed it was the y-e-w tea, but he didn't know for sure until a couple of weeks ago."

"How'd he find out?"

"At the university library," Butch said. "He couldn't go there last year. It's the only change he likes. He hates the new teacher."

"Umm, that would be me."

"Oh, sorry." Butch said. "He didn't mention you. The other guy."

"Father Fox?"

"Yeah, that's him."

"*Hates* is a pretty strong word, especially because Dave doesn't have any classes with him."

"Yeah, maybe. He's just doesn't like some things about him."

"Like what?"

"Like he teaches history backwards."

"Like I said, he doesn't take history. So what's the deal?"

"He heard that he brought up concentration camps in Germany and made a big deal homosexuals in the camps."

"Well, there were," I said. "But there were mostly Jews, and some Gypsies too. Even some Christians. It was bad. Remember, I got a first hand look at some of it during the war."

"I guess. Maybe BJ mentioned ..."

I grimaced. The awkward nickname was already in play. "Don't call him that."

"That's what Dave calls him."

"Just don't." I didn't feel like explaining to him. "Just don't. Call him 'Father Fox'."

"So, okay," he looked at me, puzzled. "Anyway, Dave heard that he brought up the queers in Germany and ..."

"Don't use that word ..." I said, issuing a correction I thought I should make, even though I wasn't sure what word he should use. "Gay" hadn't come into use yet, and there wasn't much out there except insults and denial.

"Uh, okay. Homos ... uh sexuals," Butch stuttered. "It's getting hard to communicate here. Anyway, Dave didn't like it."

"He didn't think it was true," I offered.

"Dunno. Maybe he just didn't like, um, Father Fox, bringing it up."

By then, Sissy had finished her shower, dressed in her change of clothes, and had exited the bathroom with a demand: "Dad, where's your hair dryer?"

"Geez, Sissy," I said. "Do I look like I need a hair dryer?"

This amused my son no end. "Look, Sissy, Dad's got a 'butch'!"

Sure enough. Earlier in the week, I had gotten a short haircut from the house barber. Not a buzzcut, exactly, but short. It wasn't a great look for me. Nothing was, I thought. I had an unfortunate colic in front that made the flattop I had always wanted impossible. If I grew it out, I could comb it, sort of. "Sis," I said, "I'm afraid you're going to have to use the 'air' dryer."

"Ooh, good one, Dad," said Butch. We were back to bonding over puns. With that, Butch got up, went into the bathroom for his shower.

Meanwhile, Sissy plunked down on my easy chair, folded her arms, glared at me, and didn't say a word. I really wanted to talk to her. Unlike Butch who had good information on one seminarian, Sissy would have a fix on a raft of them. But I was going to have to wait.

Fortunately, Butch finished his shower in world record time, and we went downstairs for dinner.

Seating on Sunday wasn't assigned, which meant there was a small commotion as the boys negotiated who was going to sit at Sissy's table—and somehow it did become "Sissy's table," even though she was the guest. Butch was another story. As soon as he saw Dingo Dave, he made a beeline for his table and sat next to him. I was expected to sit at the priest's table and couldn't hear the conversation, but Sissy's table was clearly the most animated.

The same scenario, more or less, developed after dinner when everyone assembled in the auditorium for the movie, *North by Northwest*, starring Cary Grant and Eva Marie Saint. This time, though, the seating was in rows, which meant there was a premium on who would get to sit next to Sissy. One of the boys tried to position Sissy for himself, with Sissy in the aisle seat and himself next to her. Sissy was having none of that and sat down on an inside seat so that she would have boys on either side of her, leaving it to the boys to figure out who would sit where. Calm for her, chaos for them. Right where she wanted them.

Butch, less socially skilled, sat next to Dingo Dave, who had taken an aisle seat.

Chapter 16

Sunday, September 27, 1964

Sunday dinner went better than I expected. Sarah had taken me aside last night, after I returned the kids, and invited me. It had been a family tradition, busted up by my misbehavior and forced emigration from the house. Sarah had kept her distance for months, interacting with me only as much as necessary, handling legalities and the logistics of allowing me to see Butch and Sissy. The only hint of a thaw had been the other day, in front of the library.

It was late afternoon. I sat in my room, lit up a Hav-a-Tampa Jewel, and bit down on the wooden tip. I knew I should check in with Hank, but I needed to think about my day, which had been a surprise. My expectations for the family gathering had ranged from disaster to nothing good. It wasn't horrible, better than a poke in the eye with a sharp stick, as my father was fond of saying. Sarah clearly had put some effort into the meal itself and into her conversation, which was not substantive but mainly facilitated my interaction with Butch and Sissy. They were uncomfortable at first, but Sarah shepherded the three of us onto safe terrain. They told Sarah about yesterday's activities, I told Sarah about my teaching activities (skipping the secret reason I was there), and they told me about their school activities. The last subject was a little ticklish, given that Sissy was still smarting about being forced to switch from St. Joe

EVIL SPEAKING

High to Adams High, but Sarah gave her "the look" and she dialed it back. The family interplay wasn't much, but it was better than we had managed in five years.

By the end of the meal, I realized Sarah had been acting more like a hostess than as my wife, which was a smart play on her part. It hinted more at a beginning than a return to the past, which was not where either of us needed to go.

With that thought in mind, I stubbed out my cigar and headed to the faculty lounge.

As I expected, I found Hank there, watching a football game and enjoying a glass of scotch. Brother Rufus was there as well, which confined our conversation to sports chatter. When the half ended, Brother Rufus excused himself, at least for the next fifteen minutes, and left the room. That gave us a chance to talk.

I filled him in on what I learned yesterday, mainly about Dingo Dave. I had nothing new to share, but I pointed out that I now had a "man on the inside" in the form of my son. Hank approved.

I also told him about my surprise Sunday dinner.

"You think you're getting back together?"

I wasn't sure whether Hank really cared or he was nervous about losing his inside man on the premises. "I have a hard time imagining that she'd let me back on the house," I said. "On the other hand, I'm thinking she may not want a divorce."

"She's a serious Catholic, right?"

"Oh yeah," I said. "To the point of rigid. Divorce may not be in her vocabulary."

"It's getting easier to get an annulment, you know," Hank said. "I could help."

"Maybe, but I doubt it," I said. "Of course, I'm at a disadvantage here because we haven't talked about it. At all."

"That would be a start."

With that, I changed the subject, asking if he had any news about the Jimmy Parker funeral.

"News to come, perhaps," Hank said. "Bernie Fox is giving the eulogy at the wake, which is tonight. That should be interesting. Joe Ferry will be there and will report back. He'll be attending the funeral and the gathering at the house afterward. I've asked him to keep his ears open."

"How's he doing? This had to be rough on him."

"You betcha," Hank said. "I spent the better part of the evening with him yesterday, and he got pretty sloshed."

"And you of course were sober as a judge." I probably shouldn't have said that.

"Years of practice, my man," he said, not appearing to take offense. "Anyway, it wasn't so much dealing with the grieving parents. That's always tough, but priests are used to being in the thick of grief. Some of it was that he felt responsible—*in loco parentis* and all of that. But for him, the worst of it—and some ways the best of it—was just finding Jimmy's body like that."

"The worst of it. I get that. But the best of it?"

"You were in the war," Hank said. "You saw death up close and personal. Joe and I were pretty sheltered in that respect. We went into the seminary in high school and came out as priests. Like I said, we've done a lot of funerals. We've sat with people in their grief. But seeing an eighteen-year-old, someone you were responsible for, hanging from a tree and facing a crucifix. That got to him. And taking the body down from the tree, that did him in. I dunno, maybe it's a good thing, somehow."

"Maybe," I said. "Somehow."

Chapter 17

Tuesday, September 29, 1964

After dinner, I drove Hank over to St. Joe Hall for a debriefing from Father Joe Perry on Jimmy Parker's funeral. Driving the equivalent of four blocks seemed silly, but Hank resisted the idea of walking and I didn't want to argue about it. On the way, Hank informed me that he had approached Bernie Fox to get his take on the funeral, but Bernie didn't want to talk about it. Surprise.

As soon as we walked into Father Perry's office, he flipped me another packet of Three-Star Blue. Apparently, his campaign to get me to trade in my cigarettes for a pipe was serious. I didn't mind. I had a chance to sample the tobacco and was impressed.

Then, without asking, Joe made Hank a scotch rocks and two club sodas with lime for himself and me. Hank just looked at him.

Father Perry answered Hank's implied question. "I'm exhausted," he said. "I need a decent night's sleep, and I find that the term nightcap is a misnomer. Doesn't help at all."

"Okay then," said Hank, taking a sip of scotch. "Whatcha got for us."

"More than I expected," said Father Perry. "Bernie gave the eulogy and led the rosary at the wake."

"Led the rosary," said Hank. "Doesn't sound like Bernie."

"It was a command performance," said Father Perry. "The family insisted. Actually, they wanted him to be preside over the Mass and to give the homily, but Bernie didn't want to do that. He offered to handle the wake instead."

"Why?" I asked.

"I asked Bernie about that," said Joe. "He wanted to do a eulogy instead of the homily because he wanted to talk about Jimmy rather than what he called the 'religious fru-fru' required in a homily."

"Religious fru-fru," I said.

"Now that sounds like the Bernie I know," said Hank.

"In any case, his eulogy wasn't religious fru-fru," said Father Perry. "It was intense—and impressive in its way. He was pretty blunt about 'certain people,' as he referred to them, who bullied Jimmy in high school."

"In high school? Not in college?"

"He didn't mention college, thank God."

"It sounds like Bernie was quite close to the young man," I said.

"Yes, but as his champion," said Father Perry. "At any rate, that's how Jimmy's parents view Bernie. They are definitely in his camp of admirers."

"You saw that?" I said.

"I heard that directly—from Jimmy's mother," Father Perry said. "She talked at some length about what happened at the high school last year. It seems three students, who had bothered Jimmy in previous years, were even worse as seniors. Much worse. They went from calling him names—she wouldn't or couldn't tell me what kind of names by the way—to playing pranks and finally to physical abuse."

"She didn't say he was a homosexual, then?" As soon as I said that, I thought it might have been a mistake. Hank and I knew the implications of the paperback, *The Charioteer*, that Jimmy had in his possession when he hung himself. It made it obvious, in our minds, that Jimmy was struggling with homosexuality.

Joe didn't miss a bit. "My guess is that she suspects, but she didn't say."

I looked at Hank. He made a slight movement with his hands, palms down, indicating "Don't worry about it. " He must have had a conversation with Father Perry that I didn't know about it. After a long pause, I asked, "Where does Bernie come into it?"

"According to Mrs. Parker, he went after the bullies—big time," Father Perry said. "When talking to them didn't work, he kept them after class. When that didn't work, he began sending them to the office almost every day. He tried talking to their parents."

"And ... "

"That was the beginning of big trouble," Joe said. "Mrs. Parker didn't know how it went for sure, but she pointed out that all three of the fathers are big wheels—one is a bank president, one is a corporate lawyer, and the third is a real estate developer. She guessed that Bernie wasn't able to talk to them—she thought he must have talked to the mothers. In any case, after he approached the families, stuff started to happen."

"Stuff?"

"Talk, especially about Bernie. This appears to have been when the accusations of, uh, impropriety started. In March of this year. Bernie wanted the principal to set up a meeting among the parents, himself, and the principal—but the parents refused."

"Outright refused?" I said.

"Yep," Father Perry said. "However, Mrs. Parker thinks they threatened the principal."

Hank interrupted. "I guess I should say something."

"I noticed you were strangely quiet," I said.

"What Joe is telling us, by way of Mrs. Parker, jives with what I had been told by our provincial."

"And you never told me, your esteemed detective," I said.

"I wanted you to start from a neutral point," he said, handing his glass to Father Perry for a refill. "At this point, I think it's pretty clear that Jimmy was the victim of some bullying. And while I can't be one-hundred percent sure that Bernie didn't engage in some, uh, sexual misbehavior, the evidence is more compelling that he went to bat for this kid and became himself the victim of bullying—in the form of vicious tale-bearing by some powerful people. That was the story I got from the provincial, and Joe's info supports it."

"So the provincial knew all along?" I asked.

"He had a strong suspicion," Hank said. "For one thing, the principal didn't buy the stories about Bernie. He stood by him, refused to fire him, or even stand him down. Do you think the provincial would have put Bernie in another boy's high school if he was a pederast? If he had any serious doubts, he would have set him up as chaplain of an old folks home or something like that."

"But you had enough doubts to hire me," I said.

"Due diligence, that's all," Hank said. "Besides, even if Bernie is innocent, which we think he is, we still have a problem."

That we did.

Chapter 18

Friday, October 2, 1964

    I didn't get wind of the depth of the problem until Friday night, after I followed the sounds of the Notre Dame Victory March to the pep rally for the first home game. We'd be playing Purdue, our interstate rival. I had no intention of getting caught up in the sweaty cattle drive into the old field house, but the Irish Marching Band was the pied piper and we were the rats. I, at least, had the strength to remain on the periphery—but I did not doubt the attraction and enjoyed being on the edge.

    I waited outside of the Huddle, my arms folded enjoying the sound of the band and the students mooing in the herd of sweating bodies entering the field house. Two seminarians, engrossed in conversation, passed right in front of me without seeing me. I had that capacity sometimes. All I could make out as they passed was "BJ and the boys." At that point, I should have known.

    When the flow of students entering the field house diminished to a trickle, I headed over to the library. I didn't expect my wife to be there, but tonight it would be quiet but not isolated. My kind of place.

    By the time I got back to HCS, it was pushing 10 P.M. The house was quieting down. The lobby was empty. I was tired and began the trudge up three flights of stairs. On the top floor, I paused, out of breath, and lost more oxygen. The door of Bernie's room was covered with a collage, similar to the first one I had seen. In th middle of this one was a giant "BJ" composed of two separate letters like a ransom note.

Yes, we had a problem.

Chapter 19

Saturday, October 3, 1964

I had a chance to talk with Hank after breakfast. We decided to meet in his office. It wasn't ideal, but the faculty lounge was occupied. The seminarians were busy doing their Saturday chores, which included cleaning faculty rooms. Because few wanted to wander around Notre Dame campus or go into South Bend—it was game day and you faced crowds or traffic wherever you went—whatever faculty remained here spilled into the lounge. Even though it was a gorgeous fall morning, Hank was averse to walking around the lake, which had its own traffic problem, and we wound up in his office.

He sat quietly while I filled him about the second collage on Bernie's door.

"That's bad," he said shortly after I finished. "Especially the BJ thing."

"I don't get it," I said. "His middle name begins with J, but do our kids even know that? Even if they do, BJ is a common enough nickname. This shouldn't be a big deal."

"Shouldn't be, but it is. And yes, Bernie's middle name is John, something we haven't publicized—precisely because he picked up the BJ moniker last year at Niles, soon after the noise about him being a molester began. Our kids are relatively innocent, but the Niles crowd knew exactly why—wink, wink—they were using it."

"I know that," I said. "But it's just so lame. You'd think it would blow over."

"Pardon the expression," said Hank.

"Geez, I can't believe I missed that."

"The problem is that it's part of his story now, however untrue," said Hank. "We'll have to tamp it down somehow."

"The kids have nicknames for everybody. You're Father Grease. I'm Bigfoot. Bernie already has a nickname in circulation—the Fox. How can we stop them from using another?"

"This is different. The other names are affectionate."

" 'Father Grease' " is affectionate?"

"It's obvious shorthand—and it wasn't invented here. I've lived with it all of my life. At least these guys are calling me *Father* Grease."

"So we could insist that nicknames for the faculty have "Father"?

"Or Mister," Hank reminded me.

"Mister Bigfoot. It does have a ring to it."

"As does 'Father BJ,' which is where it might go. Let's try another tack. Nicknames are a two-edged sword. As you said, nicknames can be a sign of affection. They can also be a sign of hostility, especially if the victim doesn't like the name and people keep using it. They can be mean, a kind of bullying, which surely is what is going on here. Our job is to train these boys to be good men, and this is really out of bounds."

"Understood," I said. "Do we know that Bernie hates the nickname."

"You're thinking he might like it?"

"Maybe he's indifferent," I said. "He's a tough guy. Sticks and stones and all that."

"Well, let's act like he hates it—or like it hurts him, which it surely does. How can we put the kibosh on its use?"

"I don't know about putting the kibosh on it, but the junior and senior monitors have a lot of influence, at least on the underclassmen."

"Great idea," Hank said. "To be honest, I think this will work with the freshman and sophomores. I'll talk with them. But what about the juniors and seniors?"

"Talk with them yourself, as a group, maybe in one of their classes. The seniors responded well to the Jimmy Parker when you treated them like grownups. Try that again."

"I like it," he said. "Do you have any influence with any of the juniors?"

"Uh. maybe." The junior that came to mind was Dingo Dave.

Afternoon

I wasn't supposed to have Butch and Sissy this weekend, but it was Notre Dame's first home game and the seminarians were graced to sit five or six in a batch on folding chairs at the top of the stadium. Hank saw no reason why Butch and Sissy shouldn't be allowed to join them "as honorary seminarians." The fact that Sissy was included amused him. The radical.

Sarah okayed the kids' attendance at the football game, but insisted they skip the soiree in the evening. She had other plans, which she probably was making up while we were gone.

Sissy was impressed with the opening ceremonies. Purdue's marching band usually was impressive, even when it's football team was not. The band was twice the size of Notre Dame's, and it's bass drum was the biggest in the world or so the university boasted. During the opening ceremonies, the tuba players had to make a deep bow and one of them fell over. To cover the mistake, the other tuba players followed suit. And so did their football team, which lost to the Fighting Irish 34–15. Notre Dame, which had won only two games the previous year, looked pretty good. Excitement was in the air.

Evening

After I returned Sissy and Butch to their mother, I thought about going to a meeting. However, the seminary schedule called for a soiree and a showing of *The Caine Mutiny*. The staff made a point of selecting first-class fare, and I thought I might as well take in the movie.

A couple of the other teachers besides me were there, but Father Fox was not among them. I didn't expect that he would be. I decided the pre-movie festivities would be a good time to socialize with Dingo Dave. As luck would have it, he hadn't arrived yet, probably to avoid the pre-movie socialization. His brother was there, not doing anything except sipping on a Pepsi.

"I heard you had a little dust-up with Father Fox," I said as I walked up to him. I was still a little weak on small talk.

He grinned.

"Tell me about it," I said.

"Aww, he brought up the holocaust again," he said.

"He *is* a history teacher."

"Backwards history," he said, "which is weird enough. Plus, he's stuck on the World War Two thing, especially the Nazis."

"And you think that's weird?"

"No, not that so much. But he keeps bringing up homosexuals, how the Nazis tried to exterminate them."

"He didn't bring up the six million Jews?"

"He did, but it seemed more like an afterthought to me," he said. "He seemed more interested in the non-Jewish victims."

"Like Christians, gypsies, and ..."

"Homosexuals."

"You're really bugged by the homosexual thing," I said.

"Well, yeah, because he doesn't have it right and I told him so."

"In class?"

"Yeah."

"And how did he react?"

"He told me to go to the library and look it up."

"And did you?"

"I didn't need to," he said. "I wasn't challenging his facts. I was challenging his emphasis."

"Point taken," I said. "But you could still go the library and find out the facts, part of which would be data about numbers killed, methods, the story behind the story."

"But I already know that."

"You think you know that, but you don't have your facts and sources lined up. Father Fox is just trying to be a good teacher. If you had challenged me like that, I might have tried to take your head off instead of sending you to the library."

"You wouldn't have."

"There were days when I would have ..."

"Oh," he looked at me and I wondered how much he knew. Then, his voice dropped. "You think I was wrong."

"You might have a point, but you might have made it another way. Like in an essay."

"BJ never ..."

"Don't call him that."

"Why, it's ..."

My voice rose. "You know why. Don't call him that."

"Okay, okay, the Fox ...." He paused and looked at me for permission. "The Fox never gives us any assignments like that. He just lectures us."

"Except when he sends you to the library."

I said nothing.

"Some guys asked me why I couldn't be more like Father Fox, who never assigns any written work."

"That's dumb, and they're lazy," I said.

"Still, you shouldn't have tried to embarrass your teacher in class," I said. "That's not too smart on your part. Everybody thinks you hate Father Fox."

"Yeah, maybe," he said. "Anyway, I don't hate him. I just think he's a lousy teacher, and they should get rid of him."

"Get rid of him?" I repeated.

"Yeah, you know. Can him. Send him to a parish or something."

"Have you told anyone else that?"

"A couple of people. Why?"

"I'll tell you what. Since you like assignments, go look up *discreet* in the dictionary."

"Funny," he said and walked away.

His brother arrived just in time for the movie to begin. I was able to catch him before he disappeared, which he was likely to do.

"Dave, we have a problem, and you may be able to help."

"Yeah?"

I explained that a problem nickname for Father Fox was circulating around the school.

Of course, he wanted to know why calling him "BJ" was a problem.

Of course, I didn't explain why it was a problem, beyond saying it was disrespectful.

Of course, he looked at me like I was from the moon.

"We need you to refer to him properly—and to use your influence, especially among your classmates."

He stared at me, seeing the moon. "Like they are going to follow my lead?"

He had a point. He was an unlikely leader—except, it occurred to me, if he was responsible for the latest collage, his classmates may already have been following his lead.

"Yes," I said, looking him in the eye.

"No worries, then," he said staring back at me

Chapter 20

Thursday, Oct 15, 1964

In some ways, there were huge developments in the past week. In other ways, I was treading water. Bernie Fox was still in place, still being talked about behind the scenes, still with no evidence of wrongdoing that any of us could pinpoint.

On the plus side, my wife and I were continuing to talk. I had been meeting her a couple times a week at the library, downstairs in the vending area for a cup of coffee or outside by the reflecting pool. She still wasn't smoking, which I was glad to see. I wished I could say the same. We had another Sunday dinner, where the conversation was less strained and subject to occasional bits of family banter. If I had experienced this in the last ten years, I would have called it "normal." It wasn't normal for me; it was completely unfamiliar territory.

On the minus side, there was the business about getting nowhere with the Bernie Fox situation. I decided to check in with Eli.

When I arrived at his office, Trudy was at her seated sentry position, and again I asked for "Mr. Bonpere."

Again she said, "Who?"

This time I nodded in the direction of his office. "The lawyer over there," I said. "I have an appointment."

Without a word, Trudy got up and led me to Eli's office.

Before she could leave, the room, Eli said, "Trudy, would you mind bringing us two black coffees?"

Trudy turned on her heels and went off to do his bidding. I like a woman who speaks volumes while not saying anything.

Eli turned his attention to me. "So, how goes it?"

I filled him in on my marriage developments.

"Are you getting back together?" he asked. He didn't look as happy as I might have expected.

"Depends on what you mean," I said. Until now, I had only talked about my relationship with Sarah at a couple of AA meetings, but it had helped sort out my thoughts. "Sarah is seriously Catholic. She'd rather cut off her arm than get a divorce. And she does, oh I don't know, love me. Maybe. At the same time ..." I paused.

"She's afraid to have you in her house."

"That," I said.

"You being a wife beater and all."

He might have been laughing at me, but I wasn't sure. "There you go with your way of words again."

"You can be married and not set up house together," he said. It bugged me that he suddenly seemed happy about this turn of events.

"Maybe." I paused. I had never faced the prospect quite so starkly. "But it's too soon to say that's how it will go. Right now, we're trying to get to know each other. For years, I didn't pay much attention to her or the kids, but now it's different."

"You're sober. You're no longer the man she threw out of the house."

"Well, I am the same man—or so my sponsor would insist. But I'm sober, at least for now, and that makes a difference."

"I should think."

"It's funny," I said. "Right now, we're circling each other. I can't tell if we're preparing for battle or, or ..."

"Courting," he said. Again he had named something I hadn't thought of. "Have you had sex yet?"

"Huh?"

"Have you had sex yet?"

"Well, that's a little personal," I said.

"As if the rest of our conversation is about national news. Have you had sex yet?"

"Well, no."

"Okay, you're courting."

Just then, Trudy brought in our coffee. This broke the conversation, much to my relief. After she left, I changed the subject. "I seem to be getting nowhere with my main task at Holy Cross."

"That being?"

"Finding out if Bernie Fox is a good guy or a creep."

"You don't know yet?"

"I know he's different. He's difficult. He's diffident."

"Spoken like a true English teacher," Eli said.

"Thanks."

"But you don't know if he's messing with the boys."

"No," I said. "There is still some gossip, but the evidence is that on his previous job he went to bat for a student who was being bullied. In doing so, he offended the parents of the bullies. The principal backed Bernie, and rumors started shortly after that."

"Suggesting ..."

"That the rumors are payback."

"Might there have been truth to the rumors?"

"Sure, but most of us don't think so."

"Most of us?"

"One of the brothers is not entirely on board."

"And his evidence is ..."

"Bias, as far as I can see."

"But you're convinced the priest is clean?"

"Let's just say I'm leaning that way."

"What are your reservations?"

"It's the suicide," I said.

"The hypothetical young man from the college seminary?"

I had talked to Eli by phone shortly after Jimmy Parker's death, mainly to consult with him about how to handle Joe Perry's discovery of the book, *The Charioteer*, signed by Bernie Fox, where Jimmy had hung himself. "The legal situation I spoke to you about resolved itself when the rector of St. Joe Hall turned the book over to the campus police, who returned it last week without comment to the parents. We haven't heard what the parents thought of it. However, the presence of the book suggests a) that the unfortunately not-hypothetical victim was struggling with homosexuality and b) that he was close to Bernie. That's discomfiting."

"Big word," Eli observed. "But the presence of the book still fits your explanation that Bernie might have been taking the boy's side. As if he was a counselor of sorts."

"Yes, and if the relationship was basically confessional, it explains why Bernie won't talk to anyone about it."

"Either that or he was messing with the boy."

"Or that."

After a pause, Eli asked, "How is the gossip situation?"

I told him about the second collage, the sudden appearance of Bernie's unfortunate nickname, Hank's plan to talk to the junior monitors and the seniors. "Our strategy is working," I said. "Things have toned down some. I talked to one of the freshman—one half of the team they call "Lois and Clark"—and he confirmed that he was being teased—his word—but he seemed to like the attention. Apparently, the teasing is this side of mean. He seemed fine with Bernie Fox."

"Part of his fan club?"

"Yeah, maybe," I said. "At any rate, he seem to like him well enough. I also talked to the newspaper editor, one of my spies. He thought most of the talk was high-school stuff."

"Most of it?"

"He said he heard that one of the sophomores—kid named Dan Johnson—really dislikes Father Fox, that they had a confrontation in class. Apparently, it got pretty tense. The seminarian took issue with his emphasis on the Nazi persecution of homosexuals."

"The student likes Nazis?"

"No, that doesn't seem to be it. I talked with him a few days ago and told him I heard he had a set-to with Father Fox. He admitted doing so and made no bones about arguing with Father Fox about the persecution of homosexuals."

"The young man doesn't think Hitler persecuted homosexuals?"

"It sounded more like a matter of emphasis," I said. "He thought the teacher should have been emphasizing Hitler's attempt to exterminate Jews instead of running on about homosexuals."

"The teacher didn't mention Jews?"

"I think he did—not enough for the kid's taste."

"Well, I have to say I'm sympathetic to that," Eli said. "So is the kid a judaeophile or a homophobe?"

"Big words," I said. "Don't know. Maybe both." I told him about what I heard on the playground, his mockery of an effeminate boy.

"Unfortunate," Eli said. "But I"m guessing not altogether unusual."

"Actually, it is." I filled him in on the theory of the seminary, whose very name refers to a greenhouse. Seminarians were fragile seedlings that needed protection. Holy Cross Seminary was no British boarding school, an institution that was notoriously dangerous for boys and generated the British propensity for profanity that focused on sodomy. When I went to Holy Cross seminary in the early forties, it was seriously sheltered. Even under Hank's more open system, the old practices survived. There was more freedom and some interaction with girls, but seminarians still took showers in curtained cubbies, still changed clothes using a bathrobe in a choreography designed to show no private parts, still avoided using a urinal next to another boy (and the urinals already had dividers), and slept in open dorms that invited public disgrace for the young man heard masturbating. Priests still wore cassocks, were called Father (mostly), and were understood to be mentors and teachers—not friends—to the young men. The system tended to do what it was supposed to do—delay puberty. Guys could go four years without confronting their liking for girls—or boys. I remember teasing—even bullying—but none of it was related to homosexuality. This was a different year, but the difference seemed entirely related to the stories about Father Fox.

"Here's my question," Eli said, after hearing me out. "Given the talk about Father Fox, why didn't the congregation's head guy ..."

"The provincial?"

"The provincial ... give Bernie an assignment where he wasn't going to be around teenagers?"

"Good question," I said. "One that's been bugging me. Hank—the seminary superior who hired me—told me this week that the provincial believes in Bernie, that he believes the talk is being orchestrated by parents of the bullies in the high school where Bernie taught last year. He thinks the parents are bullies and doesn't want to give into them."

"There's something to be said for that," Eli said. "But it's a tough call."

"That's why Hank hired me," I said. "But I don't think I'm getting anywhere. I'm inclined to agree with the provincial, but ..."

"But it's still nagging at you."

"You're the lawyer," I said. "You know it's impossible to prove a negative."

"So what's your plan?"

"Well, I've got the juniors working on Shakespeare's *Much Ado About Nothing*, in which gossip plays a key role. We're getting into some good stuff."

"That's your plan?"

"Maybe we'll study the play backwards."

Chapter 21

Tuesday, October 27, 1964

Then it happened.

I had been feeling reasonably satisfied about our efforts to tamp down "Bernie talk," the more so because my *Much Ado About Nothing* project was working so well. Juniors liked the idea of rewriting Shakespeare into modern dialogue. I had selected bits that played up the gossip angle; each group worked up dialogue that was both funny and, in some cases, pointed right at themselves. I shouldn't have been so blase.

After lunch, Hank took me into his office and showed me a letter. Well, not exactly a letter. It was more like a ransom note, cobbled together with assorted letters from magazines and newspapers. It said:

FOXES ARE PREDATORS.
GET RID OF YOURS
BEFORE SOMEONE DOES IT FOR YOU.

I read it and searched for something to say. "Mmm, okay," I said finally. "This is not good. Have you shown it to Bernie yet?"

"No, but I will. And the provincial."

Chapter 22

Saturday, October 31, 1964

Fall. The color was almost gone from the trees. The air was crisp. And right on schedule, my throat had a tickle, suggesting a bout with bronchitis to come. Every spring and fall, as the seasons changed, I got a sore throat, which after a few days went to my chest and produced a brain-rattling dry cough and lingered until it mercifully broke into a wet phlegmy cough that sounded disgusting but was evidence of healing. Someday, maybe, I would quit smoking.

The good news was that Notre Dame was playing an away game—Navy in Philadelphia—which meant I didn't have to sit through a home game feeling like crap. They were on a roll, and I would have gone to a home game, even if I had to crawl out of a hospital bed.

The Bernie Fox problem lingered like a rat two-weeks-dead inside the walls of a house. Hank had talked to Bernie, and he shrugged it off.

"A crank," he had said. "Probably a student, who doesn't like my grading."

Bernie wouldn't say which student. We had to guess, but we had our suspicions. Hank assigned me to talk to the Johnson brothers—with discretion. Great.

In the meantime, Hank had gone to see the provincial, who suggested the time might have come to move Bernie Fox to a safer assignment. Hank told the provincial that Bernie would never sit for that. "He may have to," the provincial told Hank and said he needed to think about it over the weekend.

Between that and the throat tickle, I was not in a good mood. Against my better judgment, I decided to visit the infirmary upstairs in a separate section of the building where the seniors shared rooms rather than an open dormitory. The infirmary was overseen by one Sister Angela, who spoke English quite well. Her older and heftier colleagues in the kitchen spoke German, not even trying to speak English. Some of the students swore they could understand and speak English—and were probably spies for the administration.

I had to bite my tongue whenever I heard this. I did believe they understood more than they appeared to, if only because their order was not entirely or even mostly composed of German-speakers. Case in point: Sister Angela spoke good English with an ever-so-slight accent that I didn't recognize. She was nice enough, but the word from the students was that she wasn't much of nurse, her care consisting of Coricidin, throat swabbings with Mercurochrome, and a jigger of Terpin Hyrdrate for everything from colds to sprained ankles, at least according to the students.

Sure enough, as soon as told her my symptom, she made me open my mouth, say ah-h, and hit me with a long Q-tip loaded with Mercurochrome, a practice that was discontinued a few years ago because the supposed medicine had mercury in it. Probably why I can't remember things any more. While she was choking me with the Q-tip, she inquired as to how I liked teaching at the school. When I got my voice back, I mumbled something to the effect of "fine."

"A lot of changes," she said.

"That's what I'm told," I said.

"Changes can be difficult sometimes," she said.

"That's what I'm told," I said.

With that she gave me a wee dram of Terpin Hydrate, and a small envelope of Coricidins for the road. She said they might be helpful if my bronchitis blossomed into the real thing. I had no doubt that this was in the cards..

Late morning

I left, wondering what I should do next. I went outside on the lakeside, but it was too crisp to stay out long. I was about to go back inside when I saw Dingo Dave emerging from the boathouse door.

"Hey, Dave, I thought you would be out on the lake."

He laughed. "No worries, Mate. I would, but there's nawt much to do for a sacristan on Saturday, and it annoys my mates. I lie low until later in the morning." His Australian accent was annoying and bad.

"What's up at the boathouse?"

"No worries. It's my station for tonight's shindig. Whoy dontcha have a look."

I did. The place was in disarray, though I could see the makings of an obstacle course, a combination of tunnels, things hanging from the ceiling, and upturned boats.

"Loyk it?" he asked

"Looks like an obstacle course."

"Exactly, but it will be pitch black in here," he said. "Beside that, we're going to create a ramp down the stairs." He pointed to the stairs to the upper level. The boathouse was the lower level of building set into a steep bank. The upper floor was the spudhouse,

EVIL SPEAKING

which was all about peeling potatoes for a family of one hundred.

"Really," I said. "The stairs are steep. It looks dangerous."

"Oh, we'll have mattresses and such at the foot," he said. "But it will scare the hell out of them."

I thought it looked dangerous. "Seems a little extreme."

"It'll be the best haunted house ever."

"Scaring them is fine," I said. "Injuring them is not."

"No worries," he said. "We've just got the ramp, with mattresses on the landing. Then the obstacle course, mostly crawling, which is a nice touch, I think. The sissies will be out of their minds."

I thought of one Sissy who was not going to endure this. "Sissies?"

"Yeah, freshman, the little twerps."

"My son is a freshman," I said. "Is he a twerp? You two seem to do okay together."

He looked at me. "Is he coming? I'll look out for him."

"Why should you need to look out for him?" I said. "Tonight is supposed to be fun, not dangerous." I left, having decided against letting Sissy and Butch participate in the haunted house. In addition, I went off to tell Hank that he might want to issue a warning to the juniors. Dial it back, guys.

Afternoon

Then it was off to pick up Butch and Sissy, which I had been looking forward to. Until that tickle thing. Today, I just wanted to hole up. But ... stiff upper lip, I got in the Edsel and headed out.

When I got to the house, the kids weren't ready. In fact, they seemed to be resisting the outing. Sarah explained that Sissy had been invited to a costume party hosted by one of her friends—and she really wanted to go. Butch thought Halloween was borderline "stupid" and wanted to stay home and finish building his Heathkit radio. I saw an opportunity to be gracious, selfish, and a good parent all in one. I explained that I wasn't feeling well and would be grateful if we could drop the trip to the seminary, just this once. They were delighted.

Sarah suggested that I retire to the bedroom for a nap while she dropped Sissy off at her party and went grocery shopping. Butch was left at the house, happy to work on his Heathkit, alone.

After Sarah and Sissy left, I did retire to what had been our bedroom and stretched out on the bedspread. I wasn't sure what I felt, though I decided it had more to do with hope for the future than nostalgia for the past.

I turned on the bedside radio, tuned it to listen to Notre Dame playing Navy. No problems. I dozed off. By the time I woke up the score was 40–0.

My throat was sore, and my thoughts turned to the upcoming evening. As things turned out, I was glad that Sissy and Butch had better things to do than participate in the seminarians' Halloween activities.

Chapter 23

Sunday, November 1, 1964

Today was a Sunday and a Holy Day, All Saints Day. For all practical purposes, it was the day after Halloween. That's all anybody could talk about at breakfast.

At the priests' table, Bernie Fox pointed out that a couple of the boys looked a little worse for wear, specifically Michael Clark and Louis Dzinski. One had a black eye; the other had a bump on his head.

"Oh, Lois and Clark," snickered Brother Rufus.

At that, Bernie stood up, tossed his cloth napkin onto his eggs, scanned to his right and then to his left, glared at Hank, and said, "Things get out of hand when a member of the staff doesn't know how to behave."

Hank in turn glared at Brother Rufus. "He's right, Ruf. You're not exactly modeling Christian behavior."

Rufus said nothing, but his smirk said he wasn't repentant.

The news troubled me. I wondered if the two boys had been targeted. Bernie acted like he thought so.

After we recited the closing blessing, Hank took me aside and suggested I visit "my friend," Dingo Dave, about the condition of the two freshmen.

Before I did that, on a hunch, I went back to the automatic dishwasher, where I knew Michael Clark served an obedience. He was there, doing washing pots and pans. Sure enough, he had a bump on his head, easily seen on his short haircut.

"Nice bump," I said.

He turned and looked at me, "Yeah, I guess."

"Howja get it?"

"In the boathouse," he said. "They had me crawling at one point—and stuffed something cold and wet under my sweatshirt. Seaweed, I guess. Anyway, it was creepy. I tried to stand up and hit my head on something."

"How's your buddy, Louis?"

"Okay, but he got a black eye at the bottom of the ramp. They sent someone else down before he could get out of the way. Caught him with a foot, right under his eye. Nice shiner."

Was it accidental that the two boys with noticeable bruises were "Lois and Clark"? Hard to tell. Now to find out.

Even though it was Sunday—and a holy day—most of the other seminarians had obedience chores to do, however perfunctorily. Dingo Dave was a sacristan, which meant I should be able to find him in one of the chapels. I tried the main chapel first. Dave wasn't there, but the other sacristan told me to try the sister's chapel. I did. I found him in the adjacent sacristy. He had is back to me and didn't hear me coming. When I said, "Hi, Dave," he jumped and knocked over a bottle of altar wine.

"Jee-zus!"

"I'm not who you say that I am," I said with a straight face.

"What? Sorry. Shoot." He began wiping up the wine with something that looked like a handkerchief, probably a purificator.

"You've got a pretty good startle reflex," I said. "Good thing you caught that bottle before much wine was lost. I hope you don't get into trouble."

"Not unless someone thinks I drank this stuff instead of spilled it."

"I bet that never happens."

"No worries, never," Dave said, not entirely convincingly. "What's up?"

"A couple of things. First, the faculty noticed that several of the freshmen seemed a little banged up," I said. "Seems like the haunted house might have gotten a little rough. Didn't you get a warning from Father Grease to take it easy?"

"Father Hop did that. He came down to the locker room while we were getting ready. Kind of a drag."

"So what explains the bumps and bruises? Enough for the faculty to notice."

"Got me. We took it easy—easier anyway. We kept the slide—actually it was safer than having them come down stairs in the dark. And we kept the seaweed—other than that ..."

"Seaweed?"

"Okay, technically it wasn't seaweed. It was from the lake."

"And ..."

"We just put it down the back of their shirts. Cold, wet, and creepy—but it wasn't going to hurt anybody."

"Your idea, I bet."

"Sure, I'm the resident lake expert. Like I said, it wasn't going to hurt anybody."

"A couple of guys got something to show for it."

"Kid bumps his head. Another got banged up on the slide."

"I thought you had that covered."

"Like I told you yesterday, the stairs were covered with cardboard and we had mattresses at the base of the stairs," Dave said. "No one should have gotten hurt, but maybe they ran into each other."

"Well, that shouldn't have happened."

"No, it shouldn't have. Maybe we blew it once."

"For Louis Dzinski and Michael Clark, as I understand it."

"Lois and Clark," he said.

There it was again. "See that nickname suggests to me that those two are being picked on—and your haunted house might have been the perfect opportunity."

"Well, I don't know nothin' about that."

"You know enough to call them Lois and Clark."

With that, I turned and left him cleaning up the wine. I went the two floors up to my room and lit up a Lucky. My throat was killing me, and a cigarette was unlikely to help me on that score. On the other hand, I was nicotine starved and it would help there. To address the throat problem, I decided to visit the nurse. By the time I wound my way to the nurse's station, there were only two underclassmen ahead of me, both wanting attention for scrapes.

When it was my turn, I said, "We've got to stop meeting like this,"

Sister Angela was able to stifle her mirth long enough to swab my throat again. "If you stopped smoking, we probably wouldn't have to meet at all."

"That's what I'm told," I said.

"Don't worry, that's the last time I'll mention it," she said. "If you enjoy bronchitis that much, keep smoking. It's working."

I was tired of this subject already and went in another direction. "You've been busy this morning."

"Yes, indeed. I seemed to have experienced a run on bumps and bruises."

"Anything serious?"

"Not really," she said. "But the number of patients was a little disconcerting."

"The juniors and seniors put on a Haunted House for the underclassmen," I said. "They seemed to think it was the best ever."

"And apparently they have the marks to prove it," she said.

"It bears watching," I said.

"Yes, indeed."

She gave me a jigger of Turpin Hydrate and sent me on my way.

Chapter 24

Monday, November 2, 1964

Breakfast began an hour later than usual, thanks to the incomprehensible obligation for priests to say three masses instead of one and for the even less understandable reason for the seminarians to sit through three masses. Nevertheless, it was All Soul's Day, a dark day accompanied by black vestments in a catch-all memorial for the expired sinners who weren't counted among the "saints" and collectively remembered the day before. For most seminarians, it functioned as penance for the excesses of Halloween.

The seminarians filed into the refectory with something like relief, the ordeal of three masses having been accomplished, leaving them with a ravenous hunger. The exception was a sophomore, who after grace and the delivery of gluey oatmeal befitting the day, barked two octaves below a hiccup and propelled the remains of yesterday's supper into the face of the table captain, a senior unfamiliar with such indignities. The senior yelped, jumped, and knocked over his chair, and stared at the backside of the vomit rocket who was running from the room.

The dining room was abuzz.

Once he deciphered what was going on, Hank aka Father Grease rang the bell and announced that a) the victimized table should leave the room that b) everyone should pipe down and get back to business while c) he personally cleaned up the mess.

I thought the last was a nice touch, almost Franciscan, something he would surely regret once he started mopping up the vomit. However, my thoughts had outraced the events. Hank grabbed one of the priest-waiters and immediately went into supervisory mode, sending the young man out to fill up a mop bucket, bring it along with a roll of napkins, and then begin cleaning up the mess.

Appetites had not restored themselves by the time Father Grease and his unfortunate helper were done cleaning up the worst of the mess. Therefore, while standing in the middle of the room, Father Grease said a perfunctory grace after meals and excused everyone. The room cleared of most seminarians in less than a minute, except for the food servers who had the responsibility of preparing the room for the next meal and were gathering like sour milk on the ramp to the kitchen.

"Get to work," Father Grease commanded.

"Well, that was entertaining," I said to him. "Too bad Bernie missed it."

"Speaking of the good Father Fox," Hank said after taking a deep breath, "he *is* here. He said his three masses in the sister's chapel. It's not like him to miss a breakfast. When you go back to your room, check on him."

I didn't much care for the assignment, but I was the natural choice. Bernie's room was next to mine. Procrastination, especially when it involved unpleasant tasks, was a bad habit I would address one of these days. In this case, Hank was glaring at me, and I decided to get my mission out of the way. I made the trek down the hall and up three flights of stairs, and stopped in front of the Fox's door. It was shut, which was no surprise. Bernie was a private man. I knocked and got no answer. Maybe he was in the bathroom. I went to my room, left my door cracked, and lit up a Lucky Strike. I figured smoking the cigarette would give him time to get out of the bathroom. I heard footsteps and looked out, hoping it was Bernie. It was a seminarian, coming up to do his obedience, which would consist of dust-mopping the dorms on both sides of my room and Bernie's. I stubbed out the Lucky and resigned myself to checking.

I knocked. Nothing. I knocked again. Nothing. With resignation, I tried the door. It wasn't locked.

The smell hit me, a harsh reminder of our recent breakfast. Vomit. There was a splatter trail leading from Bernie's easy chair toward the bathroom. The contents weren't abundant, but their color was a strange mix of bright yellow and streaks of blood. Bernie was in the bathroom, laying on his back in a pool of bright yellow, more bright yellow dripping from his mouth. His head was bleeding. It wasn't pretty, but I had seen—and smelled—worse in the war. The problem was—this was now and he was not moving. When I felt his neck for a pulse, I felt nothing.

I went to his phone, dialed "0", and then hung up. Bernie wasn't going anywhere. All hell was about to break loose, and it might help to face it with a plan.

I hung the do-not-disturb sign on my doorknob and did the same on Bernie's door. Then I headed downstairs in search of Hank.

Five minutes later

"Heart attack?" It was the first words Hank said after I gave him the news. The air had gone out of him, and it took more than a minute for him to speak.

"Don't think so. Some kind of stomach thing. He's in the bathroom—vomit, blood, and bile all over. He puked his guts out, literally. Looks like he might have fallen and hit his head. It's ugly."

"You sure he's dead?"

I just looked at him.

"Okay, right," he said. "You've seen your share of trauma." Twenty years ago, Hank and I had been in the seminary. He stayed put. I went to war.

"I didn't call the police," I said. "I thought about it, but this is going to throw the school into chaos. I thought we might take some time to figure out how to handle it. We've got about forty-five minutes before the guys start filing into their classrooms. Time to step up, Boss."

"Well, okay then," he said. "I'll tell you what. I'll grab my kit, run upstairs, give Bernie the last rites, and look things over. In the meantime, see if you can round up the faculty and ask them to meet me in the lounge. Umm, don't tell them anything—except that we need an emergency meeting."

"And after that," I said.

"I have no idea."

Fifteen minutes later

"Heart attack?" Father Al Hopfensperger's question broke the silence.

"We should be so lucky," I said, as much to myself as to the assembled staff.

Hank continued, describing the scene and the likelihood that something besides natural causes was behind Bernie's sudden departure.

"This is bad," someone muttered.

"What are we going to do?" someone else asked.

"The sixty-four thousand dollar question," Hank said.

"Are you going to call the authorities?" Father Hop wanted to know.

"I don't want to," Hank said. "But I think I have to."

"That's going to open up a can of worms," said Brother Rufus.

"I'm afraid the worms have been loose for some time," said Hank. "Now they are so obvious we have to deal with them."

"But how?" asked Father Hop.

Even though I was the new guy, I'd had the most time to think about it, maybe twenty minutes. I figured I should jump in. "'First things first. Let's starting with what we do right now. How do we break it to the seminarians, and then what do we do with them for the rest of the day."

"Or even just this morning," said Hank, looking at me with something like relief.

"What about this?" I said. "As soon as we leave here, let's corral everyone into the chapel for an emergency assembly."

"Good," said Father Hop. "Classes are supposed to start in twenty minutes or so. That'll be a good time to gather them. I'll stand in front the school building and redirect everyone to the chapel."

"And once everyone is assembled, someone—Hank?—can make the announcement," I said. "Probably should keep it general. He was found dead. We don't know what happened. That sort of thing."

"Absolutely," said Hank. "But I'm afraid I'm going to have to be available to the authorities. Al, as assistant superior, the job should fall to you. Bert, why don't you can handle redirecting the guys to the chapel?" I nodded assent, and he continued. "Al, keep it general, per Bert's suggestion. Don't give any details. Just say that Father Fox was found dead in his room. We don't know what happened. None of you should give out any more than that."

"After that, we can say a rosary," said Father Hop, warming to the task. "That will us buy some time. Twenty minutes, maybe. Then what."

"That's a quandary," said Hank. "I imagine it's going to take the authorities the rest of the morning—at the very least—to process the body and the scene. I'm just guessing, but I'm not keen on having the boys staring at ambulances, hearses, police cars, and whatnot. That'll just feed speculation."

"How about sending the underclassmen to their locker rooms until further notice?" I said. "Seniors can go to their rooms."

"Why not send them to study hall?" asked Father Hop. "At least they can study there."

"Because the guys in the north study hall will have their noses pressed to the windows, staring at the police cars, ambulances, comings and goings," I said. "They can't do that from the locker rooms. Besides, they are comfortable hanging out in the locker rooms. They can manage there until lunch."

"Okay," said Hank. "If you're not otherwise tied up, each of you join the boys in their space. Al, take the seniors. Bert, take the juniors. The rest of you, take the underclassmen. Everyone, answer their questions—generally please—and help them process the news. Try to control their speculating and wild theories."

"Good luck with that," I said.

After 10 A.M.

"Mr. Foote, I need you upstairs."

That was ominous. Hank hadn't visited the junior locker room all year. I was there as part of the plan, helping the seminarians process the death of their history teacher by hanging out with them. I had been there for a good hour, listening, pretending I didn't know anything when they asked me "what happened?" This part of the plan had worked fairly well. Breaking the news in the chapel, where the seminarians never spoke anything but prayers, and saying the rosary afterward had grounded everyone. Moving them to their locker rooms had worked as well. There was the expected shock of coming to terms with the sudden death of someone they had seen alive and well the day before, but the main reaction among juniors had been divided between dramatic sadness and guilty silence, the former on the part of those who liked their teacher and the latter on the part of those who didn't. Or at least I surmised as such. Dingo Dave sat on a bench, stared into his locker, and said nothing while I was around. As a change of pace, a couple of them made reference to the breakfast drama, whose perpetrator—Charles Weber—they had already branded as "Upchuck."

"Let's walk slowly," Hank said. "I have to fill you in." After getting out of earshot, we stopped at the foot of the stairs.

"Okay, shoot."

"I made two phone calls," Hank said. "One was to campus security, which generated a visit from the chief of security and the MD from the campus infirmary. After one look at the body, the doc called the time of death and the chief called the county coroner. He's not here yet.

"I made another call to the provincial, who instructed me not to tell law enforcement anything until the congregation's lawyer arrived."

"You lawyered up?"

"No surprise," Hank said. "We're not sure how much to say about Bernie and all the rumors."

"There's that. And the possibility that the murderer ... " I paused. "We're pretty sure this was a murder, aren't we ...?"

"I can tell you this: the chief waited about a second before calling the coroner," Hank said. "So yeah, I don't think anybody's gonna think Bernie ate a bad clam."

"Some clam," I said. "Then there's the possibility—even the

likelihood—that the murderer is going to be—how should I say this—one of us."

Hank looked at his shoes and then at me. "You know, I hadn't even thought of that. I guess I didn't want to."

"So what did you say to the authorities?"

"Not much," Hank said. "I told the chief that you found Bernie, came and told me, whereupon I went upstairs, checked his pulse, gave him the last rites, and went to the faculty lounge to break the news to the team and plan the logistics of the morning. I had asked the provincial if it would be okay to do that much. That's what you should do as well."

"Stick to finding the body then? What if he asks me other questions—about Bernie and so on."

"Just tell him you need to wait. The chief is waiting as well. The coroner is here. When he declares this to be a suspicious death, the chief plans to call the sheriff. He'll send out a detective, who will do the in-depth interviews. By then, we'll have talked to the lawyer."

"What do we do about the seminarians?"

"Well, while I'm here I'll go talk to the juniors. Maybe that'll help me decide what to do next."

Hank went off to the locker room, and I went off in search of the chief of security. I found him outside, sitting in his car, waiting for the coroner. He gathered that I was the person he had asked for, opened the passenger door, and motioned me to sit. I did—and waited.

The chief was mature, maybe in his early fifties, a retired city cop I guessed, not entirely correctly as it turned out. There was a chill in the air, and he was in uniform, without a coat, probably why he was waiting in his car.

"You're Mr. Foote, I assume."

"Foote" with an "e". My first name is Englebert, but everybody calls me Bert—for obvious reasons."

"I'll be calling you Mr. Foote, and you may call me Chief Ziolkowski—or Chief, for obvious reasons."

"Okay, I guess I'll be calling you Chief."

"Father Grieshaber said you found the body."

"Yes, Father Fox didn't show up for breakfast, which was unlike him," I said. "Hank, er, Father Griesehaber asked me to check on him. His room is next to mine."

"Did you have any reason to suspect a problem?"

"Other than that he didn't show up for breakfast, no."

"What did you do when you found him?"

"I checked for a pulse on his neck. Nothing. Then I left, went to find Father Grieshaber."

"Why didn't you call someone? The operator? Campus security?"

"Two reasons. It was pretty clear Bernie, Father Fox, was dead. There wasn't going to be anything we could do for him. Second, we're a boarding school. Sudden death like this is bound to create some chaos. I wanted to give ... Father Grieshaber ... a chance to think through how we were going to handle the seminarians, at least for the day. He called you shortly after a short meeting with the staff."

"You seem pretty calm for someone who found a dead body hardly more than an hour ago."

If I had been perfectly honest, I would have told the chief that I wasn't all that calm. In fact, I could have used a drink. On the other hand, strictly speaking, there wasn't anything novel about that. Even at ten in the morning. There was something odd about the situation, though. My hands weren't shaking. I was calm. Oddly so. Finally, I said, "I was in the infantry during the war. I've seen more than my share of dead bodies."

"Oh, where?"

"Europe. France and Germany, 1945, the tail end of things. Some fighting. A lot of cleanup. Maybe it wasn't the worst duty, but it was bad enough."

"Me, I was Marine MP, stationed on the U.S.S. Hornet for a while. The Hornet saw plenty of action, but we were never hit. All things considered, my job was fairly routine, mostly busting the chops of all the eighteen to twenty-two year olds who wanted to act like eighteen to twenty-two year olds."

"Sounds like it has something in common with campus security."

"In some ways, yeah," he said. "Notre Dame was a good fit for me. The only female students are across the road at St. Mary's. I figured I'd be well equipped to oversee security for seven thousand sex-starved boys." He paused. "Father Grieshaber asked if we'd wait until this afternoon for extended questioning. I said, fine, figuring someone from the sheriff's office was going to do the honors."

"He mentioned that."

"Still, is there anything you'd care to tell me before then."

"You know, I think I can tell you something. One of the boys tossed his cookies at breakfast. It made quite an impression on his table mates. In fact, we ended breakfast a bit early. It didn't occur to me until now, but there might be a connection."

"A connection? You think?"

"Well, yeah, you know. Two instances of projectile vomiting on the same morning. Same bilious contents. Could be a clue."

A clue? Who are you, Agatha Christie?"

"What, you don't want a clue?"

"I'm a campus security guard," he said. "I expect to call the sheriff soon. I'll ask him about this clue thing. In the meantime, who tossed the yellow cookies at breakfast?"

"He's a sophomore, name of Charles Weber, though I heard someone calling him 'Upchuck' as everybody filed out after breakfast."

"Poor kid, he'll have that nickname for life. I'd like to talk to him, but I've got to wait here and it's a bit of a deal to talk to minors anyway."

"The kid's in my class. How about I talk to him, find out what he's eaten or drunk in the past twenty-four hours or so?"

"Good idea, but make the timeline forty-eight hours. And find out where he's been, not just what he's eaten."

"Deal. Give me a half hour. I think he's in the infirmary." I was starting to feel like a real detective, but I didn't say that.

About 10:45 A.M.

I made the trek up to the infirmary. Father Hop had already given the seniors the news and was having a standing meeting with six of them at the end of the hallway. Others were talking quietly in groups of three to four, in the hallway or in someone's room. No one was at the nurse's station. I rang the doorbell and waited a couple of minutes until Sister Angela showed up.

"How's your bronchitis?" she said.

"Progressing nicely, thank you," I said. "Throat pain is gone, but it's migrated to my chest, waiting to break up."

"I'll give you a decongestant."

"Good, but that's not the main reason I'm here."

"Oh?"

"Is Charles Weber up here? He had an, uh, incident this morning at breakfast."

"Yes," she said. "He came in here looking a little green, but he's feeling some better."

"I'd like to speak to him."

"He's not much for conversation right now."

"It's important. It has to do with Father Fox."

"Father Fox?"

"You didn't hear?" Apparently, Hank had neglected to inform the good sisters.

"Hear what?"

"I, um ... Father Fox was found dead in his room this morning." I decided I'd best keep to the protocol.

"Oh?"

Neither her voice nor her face showed any emotion, so I said, "Maybe you didn't know him?"

"Not really," she said. "He came up here once for some aspirin. We weren't close." Her face registered something, maybe amusement, maybe curiosity. "He said the masses for us this morning. Seemed okay. Maybe a little anxious to get it over with, but it was three masses—and he's always been a quick one. Heart attack?"

"I have no idea." A little lie. "Anyway, if Charles is in your infirmary, he probably doesn't know either."

"I can tell him."

"I'd rather do it, if you don't mind. The teachers are dealing with all the students—and thanks to his little incident, Charles is out of the loop. I've been sent to rectify that." Another little lie.

"Okay then." With that she led me into a ward with a dozen beds in it. Charles Weber was in one of them. There were no other patients.

"Hey, Charlie, how are you doing?"

"Getting better," he said. "Man, something came over me at breakfast. I slept fine, served three masses in the sister's chapel, no problem. And then at breakfast, bang ..."

My antennae went up. "So you were Father Fox's altar boy this morning?"

"Yeah, why?"

"That's one of the reasons I came in here. To let you know—Father Fox was found dead this morning.'

"No! Really?" He looked shocked. No reason not to. "Heart attack?"

"No idea," I said. Third lie in ten minutes. "You might have been the last person to see him alive. Did he seem okay?"

"Yeah, well. Sure, I mean, he did the last mass really fast and then disappeared. That's his style, though. So ... the last person to see him. Whoa!"

Yeah, Whoa!

About 11:00 A.M.

Things moved quickly while I was talking to Charles. The coroner had ruled within five minutes of inspecting the scene that the death was suspicious; he called the sheriff, who gave his forewarned homicide investigators the go-ahead. By the time I got outside to talk to the chief, the homicide guys were upstairs in Bernie's room consulting with the coroner.

Meanwhile, I filled in the chief on Upchuck's activities, whereabouts, and menu for the last forty eight hours.

"Oh," was his response, which I gathered was cops-peak for "I'm really excited."

Just as I finished my briefing, another car showed up, which turned out to belong to the congregation's attorney. He introduced himself as Al Mueller, after which I offered to go in search of Hank, who the chief said had gone upstairs just before our conversation.

"I told him the coroner wasn't going to let him in the room," the chief said, "but he went up there anyway."

"Probably didn't know what else to do," I said.

"The coroner is not going to let me in there either," the attorney said. "So I'll take you up on your offer to climb those stairs and retrieve Father Grease."

"You call him by his nickname," I noticed, curious.

"Everybody calls him that," Mueller said. "Even the provincial. I don't even remember his full name."

"Grieshaber," I said, "but I call him Hank." I headed off on my climbing expedition, coughing and wheezing by the time I reached the fourth floor.

As predicted, Hank was pacing the corridor. He greeted me, almost glad to have some direction, even if it was "let's get out of here." On the way down, I told him what I had found out about Charles Weber and his morning whereabouts coinciding with Bernie's. He was aghast.

"You told the chief about this?"

"It had to do with the morning's events," I said, "which I figured was reasonable to share with the officer." I had wondered if I should say anything and felt mildly guilty about it. On the other hand, I rather relished the idea of contributing to the case. Gosh, I was sober enough to have an ego.

Mueller was waiting for us, just inside the entrance. It was a little cool, and no one was about. The seminarians were still being warehoused in their locker rooms. We huddled.

"Here's the deal," Mueller began. "I'm the attorney for the congregation. If you think you need an attorney for yourself, go get one. In my role, I'm not going to stop you from cooperating with the authorities. In fact, you have to cooperate with them. Answer their questions as best you can. Provide the information they ask for. Volunteer whatever information you think might be helpful."

"Does this include sharing our suspicions ..." Hank paused and swallowed. "... and/or the rumors about Father Fox?"

"The provincial briefed me on that," the attorney said. "Like I said, you have to be seen to be cooperating. So, yes, share this with them. You can certainly give your take on them. You didn't believe the rumors, et cetera, et cetera. However, my role is to keep the lid on what the public will hear."

"You're doing PR?" I asked.

"Yes, basically," he said. "The local authorities are going to do their investigations. They aren't going to pull any punches, but they understand the university's need—and by association the congregation's need—for discretion. It's not that they are good buddies with us. They have a natural distaste for releasing any but the most minimal information—until they identify a perpetrator."

"If there is a perpetrator," said Hank.

"Yes, of course. The point is, when that happens, reporters will be out in full force and you'll be at the mercy of events. In the meantime, though, I'll help you keep a lid on things."

"Until the cover blows off," I said.

"Until then."

After 11 A.M.

After a bit of negotiation, Al Mueller, Hank, and I convened with Sergeant Frank Hayden and Deputy Andrew Wood from the Sheriff's Office and Chief Ziolkowski from the university. The discussion had involved a quick rundown on my role in the matter and Hank's desire to have me included in informal questioning. We fit conveniently around a game table and gathered there. The sheriff's deputies weren't in uniform, unless you considered sport coats, black pants, blue shirts with no tie a uniform. Sergeant Hayden was in his mid-forties, by my guess, a notch over six-feet tall, and had a shock of very blonde hair. Detective Wood was shorter and with dark hair receding quickly, which made him look older than his partner. I guessed that he wasn't. They looked like a couple of college professors, which suggested they were the go-to team for anything to do with Notre Dame. Sergeant Hayden even took out a pipe to complete the look.

"You men need something to drink," Hank asked.

"No, thanks," said Sergeant Hayden.

"I'm fine, thanks," said Detective Wood.

"Nope," said Mueller.

I half expected Hank to go pour himself a glass of scotch. He didn't, and I tried not to register a sigh of relief.

The attorney spoke first, explaining that he was the congregation's attorney and that he had advised each of us to get our own attorneys if we were concerned about talking to the police. He explained that his main interest was in working with the authorities to ensure discretion with regard to the initial reports about Father Fox's death and the cause. "In that respect, I'd like to ask that Father Fox's room be secured in a way that does not suggest that it is a crime scene. This will reduce the speculation on the part of the seminarians and ultimately the public."

"Good idea. I hadn't thought of that," said Hank. He had that deer in headlights look.

Chief Ziolkowski jumped in. "I can handle that. I'll give the university's locksmith a call. Someone will be here within the half hour to add a keyed deadbolt to Father Fox's room, very discrete."

"And you'll hold the keys, presumably," said Sgt. Hayden.

"Yes, sir," the chief said and left the room.

After that, Sergeant Hayden took the lead, reviewing my encounter and Hank's with the body. We went through it again. With that out of the way, he asked the expected question, "Can you think of anyone who who wanted to harm Father Fox?"

Hank looked at me, then at Mueller, and said nothing.

Mueller looked back at Hank and said, "The congregation has no objection to filling them in."

Hank sighed and began by explaining that Bernie Fox had been moved to Holy Cross Seminary after rumors surfaced that he had molested a student in his previous assignment at Notre Dame High School in Niles, Illinois. "The provincial didn't believe the rumors, but he believed he had to transfer Bernie to another job."

"Why to another high school?" Sergeant Hayden asked.

"Like I said, he didn't believe the stories."

"With good reason," I interjected. "The stories began to circulate after Bernie—Father Fox—stood up for a kid who was being bullied. The bullies were the sons of prominent Chicagoans, and Bernie tried to get them expelled."

"So he made some enemies?" Sergeant Hayden said.

"It appears so," Hank said.

"But why the molestation charges?"

"Because the boy who was being bullied was struggling with homosexuality."

"How do you know that?" Sergeant Hayden asked.

"His name was Jimmy Parker," Hank said. "He entered St. Joe Hall in August. That's our first-year residence for seminarians who join us after high school or later. Jimmy committed suicide a month ago. You can check with the chief and the coroner."

"And homosexuality was an issue for this young man?"

"It appears so," I said and told them about the copy of *The Charioteer*, signed by Father Fox, that Father Perry found at the scene of the suicide.

"Doesn't this suggest that Father Fox and this Jimmy Parker had a relationship?"

"A relationship, yes," said Hank. He had a little edge to his voice. "But don't jump to the worst—and likely the wrong—conclusion. Father Fox was a teacher, as I am and as Bert is. We all have relationships with our students, relationships that are appropriate to us as teachers—and sometimes as counselors. The book didn't suggest to me that Father Fox was having sex with the boy."

"Nor to me, either," I said. "The book is about a young man struggling with his sexual identity. My first thought was that Father Fox was counseling the young man."

"And telling him it was okay to be a homosexual?" said the Detective Wood.

"Is this really your issue?" asked Mueller.

"Point taken," said the sergeant. "We're looking for a motive, but our primary issue is who killed Father Fox."

"If anyone killed Father Fox," said Mueller.

"Correct," said the sergeant. "Technically, we're jumping the gun—we don't have the coroner's ruling—but we have an expectation. That's why we're here."

Hank's jaw tightened. I thought he was going to break a tooth.

"Mr. Foote," continued the sergeant. "You found the body, but you seem to know as much as anyone about Father Fox. What's going on? Were you his best friend—or what?"

I looked at Hank and then at Mueller. "Not hardly," and I proceeded to tell them why I was hired.

"So tell us what you know," Sergeant Hayden ordered.

"I suppose you mean about Father Fox," I said.

"Yes," said the detective. "I'm not so interested in how you diagram sentences."

Good cop, bad cop, funny cop. "I think I've told you most of what I know," I said. "Father Fox tried to protect Jimmy Parker from being bullied. Because of that, he pissed off—excuse me—some powerful parents. This doesn't make him a bad guy. Quite the contrary. The seminarians gossip a bit about him, they call him BJ, playing off the rumors ..."

Hank was glaring at me.

"What's up with the nickname?" Sergeant Hayden said.

"His name is Bernard John Fox." I emphasized Bernard and John.

"So it could be innocent," Hank said, still glaring at me.

"But not so much," I said. "It's ..."

"I get it," Sergeant Hayden said. "And you don't think that's an indication he might be misbehaving."

"I get nothing from the students but gossip. No red flags on that score. But he is controversial."

"Go on," the sergeant said.

I looked at Hank and proceeded. "On the first day of class, he announced that he was going to teach history backwards. This sounded radical and thrilled some students. Others thought it was stupid. He has, um, had ... this is hard to get used to ... I'm just going to use the present tense if you don't mind."

"Always the English teacher," Hank said.

"Father Fox has a sour disposition. He hardly ever laughs," I said and stopped, thinking of my wife. "He's prone to cutting remarks, which I find hard to take, but it tickles a lot of the seminarians, depending on the target."

"And if they are the target ..." said Detective Wood.

"I suppose they might develop a bit of a resentment," I admitted. "On the other hand, some of the seminarians identify with his cynicism. He says mass in half the time of all the other priests, which makes him popular with most of the seminarians."

Sergeant Hayden puffed on his pipe and asked, "Any of the seminarians exhibit any particular animus to Father Fox."

"Animus?" Must be the pipe, I thought.

"It's Latin," the sergeant said. "I like to work university cases because I get to try out my vocabulary. Can anyone answer the question?"

Hank and I looked at each other. He shrugged, which gave me the go-ahead. "The Johnson brothers exhibit a certain, um, animus, The younger brother, Dan, he seems to be in some kind of intellectual competition with the man, but I don't think it rises to level of murderous rage." I explained Dan's class confrontation with his history teacher and his explanation of what was behind it. I added that the older brother, Dave, had expressed some misgivings about him. Nothing too dramatic.

"And that's it?" The sergeant took another puff from his pipe.

"Well, it would be, except ..." And I told the group about the collages I found on his door.

"And you think the Johnson brothers might have had something to do with that?" Another puff.

"I asked Dan about it, and he denied it," I said. "I have my suspicions, but I can't be sure."

"Sounds like someone has a certain, how do you say..." The sergeant paused to take another puff.

"Animus," I finished for him. "I guess. But I don't know who. And there is one other thing you should know." I looked at Hank and stopped.

Hank took a breath. "I received a threatening note regarding Father Fox in my mail cubby last week."

The sergeant beat the bowl of his pipe into the palm of his hand and dropped the contents into an ashtray. He stared at Hank. "Go on."

"It's downstairs in my office. It looks like one of those ransom notes, with the cut-out letters. It says, 'Foxes are predators. Get rid of yours before someone does it for you.' It was folded inside a blank envelope."

"Blank?" the sergeant said.

"Yep."

"And you didn't do anything about it?"

"Actually, I did," said Hank. "I showed it to our provincial. He had appointed Father Fox to teach here, in spite of the rumors about him. He didn't believe them. He still doesn't believe them, but the note made him contemplate moving Father Fox somewhere else, somewhere out of harm's way. He was supposed to let us know his decision today."

"I guess you should have acted on Friday," the sergeant said.

After lunch

By 1 p.m., Bernie's body had been transported to the morgue, the seminarians had been released, lunch had been served, and the staff was gathering in the faculty lounge.

Lunch had been a little quirky. The kitchen sisters were distracted and off their game, more annoyed than anything else by not having been officially informed of the day's tragedy. In fact, they had found out about it more or less accidentally from me after I had gone through Sister Angela to interview Charlie Weber.

The priest's table was subdued after Hank asked the teachers to table their questions and concerns until the meeting afterwards.

The seminarians were full of energy, which seemed odd under the circumstances. However, the underclassmen had been cooped up in their locker rooms for three hours, and they must have felt like they just got out of jail. The tragedy for them was real, but it produced what amounted to a free day for them—with conditions. Father Grease informed them they could not leave the seminary campus, a freedom that had been new this year. The lockdown was at the request of the sheriff's deputies, but Hank didn't call it a lockdown and didn't say where the request had come from.

The faculty meeting didn't consume a half hour. Hank told the staff about our meeting with the deputies, leaving out some details. He didn't mention the threatening note. He informed them that the two deputies would be back at 2 p.m to interview the staff, beginning with the cooks.

"I hope they speak German," said Brother Rufus. "Those sisters don't speak a lick of English."

"But they understand plenty," said Father Hop. "I'll be available if they need an interpreter."

"Good, but I have another job for you," said Hank. "I need you to gin up some kind of report detailing the movement of the students, beginning with the Halloween activities on Friday night until breakfast this morning."

"Hmm, I can," Father Hop said. "But it's quite a job."

"Yes it is," Hank allowed. "But the deputies are reluctant to interview 100-plus students until they have to. This will save time and give them some direction. You can group some of them, but you'll need to individualize some things, like obediences."

"That one's easy," Father Hop said. "I can give them the obedience list."

I asked how we were going to handle Bernie's history class the next day.

"I haven't thought about it,' Hank said. "Off the top of my head, let's send the lads to study hall. In the meantime, when I get a chance, I'll talk to the provincial about it. I have a feeling, we'll have to bring somebody out of retirement." With that, he dismissed everyone.

When the others had left, Hank spoke to me. "I need a drink. Do you mind?"

"I could use one myself," I said.

"Coffee?"

"Yeah, I better," I said. "And thank you for thinking of me."

"No problem," he said. getting up to pour himself a Red Label over ice. "We need a steady hand around here, and I'm feeling a tad shaky."

I followed him to the counter, grabbed a mug, and poured myself some coffee. "Be good if you can settle down," I said. "Before this whole place gets the shakes."

He took more than a sip from his scotch and let let out a deep sigh. "But hey, no pressure."

"Sorry," I made a face. The coffee was hours old and nasty. "Keep in mind, you aren't alone. You're part of a religious community, and your faculty is close."

"Hmm, one of whom could have killed their brother."

That stopped me. "I don't see that, do you? Even given Bernie's prickly nature."

"So what are you thinking?"

"I'm not getting anywhere with my thinking," I said. "It's got to be a member of the staff or a student."

"Or one of the good sisters," he said.

"Or one of the good sisters, Hard to imagine, although I am hoping for accidental food poisoning."

"Wouldn't that be nice," he said, more as statement than question.

"The detectives came alive when they found out Charlie Parker did the big barf at breakfast," I said. "I think they'll chase that tail for a while, but I don't buy it. If it were food poisoning, we'd be overrun with the puke-and-trots. We had only two victims, so it's not likely."

"Coulda been something that nobody else eats," Hank said.

"You mean like mystery squares," I said. "Nobody likes them. The legend is that the sisters serve 100 mystery squares and get back 150."

"So maybe Bernie and Charlie were the only ones who dared eat one. I like it." Hank made a sound, the distant ancestor of a chuckle, took a good pull on his scotch, and sighed.

"We can always hope, but Bernie would have had to eat a dozen yesterday," I said. "Change of subject. I could handle Bernie's sophomore history class for the next week or so. Last I heard, they were still talking about World War II. I've got a little experience there."

"What about his other classes?"

"Can't solve that one for you," I said. "All his other classes conflict with mine."

Afternoon

It seemed like the day had gone on for a week. It was only 3 P.M. I had no classes. The authorities had left, except for the detectives who were on site, interviewing the sisters responsible for preparing the food. I would have liked to have been a fly on the wall, watching their reaction to the veiled hint that their food preparation might have been responsible for the death of a priest.

The detectives were not going to talk to me until tomorrow, if then. It was a crazy day, and I needed to talk to someone. My sponsor was at work. So was my wife, but her work was at the university library. I started the walk on the cinder path, past St. Mary's Lake, and across campus, wondering what I would tell her. I hadn't even told her the details of why I was hired. And I hadn't been good at confiding in her when we were together.

I stopped at the Huddle, thinking I needed a decent cup of coffee and a relaxed smoke. Before going to the counter, I went to the bank of phone booths in the student center and called Eli, who would have to serve as my lawyer if I needed one, and arranged an appointment for later in the afternoon. I didn't expect him to make room for me today, but when I told him the basics, he said he'd stay later to talk with me. That worried me.

I decided to skip the coffee and the smoke and headed to the library. I stopped at the desk, asked for Sarah, and was pointed to the periodicals section. I found her there, got her agreement to meet me in fifteen minutes in the canteen downstairs.

That gave me time to buy a cup of coffee from the machine—not great but better than the swill in the faculty lounge—and a chance to light my pipe and relax a bit.

Sarah was as good as her word, as was her practice. She took one look at me and said, "Wow! What's going on? You look like you just stuck your finger in a wall socket."

"Yeah, well, at nine this morning, I did get a bit of shock." And I began to fill her in, starting with my discovery of the body.

"Doesn't sound like death from natural causes," she said.

"No, it doesn't. Hank ... Father Grease, the school superior ... and I are holding out for food poisoning, but it's a vain hope. Somebody poisoned him on purpose."

"Poisoned? How strange."

"You think?"

"And why would someone kill this guy, especially if, as seems likely, that the *someone* is part of the seminary landscape."

"Okay, there is something I haven't told you." And I finally told her the real reason that I, a recently sober alcoholic with no teaching experience and a dubious relationship to the Catholic church, had been hired to teach English in a high-school seminary.

When I stopped talking, she paused a bit and said, "Of course, I knew that you weren't hired for your spectacular qualifications," she said, "but I just assumed that your seminary classmate was trying to give you a helping hand."

"That was part of it, I'm sure," I said, "but he was in a jam, and he needed an outsider he could trust."

"And he could trust you?"

"He was willing to take the chance."

"So why are you telling me now," she said. "Confiding in me hasn't been your long suit."

"Yeah, right. I get that, but confiding in anyone has never been my long suit. But lately, I've been dipping my toe in the waters."

"A benefit of your meetings perhaps. But again, why me?"

"Two reasons I can think of. One, I need another person to talk to, someone not connected to the seminary, someone who can keep a confidence. Aside from not being good at the confiding thing and not being comfortable talking to you—thanks to our, hmm, situation—I had an ethical reason for not telling you why I was hired."

"And that is ..."

"And that *was* ... the need to avoid spreading tales about people, especially Father Fox. The situation was awkward."

"And now that he's gone, you can talk to me."

"Yes, but I think I could have talked to you before. My lawyer, the Jewish guy, told me that the laws against spreading gossip don't apply to sharing between a husband and wife. This is partly because a husband and wife shouldn't have secrets from each other—and they should be able to assume their confidence will be kept."

"And we are separated, so the husband and wife thing ..."

"... was up in the air," I said. "But maybe more important, I just wasn't ready to confide in you."

"And now you are?"

"I'm getting there. I'm getting there."

Chapter 25

Tuesday, November 3, 1964

The day after wasn't the adrenalin rush of All Soul's Day, but it had its own inner drama.

My meeting yesterday with Eli was both a comfort and a concern. A comfort because he didn't seem terribly concerned about my exposure. A concern because there was some exposure. He pointed out that I, along with everyone else at the seminary, would be a suspect.

"But if you're not worried, I'm not worried," he had said. "In this situation, you're most likely exposure is in how you cooperate with the investigators. On one hand, you're working for Holy Cross Seminary and might be inclined to protect your employer. On the other hand, you don't want to open yourself to a charge of obstruction of justice. As an attorney, I've got to warn you to pay attention to the latter. Cooperate with the authorities."

He pooh-poohed my belief that I was sitting on the horns of a dilemma. "Only if you have reason to feel particularly protective of your employer," he had said. At any rate, he wasn't concerned enough to insist that he be there when the detectives interviewed me again, if they did. He did point out that I could stop the process at any time and ask for my lawyer.

"And wouldn't that make them think I had something to hide?"

"Of course," he had said. "Use your judgment."

"Oh boy."

After that, I skipped dinner and went to an AA meeting, during which I shared, in general terms, about the day. I had noticed how alive I felt, something I could only compare to the time on the battlefield when the Lieutenant sent me up a utility pole to cut the communication lines. I was the target and could hear bullets whistling past me. I had entered the fray in late 1944, toward the end of things but just in time for one of Europe's coldest winters. Most of the time I was freezing, wet, or dog tired. In combat, I never volunteered. Never moved more than I had to. Yesterday was different. I wasn't cold, wet, or tired. Something bad had happened, and I was being asked to do something. The parts were moving. I felt alive again.

Today, in the morning, my first class was Bernie's sophomore history class, in which I shared my experience in the war and opened the floor for questions. I shared the same experience—the World War II part, that is—and opened the floor to questions. There were many. Were you afraid? Did you kill anyone? What was it like? And so on.

Dan Johnson raised his hand and asked, "Did the Nazis exterminate homos along with Jews in their concentration camps?"

We had discussed this in private before. It was a fair question, but the way he phrased it, in public and in the light of yesterday's event, sent a shiver up my spine. Had he researched it like I asked? I didn't challenge him, only admitted I wasn't up on the facts—and made a mental note to enlist the help of a certain reference librarian to fill me in. I did say I knew that the Nazis had executed some Christians, gypsies, and homosexuals along with roughly six million Jews.

I did tell them that I was part of the 71st Infantry Division that liberated Gunskirchen Lager, a work camp in Northern Austria. In this case, I said, there were 400 or so political prisoners, who could have been anything, but the rest of the estimated 15,000 prisoners were Jews.

Of course, they wanted to know what it was like. I did my best to explain. It was an intense experience, a mixture of horror and ecstasy. On the one hand, we were liberators, marching into a screaming sea of humanity grateful beyond words. They wanted to thank us, to touch us, to let us see their tears. In the cold, mud, and blood, we might have forgotten that this was what the war was all about. On the other hand, this human horde was like nothing I had ever seen. It was like marching in a Fourth of July Parade where the onlookers were not men, women, and children applauding politely but skeletons attacking the marchers with frantic joy. The differnce was: these humans *were* skeletons, albeit covered with a tissue of skin and rags barely showing the horizontal stripes of prison uniforms. They milled around, impeding the progress of troops and vehicles, mouthing what must have been "thank you" in different languages. Some, unable to walk, crawled toward us. One man couldn't crawl but propped himself up on an elbow and waved. People fell, knocked over by their fellows or just fainted from hunger.

To a man, we wanted to do something, anything. We didn't have much. I gave one skeleton a cigarette, but he put it in his mouth and ate it before I could light it for him. One of my buddies handed out a chocolate bar, which was consumed instantly, wrapper and all. After that, we knew to break the bar into bits, sans wrapper, and pass it around. Another soldier pointed to the left, toward a jury of human crows picking over a bloated horse that had been killed by artillery fire.

I hadn't talked about this, ever. The bloated horse wasn't the thing that stuck with me. It was the smell. We were a dirty bunch, inured to our own stink and the smell of rotting bodies, but the stench that greeted us a mile before we entered the camp sent some of us to vomit in the ditches. It was a combination of human excrement, urine, decaying bodies, smoke, and German tobacco—which worked like an emulsifier bonding the putrid with the decay into an everlasting nasal memorial. And that was the thing. The peculiar and disgusting smell permeated everything and lingered for what seemed like forever. Six hours after we left the camp, we swore we could still smell it on our clothes. It may still be there. Last night, I had a nightmare in which the images were dark and vague but the smell was there, more structure than decoration. When I woke up in a cold sweat, I sniffed my sheets, horrified at the familiarity of it. I got up early and showered for forty minutes. I didn't share my stinking dream with the seminarians.

My next class, just before lunch, was junior English. They were still wired about the death of Father Fox, so—on the spot—I assigned them to take twenty minutes to write a short eulogy for their fallen history teacher. Most had a vague idea of what a eulogy should do—say nice things about the deceased. Dave Johnson, Dingo Dave, argued that this sounded a bit phony, that a eulogy like this might not fairly describe the person.

I suggested that everyone has good and bad things about them. However, when a person dies, we bury some things but try to hold onto some things, the better things, the things we can learn from. It's the job of a eulogy to identify those things. With that, they set to work.

After twenty minutes, I invited the willing to share their eulogies. It was revealing. His "speed mass" was popular, which most thought exhibited his thoughtfulness. Several thought he was "real," citing his propensity for "telling it like it is," no matter what anybody else thought. A couple of comments, including one from

Dingo Dave, mentioned that he went out of his way to defend the underdogs.. Some felt like they were reaching for something to say — great bridge player, tough basketball coach, no homework. Nothing suggested he had been misbehaving with students.

At lunch, Hank led grace with no further comment to the seminarians but told the assembled at the priest's table that we had caught a break, albeit a temporary one. "The coroner's office completed the autopsy and determined that Bernie was poisoned," he said. "By what, they don't know. It wasn't arsenic, strychnine, rat poison or something easy. They sent the stomach contents and such to the National Poison Control Center at St. Luke's Presbyterian Hospital in Chicago, which is better equipped to determine the specific poison. More good news. The coroner prefers not to release any information until he hears back from Chicago. Meantime, we've got a few days to get our ducks in a row."

Nobody said anything, presumably contemplating what it would take to get 100 or so ducks in a row during an explosion.

After lunch

I was looking forward to a free afternoon, but Sergeant Hayden was waiting in the hallway as Hank and I left the dining room. Nobody paid him any mind. The way the sergeant dressed, he didn't look like a cop. After shaking hands with both of us, he turned to me and asked if I would mind being interviewed — now.

Answering for me, Hank said, "I expect he'll be thrilled. You can use my office."

We followed him to his office. He waved us in and left.

Sergeant Hayden scanned the room. I thought he'd take Hank's desk chair. He didn't. Instead he motioned to the guest chairs on the outside of the desk and said. "Let's do this friendly like. I'll take this chair and you take that one."

"How's it going?" I said. Great opening line.

"Fine, thanks." Informative comeback. "Tell me about Charlie Parker." Down to business.

"I assume the chief filled you in," I said.

"I'd like you to hear it from you."

"Charlie vomited rather dramatically at breakfast yesterday. After I had a chance to think a bit yesterday, I realized there might be a connection between him and Father Fox."

"Puke being the common symptom."

"Yes, along with the fact that no one else registered any similar symptoms."

"So you interviewed him?"

"Not really," I said. "As it turned out, he hadn't heard that Father Fox was, umm, found dead. I broke the news to him, let him absorb that. His reaction gave me some interesting information."

"Which was."

"He was the altar boy for Father Fox that morning."

"So he might have been the last person to see him alive?"

"Along with the sisters. But more than that." And I stopped.

"What?"

"Maybe the sister's chapel was the crime scene."

Now it was his turn to pause. "Because it was the only place the two people with stomach issues were together?"

"Exactly."

"Let's say that the young man and Father Fox ingested the poison there," he said. "How would they have done that?"

"Best guess. They drank something."

"Wine?" Sergeant Hayden didn't need to be Catholic to make this guess.

"Bingo," I said. "They could have eaten something. Unleavened bread. Hosts. But I think you can eliminate that."

"Why?"

"Multiple reasons. I'm no expert, but I think it would be hard to deliver the poison via the hosts. Anyway, if it were so, the sisters might have gotten sick."

"Okay, how about water?"

"It's a thought, "I admitted. "During the mass, the priest puts a few drops of water in the chalice. If you were trying to deliver some poison, I don't think you'd use water."

"You'd use wine."

"Yes, the more so because on this day the priest would be saying three masses and drinking multiple cups of wine."

"Might Father Fox have cut back on the wine for masses two and three?"

"Some priests do, I'm sure," I said, "To be honest, I don't know his habits in this area. I didn't think to ask Charlie about this. I'm sorry."

"And what about Charlie? Surely he wouldn't have drunk as much as Father Fox?"

"He shouldn't have drunk any, but ... have you ever been an altar boy?"

"Nope, where I go everyone drinks grape juice out of little cups four times a year."

"Well, then, you may not know that altar boys have been known to sneak a sip now and then."

"When the priest is not looking."

"They are very good at it."

"And you think, Charlie might have done so."

"I didn't ask," I said. "In this instance, I thought discretion was important. Besides, I didn't have to ask."

"Because you're certain he filched some wine."

"Ninety-nine-point-nine percent. Probably after Father Fox left, in a hurry according to Charlie."

"Can you take me to the sister's chapel?"

I paused. I wasn't sure, but I thought about Eli's warning and said, "Sure." We headed upstairs without talking, heading past a couple of seminarians in the library and into the sister's chapel. It was empty. Sergeant Hayden looked it over and asked me show him where wine might have been positioned. I showed him the credence table, where the cruets would have been and the altar where the chalice would have been. I demonstrated where and how the altar boy would have handed off the cruets and the priest would have poured the wine and water into the chalice.

"Was there only one altar boy?"

"Yes," I said. "In the main chapel, two. In the small chapels, like here, only one."

"Who else was here? Nuns?"

"Yes, that's all. They handled their own singing, I think, but we, uh, you should check that. In the other small chapels, two seminarians sometimes did the chants for a high mass. Here—I think—the sisters handled that."

"No one else was here?"

"Hmm. not during the service, no. Just Father Fox, three sisters, and one altar boy."

"You said 'during the service,' " the sergeant said. "Did anyone else have access to this chapel?"

"Well, any of the priests can come in here, but they usually don't unless they are saying the mass here. Then the sacristans, of course."

"Sacristans? What's that?"

"Two seminarians are assigned this role. Their job is to set things up for the next mass and cleanup after a mass. One usually handles the main chapel. The other handles the small chapels."

"What does this setup and cleanup involve?"

"Here, I'll show you." I took him into the sacristy, a small room at the side where the vestments, vessels, and other accessories were kept.

He was very interested in this and asked plenty of questions, including but not limited to the wine. "You said there was one seminarian assigned to the small chapels. Who was that?"

Oops. I don't know why I wasn't prepared for this. The thought that Dingo Dave might be a suspect had crossed my mind. But so, I reasoned, should have been the sisters, priests, and other staff. They all had access. I took a breath and told myself to keep to the truth, the minimum truth where possible. "Dave Johnson. His classmates call him Dingo Dave because his mother hails from Australia and he sometimes affects an Australian accent. I saw him in here the night before the, uh, unfortunate event."

"Was he supposed to be in here at the time?"

"Sure. I think so anyway. I believe the sacristans usually set up the night before."

"And the cleanup? When do they do that?"

"In the morning. After breakfast. That's when everybody does their obediences. That's our name for assigned housekeeping roles."

"So he would have had time to get rid of the evidence before Father Fox's body was found?"

"Well, actually, he probably would have been here just about the time I found the body."

"With enough time to get rid of the evidence."

This was going to a place I didn't like. Fast. "Are you assuming Dave Johnson did the deed?"

"Right now, I'm just looking at someone who seems to have

had the opportunity to do it and the opportunity to clean it up."

"But the sisters also would had the opportunity on both counts." I can't believe I said that.

"Yes, that's true," Sergeant Hayden said. "As did the altar boy, though he probably wouldn't have drunk his own poison. We'll be looking at other things too."

"Like motive?"

"Sure. Do the sisters have motive? Does Charlie Parker, who may have drank some of the poison, have motive? Does this Dave Johnson have motive?"

Oops.

Early afternoon

After I told Sergeant Hayden what I knew about Dingo Dave and his brother, I went up to my room and tried to think. I filled my pipe with Cherry Blend and tried to feel wise. It didn't help, Between coughs I felt like an idiot. I tried to tell myself that I had no choice, that I had to tell the police what I knew, but I felt like a snitch—and an idiot. I contemplated trying to find Hank and talking it over with him and decided against it.

With no better plan, I knocked the remains of my pipe tobacco into an ashtray and headed out the door, downstairs, and out and onto the cinder path, along the lake to the library. Before I reached the lake, I remembered I hadn't voted. Lyndon Johnson was going to clobber Barry Goldwater, I was pretty sure of that, but there were other offices open. It wouldn't do for a history teacher, however interim, to skip voting. I reversed direction, fired up the Edsel, and headed to a voting station near my house, Sarah's house, where I was registered. The lines were long, but I was able to do my civic duty in half an hour. I got back in the car, drove to the university library, and parked my car in the faculty lot across the road.

When I got to the library, I found Sarah at the front desk. I told her I was interested in doing some research on Nazis and homosexuality. I expected her to think this was a bit strange, but she reacted as if I was anyone coming in off the street.

"Fifth floor," she said. "But you might want to talk to Dr. Paul Schueller. He's an expert on Germany, specifically the run-up to World War II and beyond. His office is downstairs. Can't say when he'll be there. Anything else?"

"No, thanks. Talk to you later."

I worked my way down to the basement, found his office, which had office hours posted on his door. Supposedly, he'd be there at 4 P.M. It was almost 3:30. I figured I could wait. I assumed he'd be on time—with a name like Schueller and and a specialty on Nazis, he wouldn't be careless about time. I just hoped there wouldn't be a line of students.

After browsing the periodical section for twenty minutes, I went back downstairs. He wasn't there, and there were no students in line. I leaned against the wall next to his door. I wanted to be first.

And he was on time. Good German. I recognized him, probably had seen him on campus somewhere. He was short, was balding with frizzy gray hair on the sides, glasses, and a grumpy demeanor.

"You're not a student," he said, looking at me suspiciously.

I explained who I was and the surface of what I wanted.

"Pity about Father Fox," he said. "I didn't really know him. You'd think we would have crossed paths."

"Well, he's been in the Chicago area since ordination," I said. "Can you help?"

"Have your students read my book, *Nazis from the Weimar Republic until the End.*"

"Not a bad idea," I said. "At least for one student. Is it in the library?"

"Of course, but you could buy it from me." The man wasn't shy about self-promotion.

"Do you mind giving me the gist—about the homosexual part at least?"

He looked at me suspiciously. "The Cliff Notes version, then. The Weimar Republic was not very good on economics but quite liberal socially. It was fairly tolerant of homosexuality. The Nazis swam with this tide for a while, to the point where certain elements—notably the Brownshirts or Sturmabteilung, who predated the Nazis but became its early paramilitary wing—became well known for homosexuality within their ranks. Some sources think this was mixed up with a cult of virility. At any rate they were a tough bunch, not effeminate types at all. They were instrumental in bringing Hitler to power, but he turned on them. Big time."

"Because they were homosexual ... ?

"Because he perceived them as a threat—or, at any rate, because Himmler and Goering perceived them as a threat and convinced Hitler this was so. This may or may not have been true, but they apparently were trying to replace the German army, which made them serious enemies. Their leader, Ernst Rohm, was popular and influential. He surely was a threat to some. Not incidentally, his taste for young boys was well known and accepted for a time. Hitler with considerable help from the SS or Schutzstaffel, with which you might be familiar, purged them in 1934, killing most of the leadership in something called the 'Blood Purge' or 'The Night of the Long Knives.'

"Somehow the perceived threat of the Brownshirts and their reputation for homosexual behavior got mixed together, to the point where purges spread to the Hitler Youth and then to homosexuals—and suspected homosexuals—who had no connection to any of these groups. It's hard to tell how widespread the purge was, but the Nazis left the tolerance of the Weimar Republic behind. They were pretty vicious."

"Well, I'm shocked," I said in mock outrage. "Not really, but it sounds like Father Fox was onto something."

If that's what he was alluding to," Dr. Mueller said. "We just don't know the extent of it. Clearly, some people were sent to concentration camps *because* they were homosexuals."

"And I bet some were accused of being homosexual because someone wanted to get rid of them."

"Surely," he said. "Hard to know how many."

I left with a copy of his book, which I offered to pay for and which offer was accepted.

Chapter 26

Wednesday, November 4, 1964

I learned at breakfast that plans were afoot for Bernie's funeral on Friday. Hank had made the announcement at mass in the main chapel. The other priests weren't there. They had been celebrating mass in the smaller chapels. Of course, I wasn't there either. It wasn't my practice. Hank had to bring me and the others up to date at breakfast. Everyone expressed relief, Father Hop asking for the obvious update on the investigation. Hank said the only information he had was that the coroner expected to release the body for burial later in the day. Obviously, he didn't know how the investigation was going.

After instructing Father Hop to schedule the juniors and seniors for the all-night wake on Thursday evening and Friday morning, Hank dismissed the faculty. They dispersed, relieved for the normalcy of a funeral.

Hank took me aside privately and explained a few things. "What I told the group was not the whole truth," he said. "I probably should not tell you, but I have to tell somebody who is not suspected as the perpetrator."

"They don't suspect me?"

"Well, let's just say I choose to assume they don't," he said. "There appears to be something developing. I jumped the gun on announcing the funeral, though I had permission from everyone concerned to do so."

"That sounds opaque."

"Opaque?"

"Not transparent."

"I know what it means. Bernie's body is still in the morgue, but the coroner is planning to get clearance to release the body from the National Poison Control Center later today. He is almost certain that the center will be able to identify the poison by today or tomorrow, which normally would trigger his announcement that the death was a homicide."

"Normally."

"Well, this assumes that the particular poison would not have been ingested accidentally. Still, the normal expectation would be for him to follow the center's determination with his own ruling. However," he paused. "However, the congregation's lawyer seems to have worked out an arrangement benefiting both the congregation and law enforcement, at least temporarily. The lawyer told us—told the provincial, at any rate—that the detectives wanted the coroner to delay announcing the ruling out of fear that it might prompt the killer to flee."

"Suggesting what?"

"Suggesting that they think whoever did the deed feels safe at the moment, which narrows the field."

It took me a while, but I finally got it—to my dismay. "This means the detectives are not suspecting a faculty member."

"That's my guess. They know that the faculty knows Bernie's death is suspicious."

"And their behavior is ..." I paused.

"Normal, at least under the circumstances," Hank said. "Faculty members are shocked, saddened, and nervous about what lies ahead."

"Normal under the circumstances," I repeated. "But how do the detectives know about the faculty's behavior? Through you?"

"Some," he said. "But they interviewed everyone on the staff—at some length—and I don't think they stirred anybody up. Well, except for the good sisters."

"What? Surely the authorities don't expect food poisoning."

"They don't," Hank said. "But it's something they needed to eliminate. They talked to the cooks yesterday, and Father Hop said that it didn't go well."

"He was the interpreter."

"Yes, and he said the good sisters took considerable umbrage ..."

"Umbrage. Big word. And how can you tell? Those two are not known for their conviviality."

"Father Hop had no trouble identifying it as umbrage. He said the velocity, volume, and quantity of the German was up three or four notches—and he didn't dare translate much of what they said literally."

"I bet," I said, "Sorry I missed it."

"Despite Father Hop's best intentions, the detectives got the gist—and they weren't pleased."

"But they don't suspect them."

"Of course not, but their reaction forced them to call in the health department to check the kitchen. Today, as I understand it."

"Umm, more fireworks to come."

"You might want to eat at the Huddle tonight."

"If they aren't suspecting the good sisters, who are they suspecting?" I didn't really want an answer.

"I think they are looking at one of the students."

"Who?"

"You tell me."

"I'd rather not."

"Everything seems to be pointing to Dave Johnson."

"Dingo Dave?"

"Don't you love their nicknames? As I understand it, Dingo Dave has motive, means, opportunity."

"But they haven't even talked to any of the students yet, Dave included," I said.

"No, but they've talked to you."

"But the seminarians think it was a natural death, like a heart attack."

"Except for the um, killer, who—if he's a seminarian—feels safe because nobody seems the wiser."

"They suspect a seminarian," I said. "That's ugly."

"You think there is an outcome that is not ugly?"

"Good point."

"We've stepped in something nasty, and we're not likely to get it off our shoes for some time."

Dinner time

My classes went better than I expected. The seminarians were subdued, but returning to the regular schedule had anchored them. Lunch, which featured bologna sandwiches, was uneventful. I didn't have a history class, but I collared Dan Johnson after my sophomore English class and gave him Dr. Mueller's book to read, clarifying that I wanted it back. He seemed interested.

There was one afternoon class, and then the boys went off to recreation. Mostly flag football, the last games before attention turned to basketball.

Then, at dinner, everything fell apart. The cooks were in a foul mood, banging pots and slinging German that nobody could understand. The waiters waited impatiently for the food, which was slow to come to the counters. When it did, it featured mystery squares cooked to a black crisp, stewed tomatoes heated to room temperature, and partially boiled potatoes.

The priest table, whose fare was a notch above what the seminarians were served, got the same treatment. Something was going on. The good sisters had served up a trifecta of the most hated foods—and ruined them, which heretofore no one had thought possible. The gathering set to murmuring, and Hank sent Father Hop back to the kitchen to reconnoiter.

He returned ten minutes later to report.

"As near as I can tell," he said after taking his chair and staring for a bit at the plate of burned mystery squares, "our cooks are in rebellion, thanks to yesterday's interview with the detectives and today's visit from the health department."

"I assume they will settle down by breakfast."

"I wouldn't count on it," Father Hop said.

"I see," said Hank.

The table got very quiet, while the priest waiters poured everyone coffee, an item they controlled.

"I sense we'll be doing some snacking in the faculty lounge and in our rooms," said Brother Rufus.

"What about the seminarians?" asked Hank.

"We could do an impromptu soiree," I suggested.

"A party hardly seems appropriate under the circumstances," Hank said. "Are they getting enough to tide them over."

Father Hop responded, "While I was down there, the runners were asking the cooks for bread, at which point they threw unopened loaves of white bread at them. I think everyone got a loaf. They won't starve, but they won't be in a good mood either."

"It'll have to do," Hank said and turned to me. "You've chatted with Sister Angela?"

"Most of the time I had a tongue depressor down my throat, so I did a lot of listening."

"Well, maybe you could go up to the dispensary after dinner, such as it is, and give her a buzz," Hank said. "As I understand it, she speaks English. Maybe she can tell us what's going on with those two."

"Maybe."

After the seminarians got done tearing into the loaves of bread and exhausting the supplies of butter and honey, Hank slammed his hand on the bell and led the closing blessing. Since it focused on thanksgiving, participation was limp.

I went off on my errand. I climbed a flight of stairs to the section of the third floor that housed the infirmary and the seniors' rooms. A couple of seniors climbed the stairs with me, grumbling about the meal, planning to fire up the available popcorn poppers, and making fun of Sister Marta. Why the seminarians chose to make fun of Marta—when Sister Celia looked and behaved pretty much like her twin sister—was beyond me. They asked me what was going on.

"I don't know," I said. "I just live here." I went into the infirmary and rang the bell. The way things were going, I wasn't expecting an answer. But after five minutes or so, Sister Angela appeared in the infirmary.

"May I help you," she said.

"Perhaps. Your sisters—the cooks—were in something of a state at dinner."

She waited for me to say more, but I didn't. "A state," she repeated neutrally.

"They seemed upset. Very upset. The food was, um, they seemed very upset. Father Superior ... " I paused to let the more formal title for Hank sink in. I didn't want her to think I was here on my own recognizance. "Father Superior was wondering if anything was wrong."

"I wasn't there, of course," Sister Angela said.

"Of course," I repeated. "But you speak English, whereas Sisters Marta and Celia are a bit challenged in English, and we were wondering if you knew what is going on."

"I see," said Sister Angela. This was like watching a boat dock.

"Do you, um, know?"

"I know that this afternoon some men are coming to inspect their kitchen."

"Yes, from the health department," I said. "It is routine."

"The sisters do not think so."

"Well, okay, it is not a regular inspection, as I understand it, but it was a routine practice, given the intensity of Charlie Parker's distress."

"But nobody else was sick," she said.

I said nothing.

"And Sister Marta and Sister Celia do not like being accused of food poisoning."

"I don't think they were accused of food poisoning."

"They think so."

"Sister Angela, you know they are not being accused of food poisoning."

"I understand. I told them as much, but they would not listen."

"Can't you settle them down?"

"I'd have an easier time jumping over the moon," she said. "In any case, they ... maybe I shouldn't say."

"Would you tell Father Grieshaber if he were here?"

"I suppose."

"Then tell me," I said. "I'm his emissary."

"On their behalf, I spoke to Mother Superior and requested that we be transferred to the Mother House."

"Ouch. We don't need this."

"Mr. Foote, the point is, we don't need it either. I'm afraid the die is cast. Sisters Marta and Celia are packing as we speak, and I must attend to my own suitcase." With that, she turned and left.

A shiver went through me. I got up and headed down the stairs and to the faculty lounge, where I expected to find Hank. He was there, and I broke the news. It didn't need embellishment.

Chapter 27

Thursday, November 5, 1964

I hadn't had so much fun since, oh, marching into Germany in the driving rain.

Last night, I had connected with Hank in the faculty lounge. He looked tired, but I was relieved to find that he wasn't totally snockered. He might have been, had he not reached the provincial by phone. The provincial, perhaps more used to solving personnel problems, reacted calmly to the nuns departure and suggested that he could find some short-term solutions to the missing cooks and nurse by the next afternoon. This left today's breakfast and lunch for us to manage.

As for lunch, the provincial suggested that we send the seminarians over to the university's south dining hall, which had a section serving the public and could accommodate 100 or so extra visitors if we sent them over in shifts. As for breakfast, well that fell on me.

I was to take over the kitchen while the seminarians were at morning mass, earlier if I wanted to.

I wanted to and showed up at 5 A.M. As it turned out, I needn't have showed up this early, though it did give more time to fret. At Hank's suggestion, I decided to keep it simple, forgoing any cooking. Thus, the job consisted mostly of finding the supply of individual-sized boxes of cereal, fresh fruit, and bread. It would be a little

EVIL SPEAKING

light, but no one needed to starve.

For bread, I found bags of hard rolls, which the seminarians liked. Boxes of individual butter pads were in the large refrigerator. The next task was to arrange the food for the runners to take to their respective tables. Under a counter, I found stacks of red plastic baskets, good for holding dry items, and began putting cereal boxes in one basket, bananas and apples in another, and rolls in another. I wasn't too sure how many items to put in each basket, deciding to put nine in each basket, one extra item for each table. I had to go out to the dining room to count the tables.

By 5:55, the seminarians were just getting up and I was good to go. I might have gone upstairs to mass, but I decided to stay here and fret.

The fretting took a solid hour, during which time I made some real coffee for the priest's table—they would have to survive on the same food everyone else was getting—and drank three cups myself, which prompted two trips to the latrine. I also smoked five cigarettes, regretting each one.

The seminarians didn't know the sisters had left, though there was some talk because the sisters didn't make any attempt to hide their departure, which was accompanied by what sounded like cursing in German and much slamming of the trunk of their car and all of its four doors.

The first to arrive were the priest-waiters, seniors who waited on the head table. When they saw me and what I had to offer, they wanted to know what was going on. I told them they'd find out soon enough. The next to arrive was the "milk man," a junior who muscled the farmer cans onto a cupboard of sorts, which held the cans and a plastic spout at the bottom, allowing table runners to fill up pitchers with milk. He was on autopilot, did his job, and didn't ask any questions. The next to arrive were the table runners who wanted to know why Mr. Foote was setting up the baskets intended for the seminarians' tables. I gave them the same noncommital answer, which did nothing to limit their speculations.

"The sisters quit." Good guess.

"They don't like Father Grease." Probably true at this point.

"The health department rejected their mystery squares." Not exactly.

"They were mad about the visit from the health department." Right on.

"The health department accused them of poisoning Upchuck." Nope.

Comments about the visit from the health department won the immediate popularity contest, which was interesting first because it was basically correct and second because they weren't supposed to know about it. The sisters own noisy reaction contributed to the rumor.

By the time they came back to pick up the baskets of buns, they were complaining about the meager breakfast.

"Is this all we get?"

"We're gonna starve."

"How are we supposed to survive on cereal? Half my table won't even eat cereal."

And so on.

I was busy and didn't hear the announcement about the sisters. The meal went on with gossip, speculation, and griping. The meal ended in a foul mood all around.

One benefit of the meager pickings was that the cleanup was easy. My cleanup team—two seminarians—had nothing to do except grill me on what they were going to have for lunch."

"I have no idea," I said.

"Well, we gotta have something."

"I suppose that's true," I said.
"I bet they're arranging something,"
"I suppose that's true," I said.
"We're not going to starve!"
"I don't suppose so."
"You're a lot of help, Mr. Foote."
"You're welcome."

Lunch time

Morning classes had a similar flavor. Everyone wanted to know what was up with the cooks. Speculation was rife that the good sisters were suspected of food poisoning, though I did my best to undermine that theory, telling that only one person (as far as they knew) had shown any symptoms of food poisoning, which made it unlikely that food poisoning was an issue, no matter what they thought of mystery squares and stewed tomatoes.

I did have the sophomore U.S. history class and was able to report on Nazis and homosexuals, mainly for the benefit of Dan Johnson. He asked a couple of questions, intended to establish that the treatment of homosexuals was not as big a deal as the genocide against Jews.

I explained as best I could that the Nazis clearly set out to exterminate the Jewish races, but it was not clear that the persecution of homosexuals rose to that level. "On the other hand," I told the class, "you didn't want to be a homosexual in Nazi Germany." Dan Johnson seemed to take this in stride.

During the last morning class, an English class for juniors, a senior came in with the announcement about how lunch was to be handled. We were to report to the public cafeteria in the South Dining Hall, freshmen at 12:30, sophomores at 12:45, juniors at 1:00, and seniors at 1:15. All anyone had to do was show his student ID. The messenger added that faculty would be eating with the seminarians, partly because we had to eat as well and partly to monitor the seminarians' behavior. "Pigging out," he said he was ordered to add, "would not be tolerated."

The assembled demonstrated their approval in various ways. A few applauded. Others said "great" or some other exclamation. Several joked, "What, no pigging out! Aw!" No one complained. Though inconvenient, this was not particularly bad news to the seminarians. Grumbling about the sisters' cooking was something of an art form, and eating at the public cafeteria on campus would be a welcome relief—at least in the short term. Aside from that, they tended to look for opportunities to visit the Notre Dame campus.

Then, the messenger said he had another announcement. He read from a sheet explaining that there would be a wake tonight for Father Fox at Moreau Seminary chapel, beginning at 7 P.M. The wake would include a rosary, followed by a eulogy from one of his fellow priests, and then most of the group would repair to the dining room for a cafeteria style dinner. Holy Cross seniors and juniors would keep vigil over the body in thirty minute shifts until midnight, at which point St. Joe Hall seminarians would take over until 7 A.M. the next morning. The messenger said the schedule would be posted on the bulletin board outside the seminary's bookstore.

The news that some of them would have to keep vigil over a dead body for thirty minutes cast a pall on the room, though it was not unexpected. It was the normal custom when a member of the Holy Cross order had died, but the fact that this was a vigil over one who was truly their own made a difference. Holding the wake at Moreau Seminary was an aberration, designed to accommodate the Holy Cross seminarians who would not normally have attended the wake and following meal. Moreau was a large facility that could easily handle the extra mourners.

After class, everyone assembled at their appointed times in the university cafeteria. It went reasonably well, considering that the lines were already longer because of the visitors on campus for ND's game with Pittsburgh on Saturday. Afternoon classes had been cancelled, leaving seminarians free to wander the campus. Thanks to a winter chill in the area, most of them walked briskly back to the seminary and entertained themselves there.

I was able to check in with Hank, who by then had made arrangements for the following day. Breakfast would be the same, though he assigned his secretary at my urging to lay in extra supplies—fruits, cereal, and buns. She would prove a good soldier, even though it required an emergency trip to the supermarket and three overfilled carts through the checkout line. For lunch and dinner—and subsequent breakfasts—Hank had worked out an arrangement with the student dining hall to provide us with the same meals the students were eating. The catch was that someone was going to have pick up the trays of warm food, get them to our own refectory, and set them up cafeteria-style. This required renting a van, another job that fell to his secretary. Two seminarians would be enlisted to pick up the food. The dining hall volunteered to send a veteran helper for the first two days, assigned mainly to show the seminarians how to set up and serve the food. The arrangement wasn't intended to be permanent, but it would have to do until we found a new cook or two.

Evening

The community wake shook things up a bit. After the rosary, led by a senior, Father Mike Miller, the order's provincial, got up and announced that the wake would not feature typical eulogies, though he invited the assembled to share their memories of Father Fox whenever and wherever they wished. Instead, he explained that it was important to read a letter that might change how everyone thought about Father Fox, for the better he hoped, but possibly not. The letter was dated June 27, 1946, and was addressed to the provincial at the time, the now deceased Father Emanuel Viognier.

```
Dear Manny,

   I wish to recommend a young man to begin
attending St. Joseph Hall this fall, with the
prospect that he will wish--and the appropriate
authorities will approve--to continue on a
path toward ordination as a priest in the
Congregation of Holy Cross. Before you approve
of his petition to begin the requisite studies,
you must know his story, a story that you may
not wish to share indiscriminately.
   I befriended this young man while I was
assigned to the Vatican State Department toward
the end of the World War. At the time, I was
assigned to deal with issues related to those
who had taken asylum in the Vatican. This was
how I got to know a man who went at the time by
the name of Bernhard Johan Fuchs.
   He had come to us as a deserter from the
German army, which was still present in Italy
and charged with the task of rounding up Jews
and others for shipping to various work and
concentration camps. It took me some time to get
to know him because, like many who came to us,
he had been wounded both in body and in soul.
   As for the former, he had a noticeable scar
on his forehead and not much else. As for the
latter, the wound went deep. He hardly spoke and
when he did it was only to answer "yes" or "no",
in American English, which made me wonder if he
had roots in the United States.
  In time, I learned from him that he was the son
of an American history professor and a German
woman--and was born in the United States in
```

1920. His father, Francis Fox, was a professor of history at our St. Edward's University in Austin, a good man, who died at the relatively young age of 45 in 1928. After a year--just before the crash--his widow decided to return with her son to the village where she grew up in Germany. In the process, she Germanized her married name--and that of her son--to Fuchs and began calling her son Bernhard instead of Bernie. When Hitler came to power, young Bernhard joined Hitler youth, an association that led naturally to a role in the Brown Shirts. When the purges came, Bernhard survived --though he never told me how--and he progressed into the SS. Germany was in difficulty, and much of the population looked to Hitler for a way out. Bernhard was a kid and was swept up into places he would come to regret. Over time, the ugliness of his role wore on him. By the time he was assigned to Rome, it only got uglier. When he saw the opportunity, he made his way into the Vatican.

I had dozens of asylum seekers to attend to, but Bernhard was special. He was rough around the edges, but no more so than the other Nazi deserters. To be honest, the St. Ed's connection made a difference--to me and to Bernhard. For him, it was a way of connecting to his father, to his life in the U.S., and to me. Knowing he was born in the U.S., I was certain I could get him back into the U.S., but I wasn't sure what he would do there. After some months, he brought up the idea of becoming a monk. He saw himself as damaged goods, incapable of raising a family, and he thought this would be a way of repenting for his past. We explored this option at some length. Somewhere in the process, he expressed some interest in becoming a teacher. He didn't say so himself, but I saw this as another way for him to reconnect to his father, his American parent, and away from his unfortunate experience in Germany. It was an interesting idea.

After some thought, I suggested that

```
    rather than joining a monastery, he might
    join a religious community of teachers--the
    Congregation of Holy Cross, for instance. He
    liked the idea immediately, and we both saw how
    this might grease his reentry to the United
    States.
       And indeed it did. Once the war ended, I
    was able to get the U.S. State Department to
    expedite the processing of his passport, which
    was done under his birth name--Bernard John
    Fox--along with the warning that his past had
    put him on the watch list of more than one U.S.
    agency.
       I am now putting the ball in your court,
    with the hope that you will facilitate approval
    of his request to enter St. Joseph Hall as a
    postulate in our congregation and to begin his
    studies as a freshman at the University of Notre
    Dame. I cannot claim to know where this will go,
    but I believe it is the right course at this
    time.
```

"And this was signed by then-Bishop and now-Archbishop Terrence O'Brien, CSC."

The provincial paused to let the letter sink in. "I was vocation director at the time and, in that capacity, was shown this letter, which remains to this day in Bernie's personnel file in the provincial's office. All of Father Viognier's successors have known about this letter—and Bernie's background—but we were all instructed by our predecessor not to share the letter during Bernie's lifetime. This is the first time that anyone, aside from the provincial, has been privy to it."

He paused again. "I just want to say that, from the beginning, I trusted the judgment of Bishop O'Brien and Father Manny. I have learned of nothing since then that would make me doubt their judgment. However, I will note—as most of you know—that Bernie wasn't the easiest man to get along with. He was interesting, always fascinating, sometimes charming. He was often short with people and, on occasion, quite fierce. I noticed that his fierceness was always in defense of someone who needed a champion. Someone who might have been unpopular, for whatever reason. This characteristic sometimes got him into trouble, and people would begin to talk about him—precisely because he was defending the wrong people. Those few of us who knew his background—and his desire to make amends for the damage he had done in his earlier years—understood this behavior and appreciated him, even when it made our jobs difficult. We understood that Bernie, as a member of this congregation, embodies more than any of the rest of us the task of comforting the afflicted and afflicting the comfortable. Moreover, he understood that that no saint was never a sinner. Whatever your experience of Father Bernie, understand that he was a hard man, a just man, and a good man."

He went back to his seat and sat in silence, during which you could have heard a feather hit the floor. After what seemed like forever, he got up, invited everyone—except the Holy Cross seminarians designated to sit wake—to the dining room.

Chapter 28

Friday, November 6, 1964

Big day. Bernie's funeral was in the morning, and I had another day of kitchen duty. With a whole day's experience under my belt and supplies acquired by the school's secretary, I went through it more easily. One more time and it would be routine. In fact, everyone seemed to be going through the motions.

The seminarians were still trying to absorb what they now knew about Father Bernie Fox, and they weren't sure how to think about it. The wake soiree was subdued. No one wanted to talk, least of all the faculty who were just as stunned as the seminarians. The party, such as it was, broke up after everyone had eaten. The fact that the juniors and seniors had kept vigil in half hour shifts over Bernie's body through the night kept the mood somber. I had done this in my day, and it was always a spooky experience. And I never had to sit staring at the body of one of my teachers.

The faculty was equally stunned. They weren't talking, and I couldn't tell what they were thinking. For me, it explained everything. I understood why Bernie behaved the way he did, why he protected a homosexual student, and why his actions could be misinterpreted. I understood the origin of his prickly personality and, after all of that, I wished I had known him better.

The seminarians ate fairly quietly, at least for them, and set off to do their obediences. Afterwards, they hung out in their rooms and locker until heading off to Sacred Heart Church for Bernie's requiem mass, which was scheduled to start at 10 A.M. Compared to the wake, it was an anti-climax. Instead of an emotional surprise, it was high liturgy, complete with a procession of the cassock-and-surplice-dressed priests and professed seminarians. There was a homily instead of an eulogy, the former being more about reminding people that life was a fragile thing but that in death there was the hope of resurrection. The words were a boilerplate, but they had some resonance at a funeral where nothing was what it seemed. Not life. Not death. Not Bernie.

The procession to the grave continued the healing ritual, with priests, brothers, and seminarians walking quietly in pairs behind the hearse to the cemetery, less than a mile away. I walked just behind with the Holy Cross seminarians, basically at the end of the line. I felt, more than saw, the presence of some others. When I turned my head, I saw a man and a woman trailing at a discreet distance. Behind them were two men, whom I recognized as the detectives from the sheriff's office.

At the conclusion of the graveside service, the presiding minister—Hank—invited everyone to lunch at Moreau seminary, another quarter mile to the north. He had told me of this plan, important because it covered another meal for the seminarians. This procession was more informal, with people mouthing the usual consolations and cliches or remaining unusually quiet.

Father Joe Perry, I noticed, made a point of introducing himself to the middle-aged couple and shepherding them toward Moreau. At this point, I guessed, correctly as it turned out, that the man and woman were the parents of Jimmy Parker, the young man who had committed suicide a month before. Obviously, Bernie's death had scraped open the wound that had had no chance to heal. The woman was dabbing at her eyes with a tissue.

I lost track of Hank on the way over and didn't seem him again until most of the group had assembled in the dining room. Some had taken seats at tables, but a few were still mulling around. Father Perry was introducing the Parkers to the provincial, who greeted them warmly.

At that point, Hank came in, spotted me, and asked for a word outside of the room. "We have some news."

"I was afraid of that," I said. "What's up?"

"The poison has been identified." He paused. "It's yew."

"Me? What the ...?"

Hank tried not to laugh. "I'm sorry. "It's not Y-O-U. It's Y-E-W. Yew."

"Oh, the evergreen," I said. "Oh, Oh-oh, Oh."

"Is that significant for some reason?"

"Maybe," I said. "It's not a very common poison, is it?"

"It's a common enough plant, as the detectives explained it. It's quite toxic, but they're not sure it's ever been used to murder someone. Hardly anyone knows it's a poison."

"I know someone who knows it's a poison." Part of me wished I hadn't spoken.

"And who is that?"

I paused, "Dingo Dave." I felt guilty as soon as I said it. Guiltier still when I fingered my son as my source of information. I was going to be in big trouble on the home front—but then that wouldn't be a new deal.

"You better tell the detectives," he said.

"I suppose."

"You tell or I will."

"Are they still around?"

"I told them I wanted to talk to you first. They said they'd be out by the lake."

After a circuitous walk around the building, I found them staring at the golden dome and the Sacred Heart steeple.

"You have something to tell us?" Sergeant Hayden asked.

I told them.

Sergeant Hayden showed no emotion, just asked me to get "Father Grieshaber."

With that, I wended my way around the building, through the entry way, and into the dining hall. Most were seated and waiting for the prayer. I found Hank, who looked unusually sober, talking to Father Hop. I motioned him to step outside the dining hall.

After I briefed him, he said, "You should come as well."

When I complained about having to take what seemed like a mile circuit around the building, he laughed and directed me down the stairs and out the lakeside door. Much faster.

Sergeant Hayden was ready for us. "We'd like to search Dave Johnson's locker and room,"

"He doesn't have a room," Hank said. "He sleeps in a dorm, but there's nothing there to see. Just a bed. He does have a locker, and you're welcome to search, preferably at a time when you won't be noticed."

"Which would be now," I said.

"Mmm, it would be now," Hank agreed. "The seminarians will be tied up at lunch for an hour or so."

"We could do it now," Detective Wood said.

Hank looked at me. He seemed relieved, as if solutions lay ahead. "Okay, Bert, but my presence is needed at the lunch. Will you mind taking the detectives over there? I'm afraid you're going to have to make other arrangements for lunch."

"No worries, as Dingo Dave would say."

"And Sergeant," Hank said, "I don't mind letting you have a look around, but can you be discreet?"

"You mean you don't want us to toss the place?"

"Yeah, that."

"I think we can handle that," Sergeant Hayden said. "Thank you for your cooperation."

Hank headed back into the building. The two detectives and I went down the bank and took the cinder path next to the lake back toward the seminary. The building was open—security was light in those days—and I took the detectives downstairs to the junior locker room and to Dingo Dave's locker.

"What's this?" asked Detective Hayden, staring at a bookshelf hanging from the ceiling. I had forgotten about this. It contained plants, featuring a bizarre assortment of plants. One was a Venus Flytrap. Another was a Resurrection Plant, which in its current dehydrated state looked like a prehistoric tumbleweed. Another was an evergreen, which I now realized would be the clincher.

"Dingo Dave fancies himself something of a botanist," I said. I didn't bother with the specifics.

"Well, well. I believe we're looking at the seedling of a Yew tree," said Detective Wood. He had gotten up to speed in a hurry.

"I don't think there's enough to poison a 220-pound man," I said, trying to slow down the freight train of conclusions.

"But it's a yew tree," he said. "Combined with what else you've told us ..."

They were careful with the search of his locker, which contained a small collage of Australian pictures, a boomerang, and Dingo Dave's trademark bush hat.

"Hmm, interesting collage here," Sergeant Hayden said. "Didn't you say something to us about a collage on the victim's door?"

I said nothing, just waited for them to finish. They made a perfunctory search of the locker room, with me answering their questions about what turned out to be a "fly graveyard," a display of photos, including one for "the Cerebral Palsy Marching Band," and a popcorn popper.

"We'd like to check that island you told us about," the detective said. "Where do we get a boat?"

I had to think about that. "This might not be a good time for that. When lunch is over at Moreau, the seminarians will come back here. Classes have been cancelled for the day, and dollars to donuts Dingo Dave will change into his outback gear and row over to his island."

"How about Monday—during classes?"

"That should work," I said. "Dave will be in my class at 9 A.M."

"We could do that. How about the boat?"

"I'm thinking you could borrow the one at the retreat house. We have a boat at our pier—the one Dingo Dave uses—but you probably don't want to call attention to yourselves by using that one."

"Right," the detective said. "We'll walk over to the retreat house right now and make the arrangements."

Afternoon

I got the picture. The detectives were fixing to arrest Dave Johnson, perhaps as soon as Monday. My feelings were mixed. On one hand, I was glad the case was being solved. Everything was lined up against Dingo Dave. In some ways, it was the best of all possible outcomes, better than finding out one of the teachers was the culprit. Or even that the good sisters had served up a homicidal microbe in a mystery square.

My guess was that Bernie Fox's demise was the result of a prank that went awry. Dingo Dave might spend a year or two in a group home and then he would be released. Of course, his promising life would be derailed.

On the other hand, what if Dingo Dave didn't do it? His life was about to be ruined over a rush to justice. My head went with the first hand. My heart went with the second. I needed to talk with someone.

The best candidate was Eli Bonpere. He knew the legal ins and outs.

As soon as the detectives left for the retreat house, I went upstairs, retrieved Eli's work number, and called it. Trudy answered, told me he was in a meeting. I guessed that he was sitting at his desk, eating lunch. That was enough for me. I didn't need to be around for the rest of the afternoon, and I was on a mission. I went down the two flights of stairs, fired up the Edsel, and drove to Eli's office.

Trudy was at her desk. I asked if I could see Mr. Bonpere some time to day. "It's an emergency," I said.

"Let me ask," she said, disappearing into his office. She returned within thirty seconds. "He'll see you now."

I followed her in and took a seat across from his desk.

"I've got about fifteen minutes before my next appointment," he said. "Shoot."

I filled him in, concluding with my latest dilemma.

"Well," he said. "You cooperated with the authorities. From a legal—and ethical—point of view, that's a good thing. On the other hand, you feel guilty."

"Yes," I said.

"Tough."

Sometimes Eli could be long-winded. I waited until he spoke again." But a compassionate man would do what he could to make sure the young man had legal representation, if it comes to that."

"Any ideas," I said.

"What's the situation with his parents?"

"Divorced. His dad is in Australia. His mom lives in Fort Wayne. Manages a restaurant. Works weekends. Doesn't have much money."

"I could help in a pinch. You going to pay me?"

"Same terms as last time?"

"I'd make more doing it pro bono."

"Funny," I said. "Maybe the congregation will pitch in."

"Even though nailing this unfortunate seminarian is the best outcome?"

"They're good people," I said. "They can manage the moral complexities better than I can."

"Okay," he said. "Come Monday, if they take him into custody—and there's no other lawyer in play—give me a call. And get me his mother's phone number."

Late afternoon

After that, I worked my way back to the seminary, hoping I could find Hank somewhere. I tried his office and then the faculty lounge. He was having a drink.

"How was lunch?"

"Tasty," he said, taking a sip. "Hmm, that's good. We've been lucky, in the sense that the congregation has provided us with two meals, handy in the absence of cooks. Tonight, we'll see how catering from the student dining hall works out."

"How was the mood?"

"Interesting. Relief. Maybe a reassessment of Bernie's life. We knew him, and yet we didn't."

"Odd," I said. "The man was a Nazi, in the military, and yet ..."

"Not just in the military ..."

"Hard core," I said.

"The hardest. I get it. Still, I feel a bit better about him somehow."

"Repentance does that. Too bad he had to die to be redeemed in our eyes."

"Maybe that's true of all of us."

"Yes sir, you'll make a theologian yet." He tipped his glass to me in a salute. "This morning, the thing that moved me the most was the presence of the Parkers. Just showing up was moving enough, but they talked to anyone who would listen about what Bernie did for their boy. They sought out me, Joe Perry, and the provincial especially. They seemed to be on a mission to restore his reputation."

"Sounds like they did a good job."

"Helluva job."

I decided to change the topic. I told him that I had arranged with my lawyer—Eli—to pitch in if Dingo Dave needed some legal help.

"Legal help?"

"It looks like the detectives are going to make their move on Monday."

"Dingo Dave?"

"That's my guess. Check that, more like an informed opinion."

"Already? My, my, Mr. Foote, you work fast." He took another sip.

"I wish you hadn't said that," I admitted. "I feel guilty about fingering the boy."

"Well, thank God anyway. It's going to be a relief."

"You mean, knowing where we stand?"

"Of course," Hank said. "And to be honest, this may be the best outcome."

"You mean, nailing a student."

"I wouldn't put it that way, but yes. It's better that it's a seminarian than a member of the staff."

"I had the same thought, but is it really?"

"Well, certainly not for young David," Hank said. "But if the culprit turned out to be a teacher, that would be the end." He paused. "We're close enough to the end as it is."

"What do you mean?"

"Well, parents could decide the school is not safe, maybe pull their kids out immediately, certainly not send them back."

"No, I get that," I said. "I mean, why do you say we're close enough to the end."

"Well, you're getting into the inner workings of the congregation here, but there is some feeling among the leadership that this institution—at least as a seminary—no longer makes sense."

"How so?"

"Quite simply, it's a lousy way to produce priests—or at least healthy priests."

"You mean like you, Reverend Alumnus," I said

"I have my issues," he said, raising his glass. "But some of us have been uncomfortable with the practice for years. You get guys who have been protected from the outside world all of their lives. Then they get ordained, and you put them with regular folks in a parish, a school, or a hospital—and they have no background for it. Emotionally, they may still be 13-year-olds. At best, they know how to get along in a community of men with the same values, but outside—nothing."

"You're talking about celibacy."

"Not just that, but yeah," he said. "If you think about it, choosing to not have a family, to not have sex, to go where someone else tells you go, to not have freedoms that everyone takes for granted—it's an odd thing. If you're going to do that, you'd better know what you're giving up."

"You believe it's better to pull men into the system when they are quite a bit older."

"In a word, yes."

"So you see the congregation closing down this place."

"Not for sure," he said. "While we are in some agreement that entering the seminary at the age of thirteen is a bad idea, some of us think that this environment turns out good men, healthy men, when they don't go into the priesthood. In fact, we know it does."

"Present company excepted," I said.

"You have your issues," he said, tipping his glass to me, "but you're still a good example. At least when you're sober."

"High praise coming from you," I said, immediately regretting the insult.

Hank laughed. "You deserve it. Do you have any regrets about graduating from Holy Cross?"

"Now that you mention it, not really," I said. "The powers that be told me I wasn't priest material, which was a blow to my ego. But they were right. When I look back on the life here—the discipline, the teachers, my classmates—no, I don't have regrets. It was a good way for a boy to become a young man."

"Exactly."

"So you'd keep the institution, but you wouldn't focus on preparing boys for the priesthood."

"Correct. We'd focus on preparing them to lead."

"A boarding school."

"If this place is going to survive, that's the game."

"Makes sense."

"I think so," he said. "What I don't know is whether it will work—and whether the congregation can afford it."

Chapter 29

The Weekend, November 6–8, 1964

What a week. I needed to take a breath, I needed a meeting in the worst way. On Friday, I picked one frequented by Rick, my sponsor, hoping I could talk to him. He was there. I filled him in, trying to speak in generalities and not doing very well. I explained my quandary, my role in the likely arrest of Dingo Dave, and my decision to enlist the aid of Eli Bonpere. He congratulated me for doing what I could but suggested it might be time to "let go and let God," a common slogan in the program. It fit my need to take a breath. I didn't feel like going back to the seminary and went out to an after-meeting gathering at a diner. That helped.

In the morning, I went to breakfast, wondering how the catering routine was going to work. It went well enough. The university cafeteria food was better than we were used to, which was a nasty testament to the cooking skills of the good sisters. Let go and let God. The good sisters might not be missed.

Things got back to a kind of normal, with the seminarians doing their Saturday obediences and the local boys going off to their families and the rest entertaining themselves with games, indoor and outdoor, and hobbies. Most of the latter would gather around the radio to listen to Notre Dame play an away game at Pittsburgh

With my head having cleared a bit, I spent an hour in my room revising my lesson plans before going over to the Huddle, buying a cup of coffee and a Chicago Tribune and sitting down to relax, away from the scene of the crime, so to speak.

This was not my weekend to be with Butch and Sissy, which left me free to listen to the football game with the seminarians. The Irish did well and there was good energy in the room, another semblance of normalcy.

In the evening, I went to another meeting and another after-dinner gathering at the diner. I was feeling passably centered.

Sunday was a bit of a surprise. Sarah had invited me dinner, which went well enough, given that I was having trouble looking Butch in the face. I was still contemplating how to broach the subject of Dingo Dave's arrest.

By the time we finished, it was pushing 2 P.M. Butch and Sissy went off to their own affairs—Butch to the basement to work on his model airplanes and Sissy off to a friend's house. This gave Sarah and me a chance to walk and talk in the crisp fall air. I was able to fill her in on the week, with considerable detail this time. I shared my conflicted feelings about the impending arrest of Dingo Dave.

"It sounds like you're doing the right thing," she said. "You couldn't have covered for him, withheld information, or steered the detectives away from potential evidence. Besides, you went the extra mile—for him—by lining up Eli as a potential attorney for him."

"I get that. It's just happening pretty fast, and I'm just not sure he's the guilty guy. He's just a kid."

"But you made it sound like all the evidence points to him."

"It does," I said. "But it's circumstantial."

"Well, that could be good for the boy."

"Maybe, but probably not," I said. "Eli warned me that many convictions are based on circumstantial evidence. And there's something else that's bugging me."

"And that is?"

"When—if—it happens, my name is going to be mud with Butch. I got the most damning information from him." I told her about the Yew shrubs on Dingo Dave's island.

"I see," she said. "Well, if it's any consolation, your name was mud to him until maybe a month ago. Besides, he's fourteen. Most fourteen-year-olds think their fathers are idiots. Your relationship will just become normal."

"Great."

"Well, what are you going to do?"

"Let go and let God, I suppose."

"Sounds like a plan," she said.

"Best I got."

Before the silence became awkward, she said, "I have something else I'd like to discuss."

"Oh, oh."

She grinned. Sarah didn't laugh much, but she did a little grin when she was tickled. "It's not that bad. In fact, maybe it's a good thing."

"I could use some of that."

"In the last couple of months, we've been interacting with some regularity."

"A couple times a week," I said. "I guess qualifies as 'some regularity.'"

She did the little grin thing again. "Well, truth to tell, the interaction has been more often and better quality than we have had in several years."

"Ain't that a bit sad?"

"If you're looking at the past, yes. If you're looking at the future, maybe it's hopeful." She stopped and looked at me. This time there was no grin, more of a question in her eyes.

"Oh?" I said, after the silence became awkward. .

"It's different now," she said. "I have grown just a bit more hopeful."

"About what? Getting back together?" I ventured. It was my turn to look at her with a question.

"I'm going to be a bit blunt here," she said. "I don't see you moving back in with me, not for a long time—if ever."

This time she was looking at the ground.

"Thanks for clearing that up," I couldn't take the sarcasm out of my voice.

"You know I don't want to get a divorce," she said gently.

"Yes, but because you're Catholic—and stubborn—not because you want to stay married." I couldn't hide the—what was it? Bitterness? Frustration?

She took her time. "Yes, I'm Catholic. Yes, I'm stubborn. And maybe it's true that this is why I don't want to get a divorce. But I'm not sure about that last part. Maybe I'd like to remain married to you because ... because maybe I'd just like to remain married to you."

"But you don't want to live with me." I tried to sound like I wasn't whining.

"Truth." She waited. "I'm afraid of living with you."

"Because I beat on you. Truth, I don't blame you for throwing me out. I admire you. That's what you should have done." I was trying to sound like a man.

"And with your issues—your addiction—I can't trust that you will not fall back into that world and threaten my world—or the children's."

"So we had to separate."

"Have to separate," she corrected. "But that's not a divorce. It's not the end of a marriage. It's something else."

"What then?"

"I don't know," she said. "But it needs to be explored."

"How?" I was getting more hopeful myself.

"Well, how about dating?"

"Dating?"

She looked at the question in my eyes. When she understood, she had that little grin again. "Oh, I mean dating each other, not ..."

"Other people," I said. The air came back into my lungs. "Dating each other."

"Dating each other."

I paused. "Sounds like a plan."

Chapter 30

Monday, November 9, 1964

Monday was supposed to mean back to normal. It meant something else, especially to the Johnson brothers. Yes, the brothers.

The morning went smoothly enough. I didn't have a class, which meant I had a chance to walk out to the lake and see the two detectives rowing toward Dingo Dave's island. They landed on the south side of the island, out of view of prying eyes, and stayed there, I guessed, until the second class began.

Apparently, the search clinched things for them. By lunchtime, with Hank's help, they had spirited away both of the Johnson brothers. I hadn't foreseen their interest in Dan Johnson. In retrospect, I should have. The brothers were different. The younger brother exhibited little interest in his Aussie background and didn't share the "Dingo" appellation with his brother. However, he did express open discomfort with hints of homosexuality in both his classmates and Father Fox—it was he who began using the nickname "BJ" to refer to Father Bernard John Fox. Dingo Dave, on the other hand, appeared to be less interested in the issue. On the third hand, the detectives had found a collage in Dave's locker, which led to the idea that he might have put the offensive collages on Father Fox's door.

One thing had been bothering me about Dingo Dave's impending arrest. What was his motive? The idea that the Johnson brothers were in cahoots made some sense. At least a little.

The detectives' action had gone so smoothly that the seminarians didn't catch on until later in the day—when both were missing from their classes and their respective flag and touch football teams. Then the chatter began. This was a problem because Hank had gone with the detectives *in loco parentis* and didn't return until late afternoon. He had no news of their status, but he was the adult observer until Eli showed up and received approval from the boys' mother to act as their attorney. This didn't happen until later in the day. By then the detectives had questioned both boys separately in what Hank said was a business-like and not particularly aggressive manner. They concentrated mostly on facts, getting Dingo Dave to admit that, yes, he had a small yew tree growing in the locker room; yes, he knew there was a yew tree growing on the island; yes he knew yew was poisonous; yes, he was the sacristan and had been in the sister's chapel the evening before Bernie's death; yes he created and posted the insulting collage on BJ's door; no he wasn't responsible for the threatening note, which he claimed not to know about; and no he didn't try to poison Father Fox. When they heard this, the detectives were a bit more insistent, repeating the question in different ways, but Dave held his ground.

Dan Johnson knew his brother was the sacristan in the sister's chapel, but he claimed not to be aware of anything else, including Dave's interest in yew trees. He admitted to disliking Father Fox, questioning him in class, and teasing "homos" but to nothing else.

Eli had arrived rather quickly. After consulting with Hank, the detectives invited him to observe the questioning—even though he hadn't been approved by the boys' mother as their attorney. In fact, at this point the mother hadn't been informed that her sons were in the sheriff's custody and the reason why. The detectives had left a message for her as soon as they arrived at the station and were waiting for a callback. When she called—some time into the questioning—Sergeant Hayden left the room and didn't return for fifteen minutes. Hank said he couldn't imagine what that conversation was like. After that, the two boys, Hank, Eli, and Sergeant Hayden talked to her in that order. The round-robin discussion took the better part of an hour, during which time questioning stopped.

Hank was exhausted. With Eli okayed to act as the boys' attorney, Hank felt free to leave. He called his secretary, who phoned my room and found me in. She asked me to wait for him in the vestibule, which I did. When I saw him drive up, I went outside. "So what do you think?"

"I think the detectives think the detectives are certain they have their guy—or guys."

"Both?"

"I don't know how that will play out or what the consequences will be for either one of them. I had a chance to talk with Eli while the mother was talking to the boys. He pointed out that they are both juveniles, which means the consequences won't be near as dire as they would be if they were adults."

"You mean they won't face long years in an adult prison."

"Correct," he said. "Of course ..."

I finished his sentence. "Their lives will be changed dramatically, almost surely for the worse."

"Well, there will be obstacles."

"Obstacles?" I said. "Expulsion from the seminary. Confinement somewhere. A reputation as a murderer."

"Which they may be able to overcome."

"Really? Are you going to break into song."

"No, but it happens," he said.

"Really?"

Hank paused. "Look at Father Fox."

I thought about that for several seconds. "Keep that thought. It sounds like the Johnson family will need it."

"In the meantime, what are we going to tell the seminarians?"

"The rule is—tell them the truth, just not too much of it."

"Can it wait?," he wanted to know. "We'll probably know something specific later tonight."

"No, I think you better say something at dinner."

"How about telling them that I wondered where the Johnson brothers went and called their mother, who told me that there was a family crisis but that the boys are safe."

"That'll work," I said.

And so he did—after we said grace and sat down for dinner. And it worked, for the moment.

I knew that after dinner Hank was going to check with Eli about developments. As much as I needed a meeting, I decided to hang around the faculty lounge waiting for news. By the time Hank came in a few minutes after 7 P.M., Brother Rufus and I were the only ones still there. He looked at Rufus, then at me, and asked me to see him in his office. Rufus raised his eyebrows, but Hank just turned on his heels and left the room. I followed him.

"That was awkward," he allowed, "but Rufus is a bit of gossip and I preferred not to speak in front of him."

"So you're just going to let him think you're taking me to the woodshed?"

"Better that," he said, "than to talk in front of him or ask you to come to my room. Like I said, he's a bit of a gossip."

"Got it."

By then we were at his office. He unlocked the door, sat down, and reached into his drawer for a bottle of scotch. He didn't bother asking me if I minded. I did. Mostly it bugged me that he could do this, be lucid, and not feel like punching my lights out.

I took out my pipe and busied myself in that way while he told me what was what. Dan was released to his mother, who had arrived two hours after her phone conversation. Dingo Dave, on the other hand, was cooling his heels in a cell—by himself, at the urging of Eli—with the prospect of being charged with something related to the death of Father Fox. The detectives were going to meet first thing in the morning with the DA, who would decide on a charge and arrange for a hearing before a juvenile judge. After that, there were unknowns. Depending on the charge, the judge could do anything, ranging from letting him go, to mandating a period of confinement within the juvenile system, to turning him over to an adult court. Eli would do what he could, which might be very little. So far, the authorities were allowing him to represent the boy, but that was a gift, he told Hank, probably because of the Notre Dame connection. Someday, legal representation for juvenile suspects would be required, but this was not the case in Indiana at this time. The juvenile judge had all the power. We would know more tomorrow.

"Obviously, the detectives think Dave is the guy," I said. "What does Eli think?"

"He won't commit," Hank said. "He pointed out that the case against Dave, while circumstantial, points to him and no one else. He admits to being troubled that Dave denies anything to do with the poison."

"Wouldn't you expect the culprit to deny everything?"

"That's just it," Hank said. "He made no effort to deny the evidence. He made no effort to deny that he did the collage on his door. He admitted being familiar with the yew shrub and its toxic properties. He just denied trying to poison anybody. The detectives gave him plenty of chances to admit doing so."

"And he didn't," I said.

Chapter 31

Tuesday, November 10, 1964

I didn't usually go to mass—I didn't exactly classify myself as a believer—but I felt I had to go this time. Hank was going to fill in the seminarians.

I had to sit through the entire mass to hear him say, "Dave Johnson is being held for questioning in the death of Father Fox. That's all I can tell you. Oh, and Dan is at home with his mother."

Tell the truth, but tell the minimum. He went with that, and it was plenty, like the igniter on a bomb.

I didn't really get the sense of it until my first class, and the sophomores were on fire. "What's up with Dingo Dave's arrest?"

"It's not an arrest," I said. "He's being held for questioning."

"Yeah, right. Does that mean BJ, er, Father Fox didn't die of a heart attack?"

"Don't know." I said. A lie.

"Well, how did he die?"

"I thought he died of a heart attack," I said. Another lie. Never true.

"How did Dingo Dave kill him?"

"Who said anybody killed Father Fox?"

"C'mon, Mr. Foote. Why is he being held for questioning?"

"I guess the police think he can provide some answers. I don't know." Well, I did know. They thought he was the guy.

"They think somebody killed him."

"You don't know that." Kinda true.

"Yeah, and they think it's Dingo Dave. I knew it!"

"Stop it! You're jumping to contusions,"

"Very funny, Mr. Foote. How did Dave kill him?"

I shut off the conversation and continued with the class, as best I could.

Mid-afternoon

After classes were done and the boys were engaged in recreation, Hank assembled the staff and filled us in. The DA had decided to charge Dave Johnson with involuntary manslaughter, a lesser charge that Eli had explained was chosen in the belief that Dave's action was more like a prank gone bad than intentional murder. In other words, he had not intended to kill the priest. The detectives genuinely believed this—and it made sense to the DA.

Eli had been allowed to observe the interview but not to advise his client, a practice that was common in those days. In fact, permission to observe the interview was something of a concession. He was finally allowed to talk to Dave in the morning, after the DA decided on the charges. Eli reported that Dave was clearly agitated by the questioning and his situation, which was understandable, and he continued to deny being involved in both the threatening note and the poisoning.

The DA arranged for a preliminary hearing before a juvenile judge, but that wouldn't happen until tomorrow. In the meantime, Dave would have to spend another day in a cell by himself.

"That's tough," I said.

"It could get worse," Hank said. "A lot worse. This is a homicide case and Dave is almost 17. He could be handed over to the adult system."

"Is that likely?" I asked.

"Eli thinks it's unlikely, given the charge and the prank-gone-bad theory." Hank said. "Dave came across more as a kid frightened and confused than a hardened criminal. If the judge buys into that, he'll go more in the direction of counseling and rehab."

"So he's going to get a slap on the wrist?" Father Fish said. Of all the staff, Phil Fischer knew Bernie Fox the best. Bernie and the Fish had been on the spent a couple of years together teaching at Niles. They weren't close, but the Fish respected him and didn't buy the rumors.

"If he's found guilty, he'll probably be sent to a juvenile institution of some sort," Hank said. "But only for a couple of years."

"A slap on the wrist," the Fish repeated.

"Maybe," I said. "But his future isn't exactly sparkling."

"He killed somebody," Father Frat said. Franco Fratelli, the math teacher, spoke as if the facts added up.

"Innocent until proven guilty," I said, proud that I kept myself from shouting.

"Bert's right," Hank said. "We need to let the police, prosecutors, defense attorneys, and judges play their role. We need to hold that attitude when we deal with seminarians."

"That'll be difficult," Father Hop said.

"But necessary," Hank said. "We need to keep cool, detached, let things play out."

"So what are you going to tell them at dinner?" I wanted to know.

"Only what the authorities want people to know. To wit, Dave's been arrested in the death of Father Fox. We'll know more in a few days. That's it."

"Okay, good for now," I said. "Are you going to handle calls from the media the same way?"

"Yep," he said. "We can do worse than follow the lead of the authorities."

"Tell the truth, but the minimum."

"You got it," he said.

With those marching orders in hand, I decided to skip dinner at the sem and drop in at the homestead. Time to talk to Butch. I didn't have much news, but the little I had was big. He wasn't going to be happy.

Just before dinner

"NO!" Butch didn't usually scream. I waited, expecting him to ask for details, which he did.

"I don't have any," I said. "All I can tell you is that he's been arrested in the case."

"But I thought BJ ..."

"Father Fox," I corrected.

"I thought Father Fox died of a heart attack."

"Apparently not," I said.

"But how?"

"The sheriff's department isn't releasing any details. All I can say is that he's been arrested. They did question his brother as well, but they released him."

"So they are blaming Dave?"

"Seems like it," I said.

"Can I see him?"

"We'll see," I said. "Right now, the only people allowed to visit him are his lawyer and family. Down the road, other visitors might be welcome. Maybe."

"I can't believe it," Butch said. "He couldn't have."

Well, that was a problem. He could have, and that seemed to be enough for everybody except Butch. And maybe me. I needed a meeting.

Chapter 32

Friday, November 13, 1964

The shoe dropped today. The juvenile judge announced his decision in the morning, though we didn't get the word until the afternoon break when Eli showed up with the news.

"It's the best he could have hoped for," Eli said. "Detention in a juvenile home until his eighteenth birthday, then release."

"Not bad for a murderer," Brother Rufus said. Funny, I thought Rufus wanted Bernie gone.

Eli looked at him, a slight stare. "The judge was convinced that Father Fox's death was unintentional, the result of a prank."

"So he gets off?" Rufus said.

"Let it go, Rufe," Hank said.

"He's not being let go," Eli said. "He's being punished for what amounts to involuntary manslaughter—and in a way that takes into account his status of a juvenile and the possibility of rehabilitation."

"Like you said, the best he could have hoped for," Hank said.

"I think so," said Eli. "Basically, the judge followed the recommendation of the DA, who had no doubts about the young man's guilt but seemed equally certain that Mr. Johnson did not intend to kill your colleague."

"So we're done," Hank said. "We can tell the seminarians."

"Up to you. One more thing," Eli said. "The DA released a press release, reporting the judge's decision."

"How much did it say?" I wanted to know.

"It said what I just told you."

"Any details about how it happened."

"Yes, poisoning."

"The kind of poison?"

"Yes, it said it was something unusual," Eli said. "Yew. Y-E-W."

"Oh, oh," I said.

Night

I had been tempted to indulge in the campus pep rally. Normally, I hated them, but this one had some juice. Notre Dame was undefeated and they were playing Michigan State, their chief rival in my opinion. It would have been something to see, but I needed a meeting. More important, I needed to talk to my sponsor, which we did at a late night diner on South Bend Avenue.

"You told him that that Father Fox died of Yew poisoning," Rick said.

The DA had gone public, and I felt at liberty to fill in my sponsor on my role in the incident, including my conversation with Butch before dinner. When I sat Butch down at the dining room table and told him about the judge's decision, he said nothing. This was in character. Generally, Butch didn't show anger directly. If he couldn't use humor, he'd say nothing, stifling even a mild sulk. However, when I told him the identify of the poison, he jumped up, grabbed his chair by the backrest flung it to the floor, and ran upstairs to the room. He still said nothing, but he spoke volumes.

"I didn't want to," I told Rick. "I had to. If he heard it on the news, his reaction would have been worse."

"You know, that's progress. A few months ago, you wouldn't have had the balls to face him."

"Cold comfort," I said. "A few months ago, Butch wouldn't have had the balls to break a dining-room chair."

"We all grow," Rick said.

"You know, you are a helluva lot of help sometimes."

"We all grow."

"Stop it! Tell me what to do."

"Easy does it."

"Christ."

"If that works for you."

"C'mon," I said. "I need some help here."

"You c'mon," he said. "You're not even a year sober, and you're still on step what-is-it?"

"Six, I guess."

"So you're son suddenly looks a lot like you, and you panic. Welcome to parenthood. From what you tell me, you don't have a lot of experience at it."

"Got that right, I never got the memo."

Chapter 33

Sunday, November 15, 1964

Yesterday could have been worse. Butch and Sissy got to go to the football game, thanks to the generosity of the Holy Cross Fathers. The game, which Notre Dame won thanks to Alan Page and the defense, took the edge off of Butch's anger at me and his historical disappointment about football. The year before he had cried when Notre Dame lost to Michigan State. Beating the Spartans 28–zip was sweet revenge.

Sissy was less excited, the victory having taken her place at center stage. She found her footing at the after-game soiree, though. I thought there might be talk about Dingo Dave, but both Sissy and Butch reported that the seminarians were focused on the victory. Dingo Dave seemed to have been forgotten.

Sarah said little when I dropped the kids off, but she did give me a parting kiss, a peck on the lips. I left for another meeting, savoring and wondering at the small but clear display of affection.

Today featured a meeting with Eli at his house, in mid-afternoon. It wasn't a meal, but his wife served up some Moroccan mint tea and some kind of honey-based sweet.

"So what have you got to tell me?" I asked.

"First, I'll reiterate what I told the staff on Friday," he said. "This was a good outcome, about as good as could be expected.

It's a light sentence, considering that his behavior—or so everyone thinks—resulted in the death of another human being."

"Or so everyone thinks?"

"All of the authorities—the detectives, the DA, the juvenile judge—are convinced that he poisoned your colleague. They have no doubts."

"And you?"

"I have some doubts," Eli said.

"You think he didn't do it?"

"I said I have doubts," he said. "I have no certainty that he either did the deed or didn't do it."

"Why?"

"Back up a second," he said. "The circumstantial case against him is strong, very strong."

"But it's circumstantial."

"Most convictions are based on circumstantial evidence. You know that."

I nodded.

"Detectives look for motive, means, and opportunity. When they find that one guy has motive, means, and opportunity, they tend to stop looking. Dave had access to the sister's chapel. You saw him there the previous evening. He knew about the toxic properties of yew needles, he had easy access to them on the island—even I gather on the seminary grounds—and he had issues with Father Fox. Dave Johnson is their guy. I hardly blame them."

"I get it," I said. "So where do your doubts come from."

"From my client," he said. "Keep in mind that clients lie, especially in cases like this. But Dave hasn't come across to me as a liar. He seems upset, understandably so, confused maybe, trapped by some things he said and recanted."

"For example?"

"For example, when the detectives showed him the threatening note, he denied any involvement. After more questions, he said he "might have" put it in the mailbox. Then he admitted he put an envelope in the mail slot, but he didn't know what was in it."

"Interesting," I said. "Who gave him the note?"

"He wouldn't say, which made the detectives think he was protecting someone."

"Like maybe his brother?"

"They pressed him on that, but by then he wasn't talking. Dan denied knowing anything about a threatening note or an envelope."

"So Dave admitted what exactly about the note?"

"He said someone gave him the envelope, but he wouldn't say who."

"He's protecting someone."

"Maybe," Eli said. "It's a problem."

"So what makes you think he might not be guilty?"

"Something he shared with me," Eli said. "The detectives think he hated Father Fox because the priest was sympathetic to homosexuals and might be one himself."

"The detectives think," I said. "But you don't buy it."

"I have my doubts," Eli said. "He knew I was Jewish—from my kippah, er, yamulke. He knows a bit of Hebrew. Apparently you have a group of students who go to a synagogue, mine in fact, to learn Hebrew. He asked me some questions about that, curious in part because I'm black and he thought that was odd, which it is, a little bit. Then he started to talk about Father Fox, who he thinks wasn't sufficiently sensitive to the extermination of six million Jews during World War II."

"Interesting," I said, "but he would have only known that from his brother, who was in Fox's history class." I told him about his brother's request for information about the persecution of homosexuals in the Third Reich.

"I didn't have a private conversation with Dave's brother, so I can't speak to that. I can tell you that Dave seemed to be more upset about Father Fox's lack of interest—perceived anyway—in Hitler's extermination of Jews than in his passion about the persecution of homosexuals."

"Really, what gave you that impression?"

"Maybe it's because I'm a Jew," Eli said, "but that's what he wanted to talk about. The six million Jews. He didn't deny Hitler's persecution of homosexuals—and gypsies, he pointed out—but he said this paled compared to the persecution of Jews. He thought Father Fox just didn't care."

"Did he say his views changed when he found out about Father Fox's background?"

"As a Nazi, you mean."

"A member of the SS, yes."

"It made him think, especially his desertion, but he didn't think more kindly of him as a result. He thought it might be evidence that he was an anti-semite."

"Okay, maybe," I said. "But what was the deal with the collage on his door. That was all about homosexuality."

"Again, I'm not sure," Eli said. "He admitted doing it, but I suspect his brother might have done that and he's covering for him."

"But Dave had a similar collage in his locker."

"There's that," Eli said.

Chapter 34

Monday, November 16, 1964

Timing was awkward. The DA had held his press conference, mercifully short, late Friday after the seminarians from South Bend and vicinity had left for home.

At evening prayer that night, Hank was equally short in his explanation to the seminarians who remained on campus. The seminarians weren't supposed to talk after evening prayer; of course they did, I was told, in loud whispers. I had been at a meeting and didn't get the gist of the scuttlebutt until the next morning, when the priests agreed that the consensus was that Dingo Dave was a bit crazy, and it had been just a matter of time before he got into trouble.

The talk died down during and after the Fighting Irish blew out Michigan State.

I didn't get the full sense of things until classes began today, the townies having been given the news at evening prayer on Sunday. Most of them knew beforehand, either because someone caught the press conference on Friday night or they had been briefed by other seminarians on their arrival back at the seminary on late Sunday afternoon.

The certainty of their observations surprised me. To a person, they had no trouble pinning the deed on Dingo Dave. Some of them confessed that they knew all along, which I doubted. Others accused the administration of not paying more attention to someone who was obviously a bed short of a dormitory.

The seminarians, like most of the staff, were probably relieved that the case was solved.

Or was it?

Truth to tell, I was like everyone else. I wanted it to be true, wanted it to be over. But something was gnawing at me, maybe just the thought of Dingo Dave sitting in a group home with his life, if not ruined, then complicated into extreme difficulty.

After the afternoon class, I had a meeting with Sean O'Hara, the editor of the school newspaper. I knew what he wanted to talk about, and I wasn't looking forward to it.

He couldn't wait to see me. "So, Mr. Foote, how do we handle the Dingo Dave story?"

I had prepared for this—or tried to. I wasn't sure I had a good answer. "Do a story, front page if you'd like, but make it short and stick to the facts."

Sean was better prepared than I was. "The facts being that Father Fox was found dead. The sheriff's office investigated, arrested Dingo Dave for what amounts to manslaughter, and the juvenile judge sentenced him to a group home."

"Basically, yes," I said. "What you don't want to do is engage in speculation about motives, methods, or monkey business."

"What if we interviewed him?"

"You'd have to get permission for that, and I'm not sure it can happen—or that he would want to."

"Oh, he'll want to."

"Perhaps, but the powers-that-be won't sit for it," I said.

"The powers that be. Like who?"

"Like Father Grease. And the provincial."

"Am I not a journalist?"

"In the end, you're a high-school seminarian with other authorities to answer to."

"I don't like that."

"If you continue down the path to the priesthood, you will take a vow of obedience. Think of this as a practice run." I can't believe I said that.

He looked suitably sour. "You're not a priest."

"Nor am I thinking of being one, but I still have a boss."

"Father Grease?"

"Would you like me to check in with him? He might not want you to even publish the short bit on the front page."

He paused, looked thoughtful. "No, never mind."

"Okay," I said and then looked at him. "But it didn't hurt to ask. Nice job."

Late afternoon

The conversation with Sean did give me an idea. I called Eli's office and made an appointment to meet him at the end of the day to discuss my idea. When I got there, Trudy gave me her usual sour greeting but told me to go right in.

"Coffee?" Eli asked.

"Black."

"Give me a second," he said, getting up out of his chair and grabbing his personal mug from his desk. "I'm going to get it myself. Trudy's a bit grumpy."

"How can you tell?"

Eli smiled to himself, left the room, and came back in less than a minute with two filled mugs. "What's up?"

"An idea," I said. And I told him how I wanted to talk to Dingo Dave.

"I think I can arrange a visit."

"But that's only the first part. I'd like Butch to come along."

"Your son? Why?"

"He's taken a liking to Dave. The thing is: Dave is a loner. He doesn't appear to be close to any of the other seminarians."

"But he likes Butch."

"He does. Butch may be able to get him to talk in a way that I can't—or anyone else for that matter."

"Interesting. What's he's going to do with that information?"

I went on to talk about Butch's anger at me about the arrest, about my participation in it, about the necessity of keeping gossip down at the seminary. "My plan is to pull Butch into the team, you might say, in return for keeping his mouth shut among the seminarians. I'm sure he can help me find out the truth—at least with respect to Dingo Dave and his involvement. My main problem is keeping some control of him ..."

"So he doesn't share his knowledge with the other seminarians and mess things up."

"Yes. If I can make him feel like he's part of Dave's team like you and I—and he really would be—he'll stick with the discipline."

I didn't add that it would be a way for me to make amends with my son.

Chapter 35

Thursday, November 19, 1964

It was getting cold and starting to snow. It was only a few steps from the main building to the Butler Building, but in our blazers it felt like miles. There wasn't much discussion of Dingo Dave anymore, just the surety that he was scum.

In the afternoon, I called over to Eli's office. Trudy answered, put me on hold, and Eli came on the line. That was unusual.

"It took a while," he said, "but I have good news and bad news."

"Bad news first."

"Dave wants nothing to do with you."

"Okay, I probably deserved that. What's the good news?"

"He wants to talk to your son."

"Let's do it," I said.

I had some logistical work to do. I called the juvenile home, talked to the house mother, and set up a visit between Butch and Dingo Dave on Monday. Then I put on my winter duds and braved the snow and wind on the walk over to the library, where Sarah asked if I would like to spend Friday night at the house. It made sense. The kids were scheduled to go to the ball game, so the less back and forth the better. Besides, the weather promised to be poor. I accepted, figuring I would be on the couch.

Chapter 36

Saturday, November 21, 1964

It snowed all day yesterday. Today began sub-zero with the prospect of the temperature climbing to ten above. I had a new reason to be happy about Sarah's invitation, but I wondered if the kids were going to want to go to the ball game.

I talked it through with them, and they both wanted to go. I thought Sarah might have objected, but she didn't. She did insist on appropriate clothing, hovering over them like a mother hen as they bundled up.

Last night, before the kids went to their rooms, I took Butch aside and told him about the prospective meeting with Dingo Dave. Not surprisingly, he was excited.

"Not so fast," I said. "This is tricky." I told him the visit was conditional. If he chose to visit, it would make him an official part of my team, the team being the only entity invested in finding out who really killed Father Fox. He would have to keep his mouth shut around the other seminarians and pretend that he had no special "in". He resisted this at first, but the idea of being part of an investigative team appealed to him.

Miraculously, the Edsel started on the first try, but it took fifteen minutes to warm up enough for me to want to drive. And the driving wasn't easy. The day was crisp, to say the least, and sunny, which meant the roads were icy. I took my time, which I would have had to do anyway. The weather held down the traffic, but there was still a jam of tailgaters. I was able to pass through the gate with my faculty pass and get to the seminary.

I set up Butch and Sissy in the junior rec room, where they could play pool or ping pong while they waited for seminarians to drift in from their morning work. I said goodbye and got a look from Sissy.

"Where are you going?"

"Back home," I said. "If you think I'm going to sit in this weather for three hours, you've got another think coming. If you find you can't handle it, leave and come back to the seminary. You can make pit stops at the library and Huddle to warm up. I'll be back here at five." I turned around and left.

The ride back was easier. No traffic in that direction.

Sarah met me at the door, gave me an affectionate kiss, and said, "We'd better get busy. You're not going to want to miss the game."

The thought had occurred to me, but I still wasn't with the program. "Get busy doing what?" I had visions of various tasks laid out before me, none of which I would be very good at and none I would enjoy.

She looked at me with her trademark grin, grabbed me by the hand, and led me to her bedroom, gave me another kiss and began removing my shirt.

"Wha-at?"

"It's a propitious time of the month, Silly."

I finally caught on. Sarah, being a good Catholic wouldn't use the pill, which was just coming into its own. She had used the "rhythm method" to get pregnant the first two times and then, having almost died giving birth to Butch, used it to avoid getting pregnant. As time went on, and my alcohol habit developed, we had less and less sex anyway. Apparently, this didn't mean Sarah's sex drive had disappeared. It meant I had become unattractive.

Something had changed. "Just because I'm about to have my way with you," she said after she removed my shirt, "doesn't mean that you're moving back in with me."

"What does it mean?" I asked, after kicking off my shoes.

"That I love you, you're my husband, and the time is right."

"Propitious," I said. Sometimes, it's good to let the woman take the lead.

I still slept on the couch that night, which was a little weird under the circumstances. I hadn't planned on staying the night, but it was so damn cold, and I had already made two round trips in the Edsel. Sarah insisted I stay on the couch. She wasn't ready to sleep together, not literally, not in front of the kids.

Besides, she said, "it was fun sneaking one in."

Chapter 37

Monday, November 23, 1964

Yesterday was the anniversary of the assassination of President Kennedy. The news media was all over the story, replaying the assassination and the funeral. Hank had the TV on in the faculty lounge for most of the day. Ordinarily, TV was limited for the seminarians, but November 22 was no ordinary day. They were allowed to watch the TV in the auditorium. Everyone was there at some point. A few were there for most of the afternoon, including one fellow who spent the entire day there.

On Friday, I had assigned each class to write something about Kennedy, the assassination, the funeral, his legacy, or whatever. Even though the country was moving on, it was still a raw memory.

Today, the seminarians read from their essays. Everyone had a chance to read at least a paragraph, and we had enough time to talk about the event and its ramifications. Nothing about Dingo Dave came up.

But today was a big day on that score. I picked up Butch at home at 3:30 and headed towards Fort Wayne, where the judge had sent Dave, doing a kindness for his mother who lived in the area. The house was victorian style, no visible bars or restraints. The rule was that anyone who escaped—or tried to—would be shipped to a different, more institutional setting. The home director met me at the door and ushered the two of us into a waiting area. He explained the procedure, which consisted of me staying put in the waiting room and Butch visiting with Dave in a separate room, where he would be chaperoned by an adult attendant standing out of earshot.

The director and Butch left, while I picked up a magazine. Little more than a half hour later they returned.

"So?" I said, once we were in the car.

"Isn't my visit supposed to be confidential?"

"Yes and no," I said. "Yes, by my agreement with you, you are to keep the visit confidential with respect to the seminarians and almost all others. No, you do not have to keep the visit confidential from me, and that's also by agreement."

"How so?"

"My deal with you is that you could visit Dingo Dave with the understanding that you are a member of the team, the only team that is interested in finding out the real truth about what happened. You understand that?"

"Yes."

"You are free to keep your visit confidential from me—that's your choice. But I would take that as your decision to not be part of the team. Does that make sense?"

"What if I think it is in Dave's best interest to not share what he said with you?"

"That could be the case, but it would make it tough for me to rely on you to do anything else."

"You're relying on me?"

"Isn't it obvious? I can't talk to Dave. You can, and you did."

Silence. Then, "He didn't do it."

"What makes you say that?"

"He's not a liar, Dad. He admitted what he did and denied what he didn't do. I believe him."

Good point. I suggested that we accept, for the moment, that Dave was telling the truth. In this case, we would accept that he could have poisoned Father Fox but didn't, that he created the collages that went up on the priest's door, that he placed an envelope containing something into Father Grieshaber's mail cubby. This was quite believable, but it left me with two questions for Butch

"First," I said, "Why did he do those collages?"

"He did them for his brother," Butch said.

On a simple level, this seemed obvious, based on what the two admitted to. But it didn't explain why. What was going on in their heads? Dan clearly had an issue with Father Fox, but Dave didn't have him as a teacher and didn't appear to interact with him. And why would he help his brother out in this way? Butch agreed to pursue this on his next visit.

"Second," I said. "Who gave him the envelope, which we assume contained the threatening note?"

Another good question. "Yeah, maybe," said Butch.

"So it could be complicated. Maybe Dave helped his brother out, participated in some way, but he wasn't the instigator."

"His brother?"

"Yes, but ..."

Butch finished my sentence. "Dave was the one that stuck it to the door."

"But you don't think he worked alone," I said. "Why not?"

"Didn't the collage make fun of Father Fox as a queer?"

"Homosexual—and we don't know that."

"You don't know if the collage made fun of him as, uh, homosexual?"

"No, I mean, yes we know it did," I said. "But we don't know that Father Fox was a homosexual."

"Oh, okay. The thing is Dave didn't care that much about the homo, uh, homosexual issue. It was just something he got from his brother. For Dave, it wasn't that big a deal. Dave didn't have him in class. I don't think Dave ever said 'hi' to him."

"So that's why you don't think he was, let's say, the instigator of the collage. Okay, I think the detectives believe his brother was involved in that, so it makes sense. What about the threatening letter?"

Butch look puzzled. "He told me he might have done that."

"Might have? That's weird."

"Well, he said he put something in Father Grease's mailbox for someone—he didn't know what it said and he didn't know who he did it for."

"For whom."

"Really, Dad. You're doing a grammar lesson?"

"So he delivered the message," I said. "Maybe he didn't know what the message said, but he had to know who gave it to him."

"He's protecting someone," Butch said.

"Who?"

"Whom," Butch said.

"Got me. Good one. For whom did he do it."

"He wouldn't say."

"Okay, good. Perhaps his brother again. Or someone else. We're onto something. Nice work. Remember. mum's the word. Not even to your sister, especially not to your sister. I haven't brought her into this game—yet."

By the time we got back to South Bend, I was convinced that Dave's brother, Dan, was the instigator of the collage episode and was motivated by his fears about homosexuality. I was equally convinced that someone else was involved in the threatening letter, someone who might be the clue to Father Fox's murder.

Chapter 38

Friday, November 27, 1964

We were on Thanksgiving break, and I took the opportunity to set up a meeting with Dingo Dave's mother. Eli had greased the skids, notifying Diane Johnson by phone that I might be contacting her and assuring her that I was on Dave's side when precious few others were. Even so, she wouldn't go along with the deal until Eli reminded her that I was Butch's father. Until he mentioned that, she didn't put together that the guy who told the cops about her son and the father of Dave's only friend were one and the same.

It was still a little tricky, but she did agree to see me at the restaurant after 3 P.M. I wasn't looking forward to another drive to Fort Wayne, but at least the weather had cleared and warmed some.

When I got there, she waved me over to a booth, asked if I wanted coffee. I said yes, and she set us up with two mugs and took a seat across from me.

"How are you doing?" I asked.

"Exhausted. It's not so much the work as this thing with Dave. I guess I'm depressed."

"There's nothing wrong with you. This is depressing."

"Thanks, I think," she said. "Mr. Bonpere said you didn't think Dave was guilty."

"Not of poisoning Father Fox," I said. "Even there, it's more accurate to say I have my doubts."

"Why?"

"All of the external evidence points to him, which is what the authorities have locked on. But the motivation and intensity doesn't fit. As far as we know, Dave didn't have that much interaction with Father Fox. He didn't have him for a class. He didn't play bridge with him—or basketball. Dan was the one who had some run-ins with him."

"Yes, Dan told me about that. He didn't like that Father Fox taught history backwards, and he didn't like that he said so much about the Nazi persecution of homosexuals."

"Was it the homosexual issue that was bugging him?"

"Maybe. I don't know. Dan is intense. He thought that teaching history backwards was nutty. When Father Fox brought up the persecution of homosexuals, he thought that was nuttier. When Dave told him that Father Fox should have put more emphasis on the genocide against Jews, that just gave Dan more ammunition."

"Dave was the one who told him that?"

"Of course," Diane said. "Dave identifies with Jews. He is, was, taking Hebrew classes over at the synagogue, you know."

"Dave feels pretty intense about that?"

She looked at me. "Yeah, I guess, but not enough to poison the man."

"Sorry," I said. "That doesn't make sense to me either, but then nothing about this situation makes sense. Eli, Mr. Bonpere, told me we're not going to be much help to Dave until we figure out what really happened."

"You mean who really did it."

"That," I said. "And we don't have much to work with. Two things bother me. The first is that your boys admitted posting an insulting collage on Father Fox's door. Twice."

"Insulting in what way?"

"The content suggested Father Fox was a homosexual."

"Was he?"

"I have no evidence of that," I said, "and it's not the point."

"It isn't?"

"Mrs. Johnson, it sounds like you're justifying what they did. Do you know something?"

"No, it's just ..." She stopped, and there was an uncomfortable silence.

I had my answer and decided to press on. "The other thing is that Dave admitted putting an envelope in Father Grieshaber's mailbox. It turned out to contain one of those notes that uses cut-out letters—like a kidnap note. This one suggested that harm might come to Father Fox. Dave denied creating the letter—or knowing what was in the envelope—which I'm inclined to believe." I stopped and looked at her. She squirmed, and I continued. "Your son doesn't strike any of us as a liar. He admitted all the things that led to his arrest, but he clammed up on a couple of points. I think he was protecting someone."

Mrs. Johnson went white at this, looked down, and said nothing.

"You?"

"I think, maybe." She was holding the coffee mug in both hands. Her grip was so strong I thought she might break it. "Okay, I gave him the envelope, but someone gave it to me, thinking I could get it into Father's mailbox through one of my sons if nothing else. I didn't know what it was. It was sealed, and I didn't open it. She said it was important to put it in the mailbox, that I not be seen."

"She?"

"Um, well, yes."

"Who?

"I'd rather not say."

"You may have to," I said. "Didn't you think it was odd that she didn't want you to be seen."

"Not really. I thought it might be a donation. You know, anonymous. She didn't want her identity known, and she didn't want Father Grieshaber to grill me."

"Like I'm doing now," I said. "I get that, but it's a different kettle of fish if the contents were not an anonymous donation but a message threatening harm to Father Fox."

She looked like she had seen a ghost.

"It's important," I said. "This could help your son."

"I know. I know. But I can't. I can't."

And she got up and went into the kitchen. I finished my coffee and left, knowing I was onto something but not sure where to go next.

Chapter 39

Saturday. November 28, 1964

"Why are we in a bookstore?" Sissy wanted to know.

"I thought I might get your mother a book."

"Dad, she's a librarian," said Sissy. "Get her something personal."

"Good point," I said. "But if I'm going to get her something personal, I'm not going to do it in front of you."

Sissy giggled. "Well, maybe not that personal."

Maybe the kids knew more about what was going on than I did. I made a motion to leave, but Butch resisted. He was over by the nature-and-gardening section, thumbing through a book on trees and shrubs.

"Look, Dad. There are a couple of pages about yew trees. They are a pretty common shrub."

"So they are," I said. "If you want to find out about yew trees, ask your mother."

"What's the deal about yew trees?" Sissy wanted to know.

Butch, ever the quick thinker. "It's for me to know, and yew-w-w to find out."

Sissy just looked puzzled.

I laughed. "Let's get out of here."

We headed toward Penney's, where Butch and Sissy each

found something for their mother.

I took the kids back home for an early but light dinner, in consideration of taking the two to a soiree and a movie at the seminary. On the way, Butch and I took bets on who was going to sit on either side of Sissy, much to her embarrassment. After a gap in the conversation, I suggested to Sissy that she might use her powers for the good, by turning her favors to two of the shyer boys.

"Oh, Dad."

She was embarassed again, but I was proud that she did exactly as I suggested for the movie. The movie was *Heaven Knows Mister Allison*, but the two favored boys hardly noticed.

We got home late, and the two kids retired to their rooms. That gave me time to talk to Sarah before I retired, at her invitation, to the couch. I told her about my talk with Diane Johnson and my hunch, better than a hunch I thought, that a relative or a close friend had used her to deliver the anonymous threat to Hank's mailbox. She thought my logic was good and pushed me to think about where the threat might lie. I had to think some, but it occurred to me that it might lie in Chicago, somehow related to the slander against Father Fox associated with the high school.

"If so," Sarah said, "We're looking for someone who is related to Mrs. Johnson."

"Sounds good, but how do we figure that out if she's not talking?"

"She's not talking—yet. She might down the road. Didn't you get the name of the Niles boys who were disciplined for bullying the supposedly homosexual boy."

"I didn't, but I know where I can get it."

"Look there for a relationship."

I had no idea how to do that, but it occurred to me that a librarian might. I told Sarah so, and she told me to get her the name of the parents involved in the mess at Notre Dame high school and Diane Johnson's maiden name. I told her I could do the former, probably not the latter. Not easily.

"That makes it harder, not impossible."

Chapter 40

Sunday, November 29, 1964

On Sunday afternoon, I called Jane Parker, the mother of Jimmy Parker. To my surprise, she answered the phone right away.

After answering my query about the health of herself and her husband in the aftermath of their son's suicide, she asked me whether we had found the murderer of Father Fox.

I filled her in about Dingo Dave and added that I had some doubts about his guilt and the commonly understood explanation of what happened. She expressed dismay that another boy might be in trouble.

"You may be able to help," I said and proceeded to tell her why I had called.

She was all over it, giving me the name of the bully boys' parents, including the maiden name of the mother, and their occupations. One wrinkle was that the father was a lawyer, which promised to make trouble but explained some of the arrogance. Neither parent was a Johnson, which was disappointing but not a surprise.

I could have waited to talk to Sarah when I went over later for dinner, but I was excited and didn't feel like waiting. Assuming correctly that she would be at home, I phoned her and gave her the particulars.

"That helps," she said. "Now all I need to do is find out Diane Johnson's maiden name. I'll see what I can do after work tomorrow. It might take me a couple of days."

Chapter 41

Monday, November 30, 1964

School was back in business on Monday, always a difficult time for teachers. As far as the seminarians were concerned, it was like nothing had happened in the last month.

Not so for me. I couldn't wait to hear from Sarah. I didn't expect instant action—and didn't get it. When I didn't hear from her by 7 P.M., I called the house. Sissy answered the phone, chatted a bit about her day, and turned me over to her mother.

"Anything?" I asked.

She did have something. "Your tip was the ticket," she said. "The bully at Notre Dame high school was David Kelly. That's a common surname, but his mother was a Guilfoyle, which is less common. I figured that if I found a connection from Diane Johnson to a Guilfoyle, I'd have something. It took a while, mainly because I was looking for a marriage record and I didn't know where she was married. I tried Indiana, found several Guilfoyles but none in the right time frame, and no females marrying a Johnson. I struck gold in Chicago, where a Diane Guilfoyle married a Duane Johnson on January 17, 1946."

"Sounds good," I said. "But it could be a coincidence."

"Could be, probably not, not when one of the witnesses is a Sandra Guilfoyle, the maiden name of the mother of the high-school bully."

"Okay, then. Nice work."

Now I needed to figure out how to handle it.

Chapter 42

Tuesday, December 1, 1964

My first thought was to give my news to the detectives, but connecting with them wasn't easy. I tried the phone, but they were never in. Asking them to call back wasn't going to work. I thought I might drive the Edsel to the Sheriff's office, but that was some trouble with the prospect of failure.

A better bet was to reach out to Chief Ziolkowski at Campus Security. I liked him. I didn't think he'd be able to help directly, but he might give me advice.

It *was* a better bet. He was in the office. It must have been a slow day in the cold weather. He offered me a cup of coffee, which I accepted, and sat down across from his desk. I told him what we had learned.

"You haven't learned it for sure," he said. "You just think you know."

"True," I said, "but it's a good bet that we know the who and the motive."

"But you don't know whether this works in Dave Johnson's favor."

"No I don't," I said. "Odds are it doesn't help him. But this should help us find the truth."

"*Some* truth. Let's say you find out—somehow—that this Guilfoyle Kelly woman instigated the threatening note. Even then, you don't know that the note is connected to the poisoning."

"I understand, but isn't it worth pursuing?"

"I'll say this. On your part, you should let the detectives know. But that's the end of it. It's up to the detectives to decide what to do with the information, but ..." He paused.

"But?"

"But don't hold your breath."

"Right now, the problem is that I can't reach them."

"I'll tell you what. You contacted me, which is a reasonable step. I'll pass on your information to them. After that ..." He paused again.

"After that?"

"Don't hold your breath."

Chapter 43

Saturday, December 5, 1964

It had take three days for Chief Ziolkowski to get back to me about the Guilfoyle connection. He said the detectives were grateful that I had passed the information onto them, but he warned me again not to expect much. "They have closed the case. Cops are not anxious to reopen a case, once closed, unless something jumps up and bites them in the butt."

"So this didn't rise to the butt-biting level."

"Not even a gnat to be swatted away."

Bad but not unexpected news. Time for plan B.

The weather was clear, the roads were fine, and I decided to try another run to Fort Wayne in hopes of catching Diane Johnson at the restaurant. I figured she would have talked to her sister or cousin, whoever she was, about the "favor" and probably—or maybe—gotten the scoop.

Since it was an ambush of sorts, I thought I might mitigate the negative by taking Butch along. Mrs. Johnson would know, at least when I introduced him, that Butch was a friend of Dave, the only one he had asked to see. With that in mind, she might not perceive me as her enemy.

Of course, I could have phoned her first. That would have been the polite thing to do. It would also have given her the chance to avoid me. I wasn't sure she would be working today, but she worked more hours than anyone else.

It was a good bet. She was there. When she saw me, her face did not express delight. I went up to her, Butch at my side, and introduced the two to each other.

Her face registered something more complicated. "Thank you for visiting Dan," she said. "It meant the world to him. I hope you will visit him again."

"I'd like that," Butch said.

"We're going to take a seat," I said. "When you get a chance, could we have a short chat? I have some news, and I'd like to check a couple of things with you."

We took our seats at a table for four and waited. In a few minutes, Diane came over as if she was taking our order. "I can't take a break for a while, so order something. Maybe we can manage while I'm standing here."

I filled her in on what we discovered about her relative, our strong suspicion that she was the one who wrote the "ransom" message. Diane looked surprised.

"How did ... ?"

"Long story," I said. "We think, I think, this was coincidental, not related to the murder, hmm death, of Father Fox. Can you confirm that?"

She took some time to answer. "I think so. She's my first cousin. We grew up together. She's a good person, but she was angry about Father Fox's role in getting her son suspended. I tried to get her to let it go, but she couldn't. She thought he was a bad guy and that he shouldn't be teaching. But I don't believe she wanted to kill him."

"If she did, she would have gone through one of your boys," I said. "That's what's making us nervous."

"It made me nervous too," Mrs. Johnson said. "I talked to

both boys about it. They denied having contact with her in several months, and I'm inclined to believe them."

"I think Butch and I are so inclined as well," I said. "It explains Dave's apparent confusion about being involved, not involved, and so on. He was involved, to the extent of popping the envelope in the mailbox, but he didn't want to explain that you gave him the envelope."

"Right."

"Did you know what was in the envelope?"

"I didn't look at it. I assumed it was a letter to Father Grieshaber, stating her case. It didn't bother me. I thought it was a reasonable thing to do, under the circumstances. I had no idea it was an anonymous threat. That took me by surprise. Frankly, I'm embarrassed about it. But again, she just wanted to get the man fired, not killed."

This explained the threatening letter affair in a way that was good news for her two sons. And it made sense. On the other hand, it didn't provide a clue as to who might have poisoned Father Fox, accidentally or otherwise.

"What do I tell my cousin? She's not exactly my biggest fan at the moment."

"You can tell her that the St. Joseph County detectives did not seem very interested in this affair—and she should relax." I thought about telling her what I thought about her cousin, but I decided not to stir the pot.

On our way home, I turned down the radio and asked Butch what he thought.

"Her cousin needs a program," he said.

I laughed. He had heard me use this language when I saw people clearly in the throes of dysfunction, alcoholic or not. "I think you're right."

"Mrs. Johnson said Dave would like me visit again. Can I?"

"It's the least we can do." I turned the radio up.

We got back to the house in time for an early dinner. There was no soiree planned, so I figured I'd go to a meeting. At dinner, we filled in Sarah and Sissy on what we learned. The conversation effectively made Sissy part of the family investigation team, which was a concern but the only way to go at this point. It would, potentially, at least bring the family together.

Sissy was a good sport about being the last to know and immediately got on board with questions. "If this Guilfoyle woman did not poison BJ, then who did?"

"Please call him Father Fox."

"Well, that's what the seminarians call him—or did."

"Did, right. He's gone now, and I'd like you to be more respectful."

"And professional, now that you're part of the team," Sarah said.

"Excellent point," I said. "Now to your question. Thoughts anyone."

"Gotta be the nuns," said Butch.

"What? You're going to blame it on women?" Sissy asked, genuinely irritated.

"Sissy, Mrs. Johnson's cousin is a woman," Sarah pointed out, "and she's our only other suspect, sort of."

"Oh, yeah, right." Sissy said, chastened a bit.

"Anyway, I was wondering about the sisters, myself, or one of them," Sarah said. "But why?"

No one said anything.

"Maybe it's one of the priests," Sissy said.

"Or brothers," I said. "Brother Rufus made fun of Father Fox every chance he had."

No one knew Brother Rufus, so I had to explain. "The maintenance guy. Impish personality, not altogether kind, especially to Father Fox."

"Is he a killer?" Sarah asked.

"Nobody on the premises appears to be a killer," I said. "They are men of God, after all."

"And women of God," said Sissy.

"And don't forget the seminarians," said Sarah.

"Hard to forget that," I said. "One of them is taking the fall."

"You know, I don't think I know the whole story," said Sissy. "BJ, Father Fox, was poisoned, right?"

"Right," I said. "The poison was identfied as an extract from the yew tree, which is rather available around here."

"And the detectives picked on Dave because he knew it was toxic," said Butch. "But there are yew bushes along the front of the building. Anybody could have done it."

"That's correct," I said."Dave got fingered because he had the the interest and the knowledge about yew trees."

"Dave knows lots of stuff," Butch said, a little loudly. "That's what makes him an interesting guy."

"Let's look more closely at the method," I said. "As I understand it, poisoning is a method more common among women."

"There you go again," said Sissy.

"I think that's true," said Sarah. "I'd have to check on it."

"The nuns!" cried Butch.

"Settle down there, Partner," I said.

"Are the nuns the only women on the premises?"

"Yes, no," I said, correcting myself. "The secretary is a woman. Hmm, the secretary quit a couple of weeks ago, supposedly under stress. Apparently the goings-on were too much for her."

"Timing seems suspicious," said Sarah.

"Good point," I said.

We were getting nowhere, with more leads and little evidence. On the other hand, we were getting somewhere as a family. I still needed a meeting.

Chapter 44

Sunday, December 6, 1964

Sundays were for work, at least for me. I made myself scarce in the morning, staying in my room and preparing the next week's classes. It took a couple of hours, less than it used to. I had gotten the hang of things by then.

Sarah had invited me for Sunday dinner, a late midday thing. However odd, we were becoming a family again, or maybe for the first time. We no longer scheduled my days with the kids. I was now a regular part of their lives, something made possible by the death of Father Fox. Ironic.

Having finished my class planning, I still had some time to kill. In the fall, I could wander around the lake. In December, it could be a little unpleasant. Nevertheless, I put on my winter coat and went out the back door, thinking I would walk over to the Huddle or the library. Sarah wasn't working today, but it wasn't a bad place to kill time.

After exiting the back door, I could hear a radio going in the boathouse. News was on, focusing on the anniversary of Pearl Harbor. The door was open. I went in and went down the stairs to the boathouse. Brother Rufus was there, scraping the paint off a rowboat.

"Sunday is not a day of rest for you," I said.

"This *is* rest for me," Rufus said.

"Scraping the paint off a rowboat? What do you do for serious fun?"

"Paint it with primer," he said.

"Of course." I paused. "Mind if I pick your brain."

"Be careful. It's an untouched wilderness in there."

I laughed. I wondered if I had misjudged the man. "I was wondering if you had any thoughts on the death of Father Fox."

"A-k-a BJ," he said, behind a hint of a smile. "Why do you ask? Isn't it locked up."

"That's why I'm asking. Man dies, probably murdered, possibly killed accidentally. Boy goes away to a sinkhole called juvenile justice. Now nobody talks about it."

"Too easy, you think?"

"I'm thinking. It bothers me, that's all. Tough on the boy, especially if he didn't do it."

"Boy didn't like BJ, I heard."

"He wasn't a fan, but I don't think he hated him, not enough to kill him."

"You've talked to him?"

"Smart boy, a bit confused by events." Okay, I hadn't talked to him recently, but Butch had. I didn't want to go into that with Rufus.

"Aren't we all?" Rufus continued. "Boy takes the fall. You don't have to think about the confusion anymore."

"You didn't like BJ, er Father Fox, did you?"

"Nope."

"Why not?"

"Horse's butt."

"That's not an answer."

"I hear he was, you know, three-gaited."

"A homosexual?"

"No, liked boys."

"What's the difference?"

"Look, we're a congregation of men. Lotta guys are here because marriage ain't for them. Why do you think? But they keep their liking to themselves, and it works out. But if they like boys, and do something about it, it's not so good. And if the boys they like ..."

"Are boys," I said. "I get that. It's trouble. But why do you think he, um, liked boys."

"It's what I heard."

"What you heard. From where."

"Around."

"C'mon, Rufus. The only evidence for what you say is gossip. Malicious gossip at that."

"Yeah, sometimes malicious gossip is true."

"In which case, it's slander. You know better than this. Any of the other staff share your views?"

"Naw, they're all priests. Political guys. They're trained to be nice, whereas I'm trained to unplug toilets. I know shit when I see it."

"Nice. You're chances of getting the Mr. Congeniality award this year are poor."

"Yeah, I don't suppose I'm in the running for that, but then BJ wasn't in the running for that either."

"So you had something in common with him," I said.

"Now, who's being nasty?"

I decided to change the subject. "You're in charge of tidying up the grounds."

"Yeah, why?"

"You prune the trees and shrubs?"

"Only when I have to."

"Not your favorite."

"I like carpentry, plumbing, handyman stuff. Gardening ain't my thing."

"What about the yew shrubs at the front of the building?"

"The what?"

"The shrubs in the front of the building. They're yew trees."

"You, what? Pain in the ass is what I call them."

"Thanks for answering my questions."

The wind had picked up. I decided a walk wasn't in order. I got in the Edsel and headed home.

Sunday Dinner

Over roast chicken, I explained that I had talked to Brother Rufus, who was incorrigible in his dislike for Father Fox but an unlikely candidate for poisoning. If Bernie Fox had died from a blow to the head with an iron pipe, I might have suspected Rufus.

So what are we going to do, the team wanted to know.

"Well, we've got to check out the former secretary, the staff, and the nuns."

"Well, that sounds easy," Sarah said dryly.

"What we need is good librarian," I said. "Oh, I know one."

"What do you want me to do?"

"We need background information on everyone. Let's see. The teachers."

"Well, I can check the official Catholic directory, get ordination dates, maybe check bios that appeared in connection with the ordination."

"Good," I said. "I'll go back and talk to Rufus. He loves gossip and might fill me in on informal stories about where everybody came from."

"What about the secretary?" Sarah wanted to know.

"I'll have to talk to her personally," I said. "If I can find her."

"And the nuns?" Sarah asked.

"Don't you have some connections with the sisterhood?"

"There is no *sisterhood*," she said, emphasizing the singular. "There are *sisterhoods*, but yes, I do have some connections."

Chapter 45

Monday, December 7, 1964

Pearl Harbor Day. I had assigned students to write a short story, somehow related to the event. Volunteers read their version in class, which was relatively successful. The project got them into the human aspects of the tragedy.

I had two things on my agenda, finding out about the school's ex-secretary and seing what else I could pry out of Brother Rufus. For the first, I spoke to Hank, with some trepidation, asking him if it wasn't odd that Judy—the secretary—had left shortly after Father Fox left us in an untimely manner.

"Not at all," he said. "At least I didn't think so at the time. She couldn't concentrate after Bernie's death, especially the possibility that it was murder. I rather expected something like that, the nuns the same thing. They were spooked. Are you still on this thing?"

"I'm bothered, that's all. We didn't really talk about Judy as a suspect, especially for that threatening message left in your mailbox."

At that point, I had dug myself a hole and felt compelled to tell him what I had learned from Dingo Dave's mother and how that had played out—or seemed to."

"You are still working it," he said, for what passed as anger from him.

"I'm just not satisfied, that's all. Clearly, Dave made a mistake. He was an unwitting accomplice in the threatening note, or seems to have been, and in the collage. Even that had more to do with his brother. But I don't like him for the poisoner. I think he—or she—is still out there."

"Really." Hank didn't know where to go with this.

"Look, you want it to be over. I get that. But I know you too well to think you'd be satisfied with a convenient untruth. So yes, I'm still trying to do the job you hired me for. But I'm trying to be discreet. I promise."

"You better be."

I left the room, thinking that talking to Rufus was not a good idea, not if I wanted to be discreet.

After classes were over, I walked over to the ND library, checked at the desk for Sarah's whereabouts, and found her on the seventh floor. I didn't need a meeting. I just gave her the name of the school's former secretary and asked her if she could find her address. It was a bother for both of us, but it was better to not go through channels.

Chapter 46

Wednesday, December 9, 1964

Sarah made short work of the task of looking up the ex-secretary. Her name was Dorothy Price, and she lived close to the university on Corby. I decided to try her around dinnertime, thinking she probably had taken a new job and that, as secretary, it would be a nine-to-five job rather than an odd-hours thing.

I was right. She came to the door herself, her husband not having a nine-to-five job. She was wearing a blouse and skirt, suggesting that, yes indeed, she had taken on another office job. I introduced myself, which wasn't entirely necessary. She knew who I was, even though we hadn't had anything but the briefest encounter. I told her I wanted to ask her a few questions related to Father Fox and his death. She let me in without hesitation.

"You know, you're the first person who asked to talk to me about Father Fox," she said. "I'll be happy to tell you what I know."

"You left shortly after Father Fox died," I said. "What's the story?"

She explained that she had been thinking about leaving for a couple of weeks before. She had heard things, mainly from a couple of people with ties to Notre Dame High School in Niles. The gist was that Father Fox was molesting boys.

"Did you believe it?"

"It was gossip, as far as I could tell," she said. "But I listened. And then I got a phone call saying that Father Fox was a dirty homosexual, only he didn't say homosexual, and that he'd better watch out. And he hung up."

"He?"

"Yes, he sounded young. A teenager. That's when I started to think about leaving."

"You believed him?"

"Not necessarily, but it bothered me. I was already uncomfortable with Father Fox being around. It's not that I thought the rumors were true. It's that I thought the congregation shouldn't have been taking chances like this, posting him to the minor seminary. They should have found a different job for him."

"Even if they were sure he was clean?"

"Yes. If they were sure he was good, they didn't have to toss him out of the order or give him a rotten job. Just something that wasn't around kids."

"I understand? So you decided to leave?"

"Pretty much. I was looking for another job, and then he, um, died. I couldn't think after that. I was getting all kinds of calls from detectives, lawyers, the provincial—asking for Father Grieshaber. I knew it was bad. I stayed for another week, until I couldn't take it any more. Even though I hadn't found a job, I gave notice. Father Grieshaber let me leave right away. That was a kindness."

"You told him why?"

"Yes. He looked sad, told me he understood."

Interesting. Hank didn't tell me he knew why she left. "Did you tell him about the phone call from the young man?"

"Yes. He looked sad, but he did tell me that he and other officials in the congregation knew about the stories that were coming out of Niles. He said he believed it was gossip, that there were reasons for the gossip, and that the stories appeared to be spiteful."

"Anything else?"

"He asked me if I recognized the voice on the phone."

"And?"

"I told him I thought so," and then she told me.

Chapter 47

Thursday, December 10, 1964

I was furious, and I couldn't wait to talk to him.

"What are you thinking of?" I almost yelled. Not quite, but close. "Is this your idea of being a journalist?"

"What?"

"Spreading gossip through the secretary."

"What gossip?"

"The rumors about Father Fox." This time I did yell. "Mrs. Price said she heard from you."

"I was just trying to do something. The man is—was—dangerous."

"You can't be sure."

"Well, I was pretty sure."

"How?"

"Everybody says so."

"Everybody?"

"Everybody I know."

"You have details, I assume. The name of a victim?"

"Jimmy Parker," he said. "It's well known."

"Not to his parents, it's not. Goddammit, Sean. What's known for sure is that Bernie, Father Fox, was Jimmy's advisor and went to bat for him when he was being bullied for his perceived homosexuality. What's known for sure is that Father Fox got the bullies suspended. What's known for sure is this began a smear campaign orchestrated by the families of these boys. What's known for sure—and this is what's really pissing me off—is that you're part of the smear campaign."

Sean looked crestfallen. Harsh words from a mentor.

"I didn't mean ... I mean I didn't ... "

"Yeah, you didn't mean to be mean. But you were, and it has consequences."

I told him a story well known in Jewish communities about a man who spread gossip about a member of his congregation. When the man realized that he had damaged his neighbor's reputation, he asked his rabbi how he could make things right. The rabbi instructed him to take a feather pillow, cut it open and release the feathers to the wind, and then return to him. The man was puzzled but did so. The rabbi then told him to gather up all the feathers and put them back in the pillow case.

I stared at Sean and delivered the punchline. "When the man pointed out that getting all those feathers back in the pillow case was impossible, the rabbi told him, 'It's easier than repairing the damage caused by your gossip.' "

Sean was suitably downcast. "So there's nothing I can do."

"Only from here on out," I said. "If you can avoid spreading rumors—or even spreading truth when it's not called for—it will be something."

"What to do you mean avoid spreading truth?"

"In your catechism, there are sins called slander, calumny, and detraction. Remember?"

"Vaguely."

"Well calumny is spreading lies," I said. "Detraction is spreading truth when no good purpose is served. Only harm to the victim.

Calumny and detraction are both forms of slander."

"Maybe I need an example."

"Suppose one of your classmates confides in you by saying that he has had homosexual dreams. Let's call him Sam. Should you go and tell your classmates that Sam has had homosexual dreams?"

"No, he probably swore me to secrecy."

"What if he didn't?" I asked.

"Well, it would be mean."

"But it's true."

"But it would hurt him," Sean admitted. "My classmates would think differently about him."

"Maybe Sam is not a homosexual. Or maybe he is. Or maybe he doesn't know. The point is, you don't know—and you don't have a good reason for spreading the story."

"What if he gave me permission to tell others?"

"Well, that would change things, wouldn't it? It would mean your classmate is ready for the consequences, which could be significant."

"Yeah, okay, I get it. Spreading gossip, true or false, is not Christian."

"Not by a long shot."

"But BJ, um, Father Fox was a Nazi. SS even."

"True, but that's a half truth. You left out something important."

"What?"

"He was a Nazi deserter."

"But weren't the Nazi's losing, at that point. He was just trying to save his ass."

"How do you know that?"

"All right, speculation on my part. But his background was kept secret."

"Correct. See our earlier discussion about not spreading tales, even when the tales are true. The congregation's leaders were trying to avoid slander, don't you think?"

"Maybe."

"Maybe nothing," I said. "That's what they were doing. They released the information only because it helps explain his behavior, as something other than predatory."

"I'm not sure I buy it."

"Then prove it—before you engage in slander. Tell me something. Do your classmates think like you do, that Father Fox was molesting boys."

"Truth. Some do. Some don't. He's always had his fans—and detractors. But," he took a breath. "He's not around. They don't talk about it so much anymore."

"What about Dingo Dave?" I wanted to know. "What do they say about him?"

"Not much anymore. He's always been an outsider, an object of fun. The guys still think he is weird, but ..."

"Out of sight, out of mind," I said.

"Something like that," he said. "But some guys think he did a service."

"Great."

Chapter 48

Friday, December 11, 1964

My conversation with Sean was depressing. I was getting nowhere, other than a growing conviction that nothing was what we thought and that Dingo Dave, weird personality and all, was the victim of misinformation.

There was something else. I had been thinking all along that the murder, if that's what it was, had to do with the belief that the Fox had a taste for boys. Sean hit on it, unwittingly. Maybe the murder had something to do with his background as a Nazi, as a member of the SS.

It was just a thought, but it kept me up all night.

TGIF. My plans after school were to go home for dinner, then to a meeting, and back to the sem. At this point, especially on weekends, I could sleep at the house—on the couch—but that was getting a little weird, at least in the eyes of the kids. So I made the trek back and forth, staying at the house every now and then. On the couch.

Dinner was welcome, appearing more normal all the time. I talked over my thought that the death of Father Fox might have had more to do with his history as an Nazi or SS member than the suspicion that he liked boys. The team was fascinated.

"It's the nuns," said Butch.

"They aren't nuns. They're sisters, or religious women," corrected Sarah. "But why are you suspecting them?"

"They're German, you know."

"Except for Sister Angela, she's Italian," I said.

"But the cooks are German," Butch said.

"Which tells us nothing," I said. "Maybe they even liked his background."

Butch was quiet for a while. "Didn't you say he deserted?"

My turn to pause. "I did. Maybe that was the problem. Perhaps we should look into the nuns' background. Correction, the good sisters' backgrounds. But how?"

"I have a few connections," said Sarah, the ex-novitiate. "Let me look into that."

"Okay, then, A couple of the priests have German backgrounds. I should look into that." I paused. "Somehow."

"What about Polish backgrounds," said Sissy. "Or French. Or Russian. Or Czech. Countries that were terrorized by the Nazis."

"You're creating more work," I said. "But good. You're going with the idea that somebody didn't like his Nazi background. Where'd you learn that?"

"Duh, World History, you know."

"Any Jews on the staff?" asked Butch.

"Not to my knowledge," I said drily. "But there is some interaction with the Jewish community. One of the major donors is a Jew. A few of the upperclassmen, including Dingo Dave, learn Hebrew at the synagogue. Maybe ..."

"Bingo," said Butch.

"No Bingo," I said. "But you do get to place a piece of corn on your Bingo card. We are going everywhere and getting nowhere. Let's go back and start at the beginning—with the victim. I think that's a rule of investigation somewhere. My understanding is that he was born in the USA to a college professor at St. Edmund's University in Austin, Texas. It's a Congregation of Holy Cross institution, so we should be able to get some information, at least on the dad. Sarah, can you pin down the names of his parents, their marriage, his birth et cetera. Once we do that, we can start looking for what happened to him in Germany."

"Good plan," said Sarah. "I'm not working tomorrow. If my offspring are not doing anything, I'll take them along and show them how to hunt, library style."

Chapter 49

Saturday, December 12, 1964

Not having anything better to do, I joined the team at the library. Sarah decided to treat the day as an education in library science. She started first with the *Official Catholic Directory*, which had the ordination date of current priests. We easily found one Bernard John Fox, CSC with an ordination date of 1954.

Next, she took us up the elevator to the 11th floor, which housed a number of items particular to the Holy Cross order. She pulled off a volume of congregation newsletters, selected one that contained newsletters between 1951 and 1961. This produced a bio of Father Fox, which said nothing about his Nazi background but did say that he was born in Austin, Texas, and attended St. Edward's High School."

"Attended, not graduated. Interesting," I said.

"You were expecting it to say, 'Father Fox served in the SS from 1940 until 1944?' "

"No, Sarah," I said. "That would be silly."

Sissy giggled at this.

Sarah smiled, looked at Sissy, and said, "Your job is to write up a to-do list for us. Here take this notebook and write down: 'Number one: Contact St. Edward's High School to verify Bernie Fox attendance. See if there are any yearbook pictures of him." Then she turned to Butch and said, "Go downstairs to where we were. Grab the current Official Catholic Directory, latest year, and take down the name and phone number of the high school. Look in the table of contents and find the section where it lists schools. We'll meet you down there."

I liked how she was getting the kids involved. "What's next?"

"Next we need to find a marriage record for Father Fox's parents, and that should give us his mother's maiden name. A newspaper notice about their engagement or wedding might provide some useful information. Then we need to get a birth record for Bernie Fox—and maybe a baptismal record."

"How do we do that?," I asked.

"County and church records should do it," she said. "That is, assuming all this happened in the vicinity of Austin, which is probably the case. If it didn't, it'll take longer. If you want copies of the records, it'll cost us something. Sissy, get out your notebook and add the following. Item: Check newspaper records for Fox marriage or engagement. Item: Check for marriage with the county clerk in Austin. Item: check parish records for marriage and baptism."

"What if none of it happened around Austin," I asked.

"Let's not get ahead of ourselves. Odds are it did. Why? Because we know that his father taught at St. Edward's Universtiy, which is a good point. We should see what we can find out about him. Do you remember what his discipline was?"

"History," I said.

"And was he a full professor?"

"Not sure."

"What's his first name?"

"Don't know. Try Bernard or John," I said, figuring the odds that the boy was junior or at least got a middle name from his dad.

"Okay, let's go downstairs and work the card catalog. He probably had to publish somewhere along the way."

We went downstairs, where Sarah showed Sissy how to use the card catalog. We found a ton of Foxes in the author catalog, including one Bernard Fox with several articles on the history of Germany ranging from 1921 until 1934. Hs seemed a likely candidate for Bernie Fox's father. The most recent article suggested that he may have retired or died shortly after 1934.

Sarah put Sissy to work writing out catalog numbers. When she had exhausted the list of articles and books by one Bernard Fox, we returned to the elevator and went to the seventh floor to look through historical journal, mainly for articles by Bernard Fox that had his bio. We each found something and compared notes. Yep, this was the man who taught at St. Edward's. He was a full professor by the 1930s, though it wasn't clear whether he had tenure. He probably did not, which was why he had so many publications.

Sarah capsulized what we knew. "So, we know he taught at St. Edward's after World War I, perhaps before, until at least 1934, perhaps after."

"Bernie the younger was born in 1920," I pointed out. "If he was the oldest—or an only child—perhaps Bernie the older got married in 1918 or 1919, which was just after World War I."

"Maybe his wife was a war bride," said Sissy.

"Maybe his bride was German," I said.

"You guys are jumping to contusions," Sarah said. "But you may be right. In any case, we'll find out, though it may take some time. Let's go downstairs and catch up with Butch."

We found Butch sitting in the reference section, flipping through the back pages of *Newsweek*.

"Why is he reading *Newsweek* backwards," Sissy wanted to know.

"Because the chances of finding a scantily clad woman are better in the feature section than in the front," I said. "Am I right, Butch?"

His face got red. He closed the book and handed Sarah a small shred of paper that had the phone number of St. Edward's High School.

"That's my boy," I said.

Sarah gave me one of her looks, trying to suppress a grin, and said to Butch, "Thank you, Sir. I'll call them on Monday."

We went down to the vending bar to discuss where we were. I coughed up some money to get drinks all around and gave it to Sissy, who took orders and fed the machine.

Sarah said, "We're on the way to getting a good picture of Father Fox's American upbringing, but tracing his Nazi background will be more difficult. If his mother was German, that'll give us a clue. It's going to take a couple of weeks to get the American info, though."

"While we're waiting for that, I'll talk to my lawyer," I said. "He's a Jew and might be able to point me to a Nazi hunter."

"There are such people?" Sissy wondered.

"It's quite a thing, from what I understand," I said.

"They are often children of holocaust victims—or sometimes survivors themselves," said Sarah. "Among other things, they have up considerable expertise in navigating German records. The irony is that Nazis, being German, tended to be quite religious about recording everything they did."

"A nation of librarians," I said.

"Watch it," she said.

Chapter 50

Monday, December 14, 1964

The weekend had unfolded well enough, though not dramatically. On Saturday, the kids had gone over to the sem for a soiree, the last one before Christmas break, for a showing of *Donovan's Reef*. They had firm instructions to play it cool, keeping quiet about their relationship to the investigation. I talked to Butch beforehand, noting that the seminarians wouldn't be surprised if he asked a couple of questions about his friend.

His report dovetailed with what I knew—or thought I knew. Some of the seminarians were sympathetic to Dave; some were not, but the consensus was that Dave had gone off the rails somehow and had done the deed. Butch handled himself well. I was pleased with his restraint.

Sissy added a more general report, that the boys were looking forward to going home for Christmas and that there was a quality of normalcy about the place.

For my part, I had been able to talk to Hank, expressing a need to talk to the provincial. Initially, he was nervous about it, but I told him we were getting close to learning something—we weren't there yet—but I would be more comfortable if both he and the provincial knew what I—we—were doing. After some conversation, he got behind the deal, and left a message for the provincial to call him.

By the end of the day, Hank informed me that he had arranged for me to meet with the provincial today. And so, I found myself in Father Michael Miller's office.

"Thank you for agreeing to see me," I said.

"Thank Hank Grieshaber," Father Miller said. "He assured me that you were doing great work, as a teacher and other things."

"And that I have been clean and sober for the duration."

"I assumed he would not have asked for this meeting otherwise," he said. "What's up?"

I filled him in on where we were and where we weren't. My misgivings about Dave Johnson as the perpetrator, the likelihood that a parent or parents of students at Notre Dame High School were responsible for the threatening letter, my doubts about their involvement in the poisoning, and our current strategy for finding out the truth.

"It sounds like all of you've got is speculation."

"Correct," I said. "But I have the strong suspicion that we've been assuming, incorrectly, that the homicide had something to do with Father Fox's reputation as an, um, abuser."

"Undeserved reputation," he said.

"Agreed," I said. "All of the gossip seems to have originated with the parents in Niles."

"Good to know."

"We don't know it for sure, but there is no evidence that Father Fox misbehaved in that way. What we know is that he came to the defense of a student thought to be a homosexual, who committed suicide and left an article related to the young man."

"Charlie Parker," he said.

"All of the gossip seems to have been in response to his defense of the young man."

"That corresponds with what I know about Father Fox," he said. "The gossip never rang true. He could be fierce, but it always was in defense of the weak. That's supposed to be what we're about."

"Comfort the afflicted and afflict the comfortable."

"That was Bernie Fox, all over. You said that his death may have had nothing to do with the gossip. If not that, then what?"

"It might have something to do with his war background."

"You were at the wake where I read the letter."

"Yes, quite interesting. Why was the assumption made that his transition from Nazi soldier to Catholic priest was sincere?"

"You think he made a commitment to a life of poverty, chastity, and obedience as a way of going underground?"

"It's possible."

"Perhaps, but I think he would have been long gone in the late fifties. Besides, out of dozens of German soldiers who took refuge in the Vatican, he's the only one who became a priest."

"How do you know that?

"It's in his file."

"What else is in his file?"

"I've said enough," the provincial said. "Are you thinking his death had something to do with his background?"

"I'm thinking someone, perhaps with a background in Germany or Italy, had it out for him."

"Hmm, so you're suspecting one of our brother priests."

"Or brother brothers," I said. "Or sisters."

He said nothing.

After an uncomfortable silence, I said, "I need to know who on the faculty might be from or have strong ties to Germany."

"Or Italy."

"Yes, good point. Do you mind if I ask Hank about the background of faculty members. He should know."

"Fine, and thank you for asking. What about the good sisters?"

"Ve haf our vays." I probably shouldn't have said that.

Chapter 51

Wednesday, December 16, 1964

I had to talk to Eli, but we couldn't work out a time until late afternoon today. The upside was that the dreaded Trudy was not there, so I just knocked on his door.

"Just a minute," I heard from inside. And it was about a minute before he opened the door for me. "Come in. Coffee?"

"Only if it's made."

"It is," And he served me his best in a Dixie cup. "What's up?"

I filled him in on my progress, or lack thereof, and my theories.

"Got the whole family involved," he said. "That does sound like progress."

"I suppose it is," I said. "But I've got a strong feeling tht Father Fox's death has to do with his background rather than the suspicion that he was molesting boys."

I had forgotten he wasn't at the wake, and I had never filled him in on his peculiar background.

"Oh my," he said, after I had made up for lost time. "Who knows whether that played a role in his death, but it's definitely an angle worth exploring. What do you need from me?"

"Know any Nazi hunters?"

He laughed. "None in my back pocket, but I might know someone who knows someone ..."

"Who knows someone," I said, continuing the sentence.

"Definitely that," he said. "What do you need exactly."

"As much as we can get on his German background. He must have gone back to Germany with his mother around 1935."

"Got a name for her."

"Not yet, but I will. We'd like anything we can get on him, particularly his military service. His outfit. Where they went. Et cetera."

"Give me a few days to find someone who can help," he said.

"Time is of the essence."

"Why? Dave Johnson is not going anywhere."

I stared at him. "That's why time is of the essence."

He looked back at me and smiled. "Good point."

Chapter 52

Saturday, December 19, 1964

This was a good day, in more ways than one.

First, Sarah had heard back from her contacts in Texas, They had found a engagement announcement in the local paper for one Bernard John Fox to one Martha Wuerth, a native of Wolterdingen, Germany, in 1919. They had also located Bernard's birth certificate, dated June 10, 1920, with the parents being Bernard and Martha Fox. The elder Bernard had been an associate professor at St. Edward's College until 1935 when he died, an event confirmed by a death certificate. The high school had come through, acknowledging that Bernard Junior had completed his freshman year there in the spring of 1935 but had not re-enrolled for the fall session.

Second, Eli had called me on Thursday afternoon to give me the name of a Nazi hunter based in Chicago who, as he said, would be happy to help. I had called him immediately and arranged to meet him tomorrow.

Third, Sarah invited me to stay the weekend at the house. I had wondered what I should do, given that the Christmas break had started yesterday and the seminary was a bit ghostly. Only a handful of seminarians were there and about half of the staff. We were closing in on Christmas, and things were a little crazy out there. I wasn't sure what to do, but we had had a fair amount of snow and the seminarians had rigged up a small toboggan run on the hill leading to the lake. Nobody was around, which left the toboggan run to myself, Butch, and Sissy. It was a little odd maybe, but they enjoyed it and so did I.

Back home we had our family supper, with some discussion of what we had learned about the Fox's background. We were still at the beginning of what we needed to know, but we had started down a good path and we all knew it. Or sensed it. I excused myself to go to a meeting, and there were no complaints. Everyone knew that my going to meetings underpinned all the good things going on at the moment. And I was able to share some of those things at the meeting and after with my sponsor at our favorite diner.

I didn't get back into the house until after ten, at which point everyone had retired for the night. I watched a bit of the *Tonight Show* and spread myself out on the sofa for a long winter's nap. I was awakened an hour or so later by a tap on my shoulder and a vision of a tall woman in a stunning nightgown I had never seen before.

"The time is right," she whispered. "Meet me upstairs."

Chapter 53

Sunday, December 20, 1964

"Dad, did you sleep well last night?" Sissy asked, trying not to giggle.

I sensed the jig was up, but I wasn't quite sure how to respond. I decided to play along. "Not so well," I said, glancing at Sarah who, thankfully, looked amused. "I woke up in the middle of the night, feeling a bit restless. It took me a while to get to sleep after that."

"I bet," Sissy said, giggling outright.

"What's going on?" asked Butch.

"Oh, you are so-o young," Sissy said, drawing out the penultimate word.

Butch stared at her, waiting for her to speak. She said nothing, just rolled her eyes.

"What?" He paused, and his expression changed. "Oh. Oh, I get it."

Sissy's eyes were still spelling out "you idiot."

"No, really," Butch stuttered. Wow! No kidding?"

I was getting uncomfortable. "I need to go to Chicago this morning—to talk to a Nazi hunter."

"Sure you have enough energy for that?" asked Sissy, who was now working on her deadpan face.

"Enough already," I said. "And you, Mrs. Foote, could give me a little help here."

"You're doing fine," she said, showing off her trademark grin. "How are you getting to Chicago?"

"The Orange Vomit," I said. "I don't think the Edsel will put up with Chicago traffic, even on a Sunday."

"Not to mention the bit of lake snow the weatherman is calling for," Sarah said.

"Gotta go," I said. "It's Sunday and there are only four trains from South Bend today."

Later that afternoon

The South Shore Railroad may have been ugly, but it was reasonably trustworthy, more than I could say for the Edsel. Trains were limited on Sundays, but it did get me into the Loop. From there, it was a hop on the El to the Rogers Park station on the north side of Chicago. I was fortunate that my contact lived there, a long mile from the train. I walked it, in a rather bitter wind, but I was pleased at the way the transit worked.

My contact, one Simon Weisberg met me at the door of his two-door apartment after I rang the bell.

"Mr. Foote, I presume," he said, extending his hand.

"Yes, call me Bert. Thank you for meeting me."

"Come in. Would you like some coffee or tea? You look like you could use something warm."

I waited a bit inside to catch my breath and let the icicles melt off my eyelashes, but I expect I still looked a sight. "Yes, indeed. Whatever is convenient."

"Coffee is made. Have a seat while I get it for you. How do you like it?"

"Black, thanks."

He came back in less than a minute with a couple of full mugs and set them on a coffee table, sitting across from me in a chair. I embraced my mug with both hands.

Weisberg began. "I understand you're looking for someone to research a priest who might have a Nazi past."

I agreed and filled him on Bernie Fox's story, noting that we were certain he was a Nazi soldier.

"I am what you might call a Nazi hunter," he said, "but this man is already deceased—so why would I want to help you?"

"Are you interested in truth," I asked, "or vengeance."

"Truth," he said, staring at me, "and justice. And if I were honest, maybe a bit of vengeance. I lost my family—parents, grandparents, my sisters—in the Holocaust. So, yeah, if I were honest, a bit of vengeance. But my work is about nailing down the story, and, really, that's the most important thing. Nailing down the story."

"Then you *will* help me nail down the story about *this* man."

"Only because a friend asked me to help," he said. "That and it should be easy. In my business, the hard part is locating a war criminal. Here, the war criminal—or the suspect, at any rate—is already located and taken care of. Looking up his war record should be a piece of cake."

"Really. How do you do that?"

"Ve haf our vays," Weinberg said with a straight face. I laughed. Apparently this was an old joke. "The Nazis were Germans, and Germans are organized, even anal. They are, were, and probably always will be great record keepers. The only trick is getting to see the records, and the post-war administration—at least the West German part—has been quite cooperative in that respect."

"We have to hope that what we need to know is not held by East Germany."

"There's that."

I gave him the necessary details, agreed on paying him $200 for his work, and left satisfied that I would be getting some interesting information in a week or so. I held a vague hope that I might be reimbursed for my expenses.

Back in the Loop, I stopped in Iwan Ries for some Three-Star Blue pipe tobacco. After that I went into Kroch's and Brentano's, where I picked up a colorful book on the Australian outback for Butch to give to Dingo Dave.

I got home after dark, too late for a meeting and got invited to spend the night with my wife and her new nightgown.

"Time's a-wastin," she said, her slight grin right where I left it.

Chapter 54

Wednesday, December 30, 1964

It was the Christmas season, which had its own rhythm, peculiar all around. I had been able to spend more time with the family, though I had taken to going back to the seminary for most of the nights. The rhythm method, in this case, would have put me on the couch, which was not all that comfortable. Besides, I rather liked my own space. And so did Sarah.

I did arrange to take Butch to visit Dingo Dave on Christmas day. Dave still didn't want anything to do with me, but the visit from Butch was welcome, or so I gathered. Butch said Dave was surprised to get two presents, one book from me and one from him. Dave's mother and his brother Dan were there. Dan just glared at me. His mother was a bit friendlier, wary because of our last encounter but genuinely grateful that I was willing to let Butch stay in touch with her son.

The Christmas season had less impact on Jews, sometimes giving them a bit of a breather, sometimes offering uninterrupted times for getting things done. This was true of Simon Weisberg, who used the time to throw himself into the task I had assigned him. By Wednesday, he called the house—I wasn't there—and left a message with Sarah that he had some details. He didn't want to give them to her, and she didn't press him.

I called him back and got much of what I wanted.

He started by explaining that he couldn't find anything under Bernard Fox or Bernard John Fox, which didn't surprise him. He tried alternative formulas using German spelling and got a hit for Bernhard Johan Fuchs, the surname being German for "Fox."

"Oh, I should have thought of that," I said. "The Holy Cross provincial said his name in Germany at his eulogy, but it's so close to the English when spoken that I didn't think anything of it. His mother probably switched it to the German after she moved back to Germany."

"Likely," said Simon.

"And when he moved back here, he switched back to the spelling on his birth certificate."

"Usually, the war criminals change their names."

"But, as I understand it, he wasn't trying to hide his identity," I said. "Not from the leaders of the congregation anyway. His given name took advantage of his father's identity."

"I'm surprised in a way," said Simon. "Your man was the real deal. It turns out he was a member of the Brown Shirts as a teenager and then segued into the SS."

I remembered the Brown Shirts from my research for Dan Johnson and their connection to homosexuality. I asked Simon about this history.

"The eventual leader was a well-known homosexual, a charismatic leader who attracted and developed a hyper-masculine—and not incidentally—homosexual culture among his troops. Hitler used the Brown Shirts for a while, but when they became too powerful, he began a purge that included a particularly vicious persecution of suspected homosexuals. If your man survived that, he would have had to put himself outside that world—by clearly not being a homosexual, by using his connections, or by turning on his fellows."

"Interesting," I said. "I like the last one, just because there is something strong about his behavior toward accused homosexuals. If he turned in his fellow soldiers, he might have built up a ton of guilt. Maybe he was trying to make amends somehow."

"Up to you," Simon said. "I'm just giving you the info."

"What about his Italian connection."

"It's there, especially in 1943 after the allies invaded Italy." Simon said. "Bernhard Fuchs was an officer under Herbert Kappler's command."

"Who dat?"

"Herbert Kappler was the head of the German police and security services in Rome in 1943. It was a stressful time, and his outfit was responsible for rounding up Jews and getting them to concentration camps."

"I wonder if that got to Bernhard Fuchs," I said. "Apparently, he deserted and went to the Vatican."

"I don't have that," Simon said. "The records say he was missing in action. But that's interesting. Herbert Kappler was the main liaison to the Vatican and tried to take refuge there when Rome fell—but he was unsuccessful. Bernhard Fuchs had better luck—if you're right."

Chapter 55

Monday, January 4, 1965

    Things were quiet. New Year's had passed uneventfully, which for me was a good thing. In previous years, I had spent New Year's Day comatose, having partied on New Year's Eve and gone out for Tom and Jerrys on New Year's Day. The latter came with a particularly savage custom, though the veneer was holiday cheer. In most places, the first Tom and Jerry was free. Of course, etiquette required that you order a second one for regular price. Then it was off to the American Legion for the same drill. Then to a VFW lodge further down the road for two more. Since each cup of the hot drink had a shot of rum and a shot of brandy, the entire escapade required drinking twelve shots of 80 proof spirit. I had built up my tolerance over the years, so I managed to make it home more or less conscious. But the the practice led to another custom, sleeping away the afternoon. This year I was sober and was able to watch a couple of bowl games, though I believe I might have slept away most of those. Habit, I guess. New Year's Day had to be one of the more boring festivals ever invented. Men did the Tom and Jerry thing and watched football. Women mostly wanted no part of it, though my wife did consider this a "Holy Day of Obligation," the Feast of the Circumcision in those days. I resolved to ask Eli about that.

Today, the unfortunate festivities were finally behind us. Sarah was back at work. The library was open for business, even though classes had not begun yet. She had plenty to do but time enough to meet for coffee downstairs and plan strategy. By now, we had a good picture of young Bernie's life as a Nazi. He had been party to a massacre in Italy and other things we didn't know about. The massacre occurred not long before his defection, so we surmised it might have been the straw that broke the camel's back. We were guessing, but the time was right. We also guessed that the massacre would have given someone a motive for seeking revenge.

However, Sarah pointed out that, as a member of the SS, Bernhard surely would have been party to other atrocities, creating reasons for revenge all along his career. His background as a Brown Shirt was interesting, the connection to the persecution of homosexuals suggesting some context for his passion on the subject. Then again, he was involved in the rounding up and transporting Jews to extermination camps, but maybe he didn't know what happened at those camps. Sarah thought this was unlikely.

Still, I was intrigued with the Italian connection. We had progressed a lot in our surmises, but we were getting nowhere with anything solid. We were back to looking at the staff, including the good sisters.

Sarah volunteered to look into the background of the three nuns. "I have a few connections." She had been a novice once, though not in the same order. Still, she knew people and people who knew people, as Eli might have said.

The rest of the staff was on me. I had managed to get most of what I needed from Hank, though he wasn't happy about it.

Father Hopfensperger, aka Father Hop, was the son of parents who emigrated from Germany near Czechoslovakia in the 1920s. He joined the U.S. Army soon after World War II began, fought in

Italy and got sent home with a wound that left him with a permanent limp.

Our religion teacher, the aptly named Mathew O'Connor was of Irish descent, something he was quite proud of, though you had to go back three or four generations to find the Irish emigrant.

Father Franco Fratelli, our math teacher, had an Italian name and was also second-generation American. His people came from the North, Hank thought.

Father George Pieczi, our physics teacher, was of Polish descent, also second generation out of Chicago.

Father Phil Fischer had a German name and a French background, his great-grandparents having come from somewhere in Alsace Loraine. Ironically, he was fluent in French and Spanish, which he taught, but not in German. He had taught at Notre Dame High School in Niles, had worked with Bernie Fox there and respected rather than liked him. He acknowledged that he could be hard to get along with but verified that Bernie had a habit of going to bat for the underdogs.

Brother Rufus Meyer, maintenance man, was American born, son of German immigrants from near Luxemburg.

Then, of course, there was my friend and patron, Hank Grieshaber, grandson of German immigrants.

The staff was American, but all had descended from Europeans and might have ties to the old country. I'm not sure what that got me. Fathers O'Connor and Fischer had worked with Bernie Fox. Neither seemed to like him, any more than I did, but both swore they respected him. O'Connor compared him to Dorothy Day, who had visited the seminary earlier in the year and had answered student questions rather sharply, almost rudely. "She's a thorn in the side of good people," he said. "A good thorn, but a thorn. Bernie was like that."

That was Bernie. Someone you could admire. And someone you wanted to avoid.

Chapter 56

Wednesday, January 13, 1965

Students arrived on Sunday, and we were back in business as an educational institution on Monday. I was a little preoccupied with that.

Meanwhile, Sarah had been working her network, trying to find a connection to the sisters who had served the seminary and left in a huff. Finally, one of her classmates, now a member of the Adrian Dominicans order, acknowledged being high-school chums with a member of the School Sisters of Notre Dame. Her friend was teaching at a high school in Ann Arbor, and Sarah had arranged to ambush her on a day trip, which turned out to be yesterday.

Sarah's contact hardly knew the two cooks, which was disappointing, but she did know the nurse. They had served together on their previous assignments. As it turns out, Sister Angela grew up in Rome and had been orphaned during the war. At one point, she shared her story. Her Catholic parents had been hiding a Jewish family. Seeing the handwriting on the wall, they managed to get the two Jewish children to a Catholic orphanage. The Jewish parents stayed behind but were discovered in an SS roundup and carted off to a camp somewhere and lost in the Holocaust. During the commotion, Sister Angela's father had protested their treatment by the SS. Sister Angela, then only eight, saw one of the officers knock him out with the butt of his rifle. Her father died before the family could get him to a hospital. Her mother died a few days later, of a broken heart according to Sister Angela, but not before telling her daughter to make her way to the same orphanage that was hiding the Jewish children.

At this, Sarah asked where she was, knowing that we would have to talk to her.

"No one knows," her friend had said. "She left the order around Thanksgiving."

"Okay, then," I said after Sarah finished her story. "I think we have a suspect."

"You still have only suspicions, but they are logical," said Sarah.

"Because of the timing," I said, my voice rising as if asking a question.

"Yes, it certainly makes you think," she said. "Plus, Sister Angela had the opportunity."

"The sisters could access the chapel at any time."

"Yes, the method fits her as well."

"Why?" I asked, knowing the answer but wanting Sarah to verify it.

"Her gender. Poisoning is more common among females."

"Moreover ..."

"She's a nurse. Even better, my contact said that Sister Angela had been trained as a midwife."

"Why is that better?"

"Because the poison might have been known to her as an abortifacient."

"And you knew that because of your work with the Right to Life Society," I said.

"I remember it from a seminar about various techniques and potions used to abort babies in the early part of a pregnancy. Yew came up."

"I came up?" I said, trying not to smile. I never could pass up this pun.

"Y-E-W, you jerk."

"You know I know."

"Stop it."

"Anyway, it seems to fit," I said. "What about the connection to Italy."

"You tell me."

"It appears she was in Rome when Bernhard Johan Fuchs was there, perhaps involved in rounding up Jews. Maybe he was the one who cold-cocked her daddy."

"And she recognized him," Sarah said.

"Exactly. I bet she remembers that scar on his face."

"Oh, I didn't know he had a scar," Sarah said. She had never met him.

"Well, a few people have scars from WW II," I said.

"But it fits. Right now, it's coincidence. But it does fit. Here's a question: Did Father Fox talk much about the Jews in the Holocaust. I thought he was focused on homosexuals."

"In retrospect, I don't think that's accurate," I said. "The Johnson brothers reacted to his sympathetic defense of homosexuals, but this was in the context of Nazi attempts to exterminate Jews and other groups as I understand it. He also mentioned gypsies. I don't know whether he lingered on the persecution of homosexuals or whether that was just in the mind of some of the students."

"So where are we?" Sarah asked.

"I think we know the story, but we don't have any proof—and our likely suspect has skipped. I'm not as juiced up about finding Sister Angela—the former Sister Angela—as on getting Dingo Dave off the legal hook."

"You think we can do that without proof?"

"Probably not, but I'll talk to Eli," I said. "My suspicion is the authorities are unlikely to budge without proof. Anyway, how do we find the former Sister Angela?"

"Would it help if you knew her civilian name?" Sarah asked, giving things away with her grin.

"Well, yeah , you don't?"

"I do. Gina Scarpelli from Detroit."

"You think?"

"Worth a try."

Chapter 57

Friday, January 15, 1965

By now, I had become convinced that no one on the staff could have, or would have, poisoned their colleague. Their biographies didn't produce a motive. Besides, Gina Scarpelli, aka Sister Angela, was looking pretty good as the culprit.

The problem was that she had left her order. While this only increased our suspicions about her, we had no idea where she was. Finding her was no walk in the park. Her family was the order. She had been raised by them, worked with them, and joined them. That's all she knew.

Somebody in the order would know where she was, I was sure. Getting that person to tell us was the problem. Sarah, who knew more about women religious than I did was pessimistic. Gina Scarpelli was family, even if she had flown the nest.

Still we had to try. The only other option was tough going. It meant searching medical institutions, on the theory that she'd take a nursing job somewhere. We didn't have a net that wide, though Sarah pointed out that this did make it more likely that someone in her order would have served as a reference and would then have a clue about her whereabouts.

Again, we had to try to crack the sisterhood.

We didn't have a strong interest in nailing Gina Scarpelli for murder. In some ways, we could have cared less. If Bernhard Fuchs participated in the death of her father, and indirectly her mother, maybe he deserved what we got. But we needed to pin the murder on somebody else in order to get Dingo Dave released. Eli had made that clear. He promised to look into Dave's release, but he wasn't optimistic. Chief Ziolkowski wasn't either, noting that the county authorities would not reopen the case without proof. And so it went. If we were to get Dingo Dave any help, we were going to have to find Gina Scarpelli and get her to confess.

Easy peasy. Yeah, right.

I talked it over with the team at suppertime. Sarah agreed to make another trip up to the motherhouse, hoping mother superior or her assistant would be forthcoming. Sarah herself wasn't optimistic, explaining that mother superior would feel an obligation to someone whose only family had been the order. Still she agreed to try.

Then Sissy put in her two cents. "Go ahead, Mom. Sure, they won't tell you right off, but when you explain that there's an innocent boy in jail ..."

"It's not really jail," I said.

"He thinks it is," said Butch.

"Okay, in a group home that feels like jail," corrected Sissy. "Anyway, you're trying to help a boy who was wrongly accused and Sister Angela, um Gina, can help. Even if they won't tell you where this Gina is, I bet they'd tell her about Dingo Dave. Maybe she'll feel so guilty she'll come forward."

"You think so?" I asked. "She could be charged with murder."

"I bet she can't carry the guilt she feels," said Sissy.

"You know, Sissy has a point," said Sarah. "We're dealing with super-Catholics here. If we use a little guilt ..."

"Something you're good at, Mom," said Butch with a straight face.

"World class," said Sissy with a not-so straight face.

"Looks like we're depending on your wiles, Sarah," I said.

"Looks like it," said Sarah.

Chapter 58

Saturday, January 16, 1965

Sarah called the motherhouse at 8 a.m., which I thought was chancy on two accounts. First, it seemed a bit early to call. Second, it gave the community a chance to turn us away.

Sarah didn't agree. "They're sisters," she said. "By eight, they've attended mass, sung Lauds and Matins, had breakfast, and started their housework. It's practically the middle of the day." She dismissed my point two out of hand. "It's polite," she said. "And why wouldn't mother superior—or her second—agree to see us?"

"Because ... Oh, never mind."

Sarah also got her way on driving up there in her car. She didn't think the Edsel was reliable. I didn't argue with her about that one.

The motherhouse was really a big house, set into a residential area. "I'll take the lead on this," she said, as we were walking up the front porch. She did let me ring the doorbell.

A sister in a white habit, probably a novice, opened the door, welcomed us inside, and sat us in a front room, simply but tastefully appointed. In less than two minutes, another sister appeared and introduced herself as Mother Lucia.

"May I call you Mother," I was tempted to ask. I did not. I just shook her hand, after she shook Sarah's hand. This was a house of women, after all.

"Perhaps we should meet in my office," Mother Lucia said. We dutifully followed her into her office, which was not much larger than the waiting room but which featured a big desk, a swivel chair for the boss, and two nice armchairs across from her. We sat in those.

"What can I do for you?" she asked.

Sarah described the death of Father Fox, the subsequent investigation, the arrest, and punishment of Dave Johnson. Then she paused.

"And the problem is ..." Mother Lucia said with her own invitational pause.

"We don't think he's guilty."

"We?"

"His lawyer, my husband, and I."

"But everybody else thinks he's guilty," Mother Lucia said.

"Not really," Sarah said. "We know that the basis for pinning the murder on Dave Johnson was flawed. Someone else did it, for a different motive. We're sure of that. Well, almost sure. And we think Sister Angela—Gina Scarpelli—has some answers."

"Explain."

Sarah said that in the beginning we all thought the murder had to do with the rumors about Father Fox molesting students. I was glad that she took pains to say that the rumors appeared to be based more on revenge than on truth. She then explained how we had begun to think that the murder might have been related to his background as a Nazi, which we had learned about later but in considerable detail.

"What's this got to do with Gina?" Mother Lucia said.

I was getting nervous. This was the essential question.

Now Sarah explained that Bernhard Fuchs was a deserter, apparently repenting of his deeds, taking refuge in the Vatican.

EVIL SPEAKING

"Something happened there in Italy."

"Something like the Nazis losing the war?"

Mother Lucia was no fool. I felt myself beginning to sweat.

"Fair question," Sarah said. "One shared by others. But this Bernhard Fuchs was clearly repentant. He didn't have to join the Congregation of Holy Cross and become a priest. Obviously he was making amends for his actions during the war. We think something about Italy put him over the edge."

"So ... "

"So, Gina Scarpelli was there, orphaned after an SS officer killed her father with the butt of his rifle. Her parents had been hiding a Jewish couple, who were taken away in the raid."

"And ..."

"We think Bernhard Fuchs might have been involved."

"And ..."

"And Sister Angela, while serving as the nurse at Holy Cross Seminary this school year, recognized him, perhaps as far back as September."

"And ..."

"And we don't know," Sarah said. "But Gina Scarpelli does."

"You think Sister Angela might have ..."

Sarah interrupted. "Mother Lucia, we don't know. We think Gina Scarlelli knows something. Perhaps it wasn't Bernhard Fuchs she recognized in September, and we're barking up the wrong tree."

"Perhaps."

"In any case, we think Gina Scarpelli knows something. Like I said, we are pretty sure that Dave Johnson has been convicted of something he didn't do. Gina Scarpelli might help us untangle that." Sarah paused. "Do you know where she is?"

"If I knew, I wouldn't tell you," Mother Lucia said.

"If you do know," Sarah said with emphasis, "perhaps you can pass along the information we've given you."

"Perhaps," Mother Lucia said. "Thank you for coming."

With that she got up, ushered us out of the room, shook Sarah's hand and then mine, and opened the door for us.

Sarah and I got in her car without saying anything. Finally, I said, "Well, that was a waste of time."

"I don't think so," Sarah said.

"How so?"

"Mother Lucia will pass on the information to Gina Scarpelli."

"How do you know that," I said. "She probably doesn't even know where Gina is."

"She probably does."

"How do you know?"

"If she didn't know, she would have said,. 'I don't know where she is.' Instead, she carefully said, 'If I knew, I wouldn't tell you.' This is a woman who can lie only with difficulty. She knows where Gina Scarpelli is, and she will tell her what we know and what we suspect."

"And how do you know that?"

"She doesn't want the unjustified punishment of Dave Johnson on her conscience," Sarah said. "I'm hoping the former Sister Angela feels the same way."

"What do we do now?" I asked.

"We wait."

Chapter 59

Friday, January 29, 1965

And so we waited. I had given up on Gina appearing. I didn't think much of the odds to begin with, and I went back to teaching, having come to the conclusion there was no happy ending to this story.

I won't say there was a happy ending, but Gina Scarpelli did appear. After lunch, I found the new secretary waiting for me outside of the dining room. She told me I had a guest in the waiting room at the front of the building.

It was Gina Scarpelli. In spite of her new status as a civilian, she looked every inch the nun. She had short hair, barely covering her ears and no makeup. She wore the same institutional wire glasses, the emblem of a religious woman.

"I'm Gina Scarpelli," she said. "You might remember me as Sister Angela."

"I do," I said. "To what do I owe the pleasure?" It seemed a ridiculous thing to say.

"Guilt," I suppose. "Perhaps despair."

I said nothing.

"I have nowhere to go," she said, choking a bit. "Well, that's not true. I've been working as a nurse, thanks to good recommendations from my order. But I'm a fish out of water. I belong in the order, but I can't ... " She stopped.

I looked at her, still saying nothing.

"It's all I know. The convent. I was raised there. It's my family, but now ..." She stopped again. "The boy? Is he well?"

"The boy? You mean, Dave Johnson?"

She nodded.

"My son visits him," I said. "He's doing as well as could be expected." I didn't bother saying that he would have nothing to do with me.

"He didn't poison anyone."

I said nothing.

"I did. The man deserved it. At least I used to think so."

"And now?"

"I watched him kill my father. He hit him with the butt of his rifle, knocked him out. Then he looked at me, turned around, and said nothing. He had this scar across his eye. Same as Father Fox. It was him. I know it was."

"And you poisoned him."

"There were yew bushes in front of the building. I knew it was a poison. Midwives used it as an abortifacient. Of course, I never used it for such, but we learned about it in nursing school. I made a tincture, a strong one, and added it to the altar wine. It was an abomination that he pretended to serve the Lord. I thought it was a good way for him to die. On the altar, poisoned by the blood of Christ. I thought he deserved it."

"And now?"

"I don't know. I confessed it, but my heart wasn't in it, and I said so. The priest wouldn't forgive me without true contrition, and I don't blame him. But ... " She paused for what seemed like a long time. "It's the boy. I feel guilty about the boy. I felt it as soon as I heard. I haven't been sleeping well. It's the boy. As far as Father Fox

EVIL SPEAKING

goes, I'll take my chances with Our Lord. But having that boy's life be ruined because of something I did, I can't do that. Not anymore. I'm willing to turn myself in if it will help the boy."

"I expect it will," I said.

"Mother Lucia said your wife was very persuasive."

"She can be," I said.

"Any chance I can meet her?"

"If you don't mind walking over to the library, we can do that." I did wonder if she might change her mind on the way, but I thought not. She had thought about this for too long. And so we went to meet my wife.

Chapter 60

Friday, March 18, 1965

It took better than two weeks for the wheels of justice to grind into a conclusion of sorts. After Gina Scarpelli thanked my wife for pushing her to do the right thing, I took her over to see Chief Ziolkowski, who I thought deserved the honors rather than the sheriff's department.

Eli then went to work, negotiating Dave Johnson's release with the district attorney and juvenile court. Eli, in consultation with me, arranged for Butch to give him the news. Butch wouldn't tell me what went on in the room, but he must have used some magic. Dingo Dave came into the waiting room, extended his hand, and thanked me for my efforts. He didn't say more than that—he seemed a bit choked up—but it was heartfelt.

Eli found Gina Scarpelli a lawyer who had her work cut out for her—or maybe not. Chances were better than even, Eli thought, that Gina would work out a plea deal that would involve pleading guilty to something in return for the lightest sentence. On the other hand, there was a chance she would want a trial—just to rub the reputation of Father Fox, aka Bernhard Fuchs, in the mud. The congregation, I expected and Hank confirmed, would much prefer the former. We'd all have to wait.

At least Dingo Dave was exonerated, quickly becoming the hero of the story. That one of the sisters was the culprit was particularly satisfying to the seminarians, who to a man swore they knew all along that "the nuns did it," and this became the partly true legend.

Dingo Dave and his brother knew better and remained a little bitter, knowing that their lives were affected by rumors. Dave harbored only good will for Butch, who soon received a package in the mail. It was an Australian outback hat, which Butch came to treasure.

Neither Dave nor Dan wanted to return to the seminary, not surprising under the circumstances. CSC officials were mortified at the injustice done to Dave and, to a lesser extent, to Dan. Hank told me on the QT that the order would probably offer Diane Johnson free tuition at Notre Dame for a year or two for both of her boys. Details to be worked out.

Butch was a little smug, but I decided to view it as an air of confidence. Sissy was glad to be able to attend more soirees at the seminary, having honed her skills at working the room.

Sarah and I were getting comfortable with living apart together—or something. As I was thinking about such things, Sarah invited me upstairs for a tete-a-tete. "The time is right," she said taking me by the hand.

We chatted a bit about how we seemed to have worked out something, living together apart. That night we took another step farther.

And Sarah laughed

Made in the USA
San Bernardino, CA
31 August 2017